John Reed S

In Her Own Right

John Reed Scott

In Her Own Right

1st Edition | ISBN: 978-3-75242-398-3

Place of Publication: Frankfurt am Main, Germany

Year of Publication: 2020

Outlook Verlag GmbH, Germany.

IN HER OWN RIGHT

BY JOHN REED SCOTT

I

"The expected has happened, I see," said Macloud, laying aside the paper he had been reading, and raising his hand for a servant.

"I thought it was the unexpected that happens," Hungerford drawled, languidly. "What do you mean?"

"Royster & Axtell have been thrown into bankruptcy. Liabilities of twenty million, assets problematical."

"You don't say!" ejaculated Hungerford, sitting up sharply. "Have they caught any of our friends?"

"All who dealt with them, I reckon."

"Too bad! Too bad!—Well, they didn't catch me."

"Oh, no! you're not caught!" said Macloud. "Your father was wise enough to put your estate into Government threes, with a trustee who had no power to change the investment."

"And I'm thankful he did," Hungerford answered. "It saves me all trouble; I need never look at the stock report, don't you know; Government bonds are always the same.—I suppose it's a reflection on my ability, but that is of small consequence. I don't care what people think, so long as I have the income and no trouble. If I had control of my capital, I might have lost all of it with Royster & Axtell, who knows?"

Macloud shook his head.

"It isn't likely," he commented, "you wouldn't have had it to lose."

Hungerford's momentarily vague look suddenly became knowing.

"You mean I would have lost it long ago?" he asked. "Oh, I say, old man, you're a bit hard on me. I may not have much head for business, but I'm not altogether a fool, don't you know."

"Glad to know it," laughed Macloud, as he arose and sauntered away.

Hungerford drew out his cigarettes and thoughtfully lighted one.

"I wonder—did he mean I am or I am not?" he said. "I wonder. I shall have to ask him some time.—Boy! a Scotch and soda."

Meanwhile, Macloud passed into the Club-house and, mounting the stairs to the second floor, knocked sharply at a door in the north-west corner of the corridor.

"Come in," called a voice.—"Who is it?—Oh! it's you, Macloud. Make yourself at home—I'll be out in a moment."

There was the noise of splashing water, accompanied by sundry exclamations and snorts, followed by a period of silence; and, then, from the bath room, emerged Croyden clad in robe, slippers and a smile.

"Help yourself," he said, pointing to the smoking materials. He filled a pipe, lit it carefully, blew a few whiffs to the ceiling and watched them slowly dissipate.

"Well, it's come," he remarked: "Royster & Axtell have smashed clean."

"Not clean," said Macloud. "It is going to be the most criminal failure this town has ever known."

"I mean they have busted wide open—and I'm one of the suckers."

"You are going to have plenty of company, among your friends," Macloud answered.

"I suppose so—but I hope none of them is hit quite so bad." He blew another cloud of smoke and watched it fade. "The truth is, Colin, I'm done for."

"What!" exclaimed Macloud. "You don't mean you are cleaned out?"

The other nodded. "That's about it…. I've a few thousand left—enough to pay laundry bills, and to board on Hash Alley for a few months a year. Oh! I was a sucker, all right!—I was so easy it makes me ashamed to have saved *anything* from the wreck. I've a notion to go and offer it to them, now."

There were both bitterness and relief in his tones; bitterness over the loss, relief that the worst, at last, had happened.

For a while, there was silence. Croyden turned away and began to dress; Macloud sat looking out on the lawn in front, where a foursome were playing the home hole, and another waiting until they got off the green.

Presently, the latter spoke.

"How did it happen, old man?" he asked—"that is, if you care to tell."

Croyden laughed shortly. "It isn't pleasant to relate how one has been such an addle-pated ass——"

"Then, forgive me.—I didn't mean to——"

"Nonsense! I understand—moreover, it will ease my mortification to confide

3

in one who won't attempt to sympathize. I don't care for sympathy, I don't deserve it, and what's more, I won't have it."

"Don't let that worry you," Macloud answered. "You won't be oppressed by any rush of sympathy. No one is who gets pinched in the stock market. We all go in, and—sooner or later, generally sooner—we all get burnt—and we all think every one but ourselves got only what was due him. No, my boy, there is no sympathy running loose for the lamb who has been shorn. And you don't need to expect it from your friends of the Heights. They believe only in success. The moment you're fleeced, they fling you aside. They fatten off the carcasses of others—yours and mine and their own brothers. Friendship does not enter into the game. They will eat your bread and salt to-night, and dance on your financial corpse to-morrow. The only respect they have is for money, and clothes, and show; and the more money, and the more show the greater their deference—while they last—and the farther the fall when they fail. The women are as bad as the men, in a smaller way. They will blacken one another's reputation with an ease and zest that is simply appalling, and laugh in your face while doing it. I'm speaking generally, there are exceptions, of course, but they only prove the rule. Yet, what can you expect, where aristocracy is based on one's bank account, and the ability to keep the other fellows from laying violent hands on it. It reminds one of the Robbers of the Rhine! Steal everything within reach and give up nothing. Oh! it is a fine system of living!—Your pardon! I forgot myself."

"It is good to have you forget yourself occasionally," said Croyden —"especially, when your views chime with mine—recently acquired, I admit. I began to see it about a month ago, when I slowed down on expenditures. I thought I could notice an answering chill in the grill-room."

"Like enough. You must spend to get on. They have no use for one who doesn't. You have committed the unpardonable sin: had a fortune and lost it. And they never forgive—unless you make another fortune; then they will welcome you back, and lay plans to take it, also."

"You paint a pretty picture!" Croyden laughed.

Macloud shrugged his shoulders.

"Tell me of Royster & Axtell," he said.

"There isn't a great deal to tell," Croyden replied, coming around from the dressing table, and drawing on his vest as he came. "It is five years since my father died and left me sole heir to his estate. In round numbers, it aggregated half a million dollars—all in stocks and bonds, except a little place down on the Eastern Shore which he took, some years before he died, in payment of a debt due him. Since my mother's demise my father had led the life of quiet and retirement in a small city. I went through college, was given a year abroad, took the law course at Harvard, and settled down to the business of getting a practice. Then the pater died, suddenly. Five hundred thousand was a lot of money in that town. Too much to settle there, I thought. I abandoned the law, and came to Northumberland. The governor had been a non-resident member of the Northumberland Club, which made it easy for me to join. I soon found, however, that what had seemed ample wealth in the old town, did not much more than make ends meet, here—provided I kept up my end. I was about the poorest one in the set I affected, so, naturally, I went into the stock market. Royster was the particular broker of the gang and the first year I did very well.—You think it was intended?" (As Macloud smiled.) "Well, I don't doubt now you're right. The next year I began to lose. Then Royster put me into that Company of his down in Virginia—the Virginia Improvement Company, you know. He took me down, in a special car, showed me how much he himself had in it, how much would be got out of it, offered to let me in on the ground floor, and made it look so rosy, withal, that I succumbed. Two hundred thousand was buried there. An equal amount I had lent them, at six per cent., shortly after I came to Northumberland—selling the securities that yielded only four per cent. to do it. That accounts for four hundred thousand—gone up the flume. Eighty thousand I lost in stocks. The remainder, about twenty thousand, I still have. By some error I can't account for, they did not get away with it, too.—Such is the tale of a foolish man," he ended.

"Will you make any effort to have Royster prosecuted?" Macloud asked.

"No—I've been pretty much of a baby, but I'm not going to cry over milk that's spilt."

"It's not all spilt—some of it will be recovered."

"My dear Macloud, there won't be enough money recovered to buy me cigarettes for one evening. Royster has hypothecated and rehypothecated securities until no man can trace his own, even if it would help him to do so. You said it would *likely* prove a disgraceful failure. I am absolutely sure of it."

Macloud beat a tattoo on the window-ledge.

"What do you think of doing?" he said—"or haven't you got to it, yet—or don't you care to tell?"

"I've got to it," replied Croyden; "and I don't care to tell—anyone but you, Colin. I can't stay here——"

"Not on twelve hundred a year, certainly—unless you spend the little principal you have left, and, then, drop off for good."

"Which would be playing the baby act, sure enough."

Macloud nodded.

"It would," he said; "but, sometimes, men don't look at it that way. They cannot face the loss of caste. They prefer to drop overboard by *accident*."

"There isn't going to be any dropping overboard by accident in mine," replied Croyden. "What I've decided to do is this: I shall disappear. I have no debts, thank God! so no one will care to take the trouble to search for me. I shall go down to Hampton, to the little property that was left me on the Eastern Shore, there to mark time, either until I can endure it, or until I can pick out some other abode. I've a bunch of expensive habits to get rid of quickly, and the best place for that, it seems to me, is a small town where they are impossible, as well as unnecessary."

"Ever lived in a small town?" Macloud inquired.

"None smaller than my old home. I suppose it will be very stupid, after the life here, but beggars can't be choosers."

"I'm not so sure it will be very stupid," said Macloud. "It depends on how much you liked this froth and try, we have here. The want to and can't—the aping the ways and manners of those who have had wealth for generations, and are well-born, beside. Look at them!" with a fling of his arm, that embraced the Club-house and its environs.—"One generation old in wealth, one generation old in family, and about six months old, some of them scarcely that, in breeding. There are a few families which belong by right of birth— and, thank God! they show it. But they are shouldered aside by the others, and don't make much of a show. The climbers hate them, but are too much awed by their lineage to crowd them out, entirely. A nice lot of aristocrats! The majority of them are puddlers of the iron mills, and the peasants of Europe, come over so recently the soil is still clinging to their clothes. Down on the Eastern Shore you will find it very different. They ask one, who you *are*, never how much money you have. Their aristocracy is one of birth and culture. You may be reduced to manual labor for a livelihood, but you belong just the same. You have had a sample of the money-changers and their heartless methods—and it has left a bitter taste in your mouth. I think you will welcome the change. It will be a new life, and, in a measure, a quiet life, but there are compensations to one to whom life holds more than garish living and ostentatious show."

"You know the people of the Eastern Shore?" asked Croyden.

"No!—but I know the people of the Western Shore, and they come from the same stock—and it's good stock, mighty good stock! Moreover, you are not burying yourself so deep—Baltimore is just across the Bay, and Philadelphia and New York are but a few hours distant—less distant than this place is, indeed."

"I looked up the time-tables!" laughed Croyden. "My present knowledge of Hampton is limited to the means and methods of getting away."

"And getting to it," appended Macloud. "When do you go?"

"To-morrow night."

"Hum—rather sudden, isn't it?"

"I've seen it coming for a month, so I've had time to pay my small accounts, arrange my few affairs, and be prepared to flit on a moment's notice. I should have gone a week ago, but I indulged myself with a few more days of the old life. Now, I'm off to-morrow night."

"Shall you go direct to Hampton?"

"Direct to Hampton, via New York," said Croyden. "There probably won't anyone care enough even to inquire for me, but I'm not taking the chance."

Macloud watched him with careful scrutiny. Was it serious or was it assumed? Had this seemingly sudden resolve only the failure of Royster & Axtell behind it, or was there a woman there, as well? Was Elaine Cavendish the real reason? There could be no doubt of Croyden's devotion to her—and her more than passing regard for him. Was it because he could not, or because he would not—or both? Croyden was practically penniless—she was an only child, rich in her own right, and more than rich in prospect——

"Will you dine with me, this evening?" asked Macloud.

"Sorry, old man, but I'm due at the Cavendishes'—just a pick-up by telephone. I shall see you, again, shan't I?"

"I reckon so," was the answer. "I'm down here for the night. Have breakfast with me in the morning—if I'm not too early a bird, at eight o'clock."

"Good! for two on the side piazza!" exclaimed Croyden.

"I'll speak to François," said Macloud, arising. "So long."

Croyden slowly straightened his tie and drew on his coat.

"Macloud is a square chap," he reflected. "I've had a lot of so-called friends, here, but he is the only one who still rings true. I may imagine it, but I'm sure the rest are beginning to shy off. Well, I shan't bother them much longer—they can prepare for a new victim."

7

He picked up his hat and went downstairs, making his way out by the front entrance, so as to miss the crowd in the grill-room. He did not want the trouble of speaking or of being spoken to. He saw Macloud, as he passed—out on the piazza beyond the porte-cochere, and he waved his hand to him. Then he signalled the car, that had been sent from Cavencliffe for him, and drove off to the Cavendishes.

II

The Cavendishes were of those who (to quote Macloud's words) "did belong and, thank God, showed it." Henry Cavendish had married Josephine Marquand in the days before there were any idle-rich in Northumberland, and when the only leisure class were in jail. Now, when the idea, that it was respectable not to work, was in the ascendency, he still went to his office with unfailing regularity—and the fact that the Tuscarora Trust Company paid sixty per cent. on its capital stock, and sold in the market (when you could get it) at three thousand dollars a share, was due to his ability and shrewd financiering as president. It was because he refused to give up the active management even temporarily, that they had built their summer home on the Heights, where there was plenty of pure air, unmixed with the smoke of the mills and trains, and with the Club near enough to give them its life and gayety when they wished.

The original Cavendish and the original Marquand had come to Northumberland, as officers, with Colonel Harmer and his detachment of Regulars, at the close of the Revolution, had seen the possibilities of the place, and, after a time, had resigned and settled down to business. Having brought means with them from Philadelphia, they quickly accumulated more, buying up vast tracts of Depreciation lands and numerous In-lots and Out-lots in the original plan of the town. These had never been sold, and hence it was, that, by the natural rise in value from a straggling forest to a great and thriving city, the Cavendish and the Marquand estates were enormously valuable. And hence, also, the fact that Elaine Cavendish's grandparents, on both sides of the house, were able to leave her a goodly fortune, absolutely, and yet not disturb the natural descent of the bulk of their possessions.

Having had wealth for generations, the Cavendishes were as natural and unaffected in their use of it, as the majority of their neighbors were tawdry and flashy. They did things because they wanted to do them, not because someone else did them. And they did not do things that others did, and never thought what the others might think.

Because an iron-magnate, with only dollars for ballast, had fifteen bath pools of Sienna marble in his flaunting, gaudy "chateau," and was immediately aped by the rest of the rattle-brained, moved the Cavendishes not at all. Because the same bounder gave a bathing-suit party (with the ocean one hundred and fifty miles away), at which prizes were bestowed on the man and woman who dared wear the least clothes, while the others of the *nouveaux riches* applauded and marvelled at his audacity and originality, simply made the Cavendishes stay away. Because another mushroom millionaire bought books for his library by the foot, had gold mangers and silver stalls for his horses, and adorned himself with diamonds like an Indian Rajah, were no incentives to the Cavendishes to do likewise. They pursued the even tenor of the well-bred way.

Cavencliffe was a great, roomy country-house, in the Colonial style, furnished in chintz and cretonnes, light and airy, with wicker furniture and bird's-eye maple throughout, save in the dining-room, where there was the slenderest of old Hepplewhite. Wide piazzas flanked the house on every side, screened and awninged from the sun and wind and rain. A winding driveway between privet hedges, led up from the main road half a mile away, through a maze of giant forest trees amid which the place was set.

Croyden watched it, thoughtfully, as the car spun up the avenue. He saw the group on the piazza, the waiting man-servant, the fling upward of a hand in greeting by a white robed figure. And he sighed.

"My last welcome to Cavencliffe!" he muttered. "It's a bully place, and a bully girl—and, I think, I had a chance, if I hadn't been such a fool."

Elaine Cavendish came forward a little way to greet him. And Croyden sighed, again, as—with the grace he had learned as a child from his South Carolina mother, he bent for an instant over her hand. He had never known how handsome she was, until this visit—and he had come to say good-bye!

"You were good to come," she said.

"It was good of you to ask me," he replied.

The words were trite, but there was a note of intenseness in his tones that made her look sharply at him—then, away, as a trace of color came faintly to her cheek.

"You know the others," she said, perfunctorily.

And Croyden smiled in answer, and greeted the rest of the guests.

There were but six of them: Mrs. Chichester, a young matron, of less than thirty, whose husband was down in Panama explaining some contract to the Government Engineers; Nancy Wellesly, a rather petite blonde, who was beginning to care for her complexion and other people's reputations, but was a square girl, just the same; and Charlotte Brundage, a pink and white beauty, but the crack tennis and golf player of her sex at the Club and a thorough good sport, besides.

The men were: Harold Hungerford, who was harmlessly negative and inoffensively polite; Roderick Colloden, who, after Macloud, was the most popular man in the set, a tall, red haired chap, who always seemed genuinely glad to meet anyone in any place, and whose handshake gave emphasis to it. He had not a particularly good memory for faces, and the story is still current in the Club of how, when he had been presented to a newcomer four times in one week, and had always told him how glad he was to meet him, the man lost patience and blurted out, that he was damn glad to know it, but, if Colloden would recognize him the next time they met, he would be more apt to believe it. The remaining member of the party was Montecute Mattison. He was a small man, with peevishly pinched features, that wore an incipient smirk when in repose, and a hyena snarl when in action. He had no friends and no intimates. He was the sort who played dirty golf in a match: deliberately moving on the green, casting his shadow across the hole, talking when his opponent was about to drive, and anything else to disconcert. In fact, he was a dirty player in any game—because it was natural. He would not have been tolerated a moment, even at the Heights, if he had not been Warwick Mattison's son, and the heir to his millions. He never made an honest dollar in his life, and could not, if he tried, but he was Assistant-Treasurer of his father's company, did an hour's work every day signing the checks, and drew fifteen thousand a year for it. A man's constant inclination was to smash him in the face—and the only reason he escaped was because it would have been like beating a child. One man had, when Mattison was more than ordinarily offensive, laid him across his knee, and, in full sight of the Club-house, administered a good old-fashioned spanking with a golf club. Him Montecute thereafter let alone. The others did not take the trouble, however. They simply shrugged their shoulders, and swore at him freely and to his face.

At present, he was playing the devoted to Miss Brundage and hence his inclusion in the party. She cared nothing for him, but his money was a thing to be considered—having very little of her own—and she was doing her best to overcome her repugnance sufficiently to place him among the eligibles.

Mattison got through the dinner without any exhibition of ill nature, but, when the women retired, it came promptly to the fore.

The talk had turned on the subject of the Club Horse Show. It was scheduled for the following month, and was quite the event of the Autumn, in both a social and an equine sense. The women showed their gowns and hosiery, the men their horses and equipment, and how appropriately they could rig themselves out—while the general herd stood around the ring gaping and envious.

Presently, there came a momentary lull in the conversation and Mattison remarked:

"I see Royster & Axtell went up to-day. I reckon," with an insinuating laugh, "there will be some entries withdrawn."

"Men or horses?" asked Hungerford.

"Both—and men who haven't horses, as well," with a sneering glance at Croyden.

"Why, bless me! he's looking at you, Geoffrey!" Hungerford exclaimed.

"I am not responsible for the direction of Mr. Mattison's eyes," Croyden answered with assumed good nature.

Mattison smiled, maliciously.

"Is it so bad as that?" he queried. "I knew, of course, you were hit, but I hoped it was only for a small amount."

"Shut up, Mattison!" exclaimed Colloden. "If you haven't any appreciation of propriety, you can at least keep quiet."

"Oh, I don't know——"

"Don't you?" said Colloden, quietly, reaching across and grasping him by the collar. "Think again,—*and think quickly!*"

A sickly grin, half of surprise and half of anger, overspread Mattison's face.

"Can't you take a little pleasantry?" he asked.

"We don't like your pleasantries any more than we like you, and that is not at all. Take my advice and mend your tongue." He shook him, much as a terrier does a rat, and jammed him back into his chair. "Now, either be good or go home," he admonished.

Mattison was weak with anger—so angry, indeed, that he was helpless either to stir or to make a sound. The others ignored him—and, when he was a little recovered, he got up and went slowly from the room.

"It wasn't a particularly well bred thing to do," observed Colloden, "but just the same it was mighty pleasant. If it were not for the law, I'd have broken his neck."

"He isn't worth the exertion, Roderick," Croyden remarked. "But I'm obliged, old man. I enjoyed it."

When they rejoined the ladies on the piazza, a little later, Mattison had gone.

After a while, the others went off in their motors, leaving Croyden alone with

Miss Cavendish. Hungerford had offered to drop him at the Club, but he had declined. He would enjoy himself a little longer—would give himself the satisfaction of another hour with her, before he passed into outer darkness.

He had gone along in his easy, bachelor way, without a serious thought for any woman, until six months ago. Then, Elaine Cavendish came home, after three years spent in out-of-the-way corners of the globe, and, straightway, bound him to her chariot wheels.

At least, so the women said—who make it their particular business to observe —and they never make mistakes. They can tell when one is preparing to fall in love, long before he knows himself. Indeed, there have been many men drawn into matrimony, against their own express inclination, merely by the accumulation of initiative engendered by impertinent meddlers. They want none of it, they even fight desperately against it, but, in the end, they succumb.

And Geoffrey Croyden would have eventually succumbed, of his own desires, however, had Elaine Cavendish been less wealthy, and had his affairs been more at ease. Now, he thanked high Heaven he had not offered himself. She might have accepted him; and think of all the heart-burnings and pain that would now ensue, before he went out of her life!

"What were you men doing to Montecute Mattison?" she asked presently. "He appeared perfectly furious when he came out, and he went off without a word to anyone—even Charlotte Brundage was ignored."

"He and Colloden had a little difficulty—and Mattison left us," Croyden answered. "Didn't he stop to say good-night?"

She shook her head. "He called something as he drove off—but I think he was swearing at his man."

"He needed something to swear at, I fancy!" Croyden laughed.

"What did Roderick do?" she asked.

"Took him by the collar and shook him—and told him either to go home or be quiet."

"And he went home—I see."

"Yes—when he had recovered himself sufficiently. I thought, at first, his anger was going to choke him."

"Imagine big, good-natured Roderick stirred sufficiently to lay hands on any one!" she laughed.

"But imagine him *when* stirred," he said.

13

"I hadn't thought of him in that way," she said, slowly—"Ough!" with a little shiver, "it must have been terrifying—what had Mattison done to him?"

"Nothing—Mattison is too much of a coward ever to *do* anything."

"What had he said, then?"

"Oh, some brutality about one of Colloden's friends, I think," Croyden evaded. "I didn't quite hear it—and we didn't discuss it afterward."

"I'm told he is a scurrilous little beast, with the men," she commented; "but, I must say, he is always polite to me, and reasonably charitable. Indeed, to-night is the only deliberately bad manners he has ever exhibited."

"He knows the men won't hurt him," said Croyden, "whereas the women, if he showed his ill nature to them, would promptly ostracize him. He is a canny bounder, all right." He made a gesture of repugnance. "We have had enough of Mattison—let us find something more interesting—yourself, for instance."

"Or yourself!" she smiled. "Or, better still, neither. Which reminds me—Miss Southard is coming to-morrow; you will be over, of course?"

"I'm going East to-morrow night," he said. "I'm sorry."

"But she is to stay two weeks—you will be back before she leaves, won't you?"

"I fear not—I may go on to London."

"Before you return here?" "Yes—

before I return here."

"Isn't this London idea rather sudden?" she asked.

"I've been anticipating it for some time," sending a cloud of cigarette smoke before his face. "But it grew imminent only to-day."

When the smoke faded, her eyes were looking questioningly into his. There was something in his words that did not ring quite true. It was too sudden to be genuine, too unexpected. It struck her as vague and insincere. Yet there was no occasion to mistrust—it was common enough for men to be called suddenly to England on business.——

"When do you expect to return?" she asked.

"I do not know," he said, reading something that was in her mind. "If I must go, the business which takes me will also fix my return."

A servant approached.

"What is it, Hudson?" she asked.

"The telephone, Miss Cavendish. Pride's Crossing wishes to talk with you."

Croyden arose—it was better to make the farewell brief—and accompanied her to the doorway.

"Good-bye," he said, simply.

"You must go?" she asked.

"Yes—there are some things that must be done to-night."

She gave him another look.

"Good-bye, then—and *bon voyage*," she said, extending her hand.

He took it—hesitated just an instant—lifted it to his lips—and, then, without a word, swung around and went out into the night.

The next day—at noon—when, her breakfast finished, she came down stairs, a scare headline in the morning's paper, lying in the hall, met her eyes.

SUICIDE!

Royster Found Dead in His Bath-room!
The Penalty of Bankruptcy!

ROYSTER & AXTELL FAIL!

Many Prominent Persons Among the Creditors.

She seized the paper, and nervously ran her eyes down the columns until they reached the list of those involved.——

Yes! Croyden's name was among them! That was what had taken him away!

And Croyden read it, too, as he sped Eastward toward the unknown life.

III

Croyden left Northumberland in the morning—and his economy began with the ride East: he went on Day Express instead of on the Limited, thereby saving the extra fare. At Philadelphia he sent his baggage to the Bellevue-Stratford; later in the evening, he had it returned to the station, and checked it, himself, to Hampton—to avoid the possibility of being followed by means of his luggage.

He did not imagine that any one would go to the trouble to trace him, but he was not taking any chances. He wanted to cut himself away, utterly, from his former life, to be free of everyone he had ever known. It was not likely he would be missed.

Some one would say: "I haven't seen Croyden lately," would be answered: "I think he went abroad suddenly—about the time of the Royster & Axtell failure," and, with that, he would pass out of notice. If he were to return, any time within the next five years, he would be met by a languid: "Been away, somewhere, haven't you? I thought I hadn't noticed you around the Club, lately."—And that would be the extent of it.

One is not missed in a big town. His going and his coming are not watched. There is no time to bother with another's affairs. Everyone has enough to do to look after his own. The curiosity about one's neighbors—what he wears, what he eats, what he does, every item in his daily life—that is developed by idleness, thrives in littleness, and grows to perfection in scandal and innuendo —belongs solely to the small town. If one comes down street with a grip— instantly: So and so is "going away"—speculation as to why?—where?— what? One puts on a new suit, it is observed and noted.—A pair of new shoes, ditto.—A new necktie, ditto. Every particular of his life is public property, is inspected for a motive, and, if a motive cannot be discovered, one is supplied —usually mean and little, the latter unctuously preferred.

All this Croyden was yet to learn, however.

He took the night's express on the N. Y., P. & N., whence, at Hampton Junction, he transferred to a branch line. For twenty miles the train seemed to crawl along, burrowing into the sand hills and out again into sand, and in and out again, until, at length, with much whistling and escaping steam, they wheezed into the station and stopped.

There were a dozen white men, with slouch hats and nondescript clothing,

16

standing aimlessly around, a few score of negroes, and a couple of antique carriages with horses to match. The white men looked at the new arrival, listlessly, and the negroes with no interest at all—save the two who were porters for the rival hotels. They both made for Croyden and endeavored to take his grip.

He waved them away.

"I don't want your hotel, boys," he said. "But if you can tell me where Clarendon is, I will be obliged."

"Cla'endon! seh? yass, seh," said one, "right out at de een' o' de village, seh —dis street tek's yo dyar, seh, sho nuf."

"Which end of the village?" Croyden asked.

"Dis een', seh, de fust house beyon' Majah Bo'den's, seh."

"How many blocks is it?"

"Blocks, seh!" said the negro. "'Tain't no blocks—it's jest de fust place beyon' Majah Bo'den's."

Croyden laughed. "Here," he said, "you take my bag out to Clarendon—I'll walk till I find it."

"Yass, seh! yass, seh! I'll do it, seh! but yo bettah ride, seh!"

"No!" said Croyden, looking at the vehicle. "It's safer to walk."

He tossed the negro a quarter and turned away.

"Thankee, seh, thankee, seh, I'll brings it right out, seh."

Croyden went slowly down the street, while the crowd stared after him, and the shops emptied their loafers to join them in the staring. He was a strange man—and a well-dressed man—and they all were curious.

Presently, the shops were replaced by dwellings of the humbler sort, then they, in turn, by more pretentious residences—with here and there a new one of the Queen Anne type. Croyden did not need the information, later vouchsafed, that they belong to *new* people. It was as unmistakable as the houses themselves.

About a mile from the station, he passed a place built of English brick, covered on the sides by vines, and shaded by huge trees. It stood well back from the street and had about it an air of aristocracy and exclusiveness.

"I wonder if this is the Bordens'?" said Croyden looking about him for some one to ask—"Ah!"

Down the path from the house was coming a young woman. He slowed down, so as to allow her to reach the entrance gates ahead of him. She was pretty, he saw, as she neared—very pretty!—positively beautiful! dark hair and——

He took off his hat.

"I beg your pardon!" he said. "Is this Mr. Borden's?"

"Yes—this is Major Borden's," she answered, with a deliciously soft intonation, which instantly stirred Croyden's Southern blood.

"Then Clarendon is the next place, is it not?"

She gave him the quickest glance of interest, as she replied in the affirmative.

"Colonel Duval is dead, however," she added—"a caretaker is the only person there, now."

"So I understood." There was no excuse for detaining her longer. "Thank you, very much!" he ended, bowed slightly, and went on.

It is ill bred and rude to stare back at a woman, but, if ever Croyden had been tempted, it was now. He heard her footsteps growing fainter in the distance, as he continued slowly on his way. Something behind him seemed to twitch at his head, and his neck was positively stiff with the exertion necessary to keep it straight to the fore.

He wanted another look at that charming figure, with the mass of blue black hair above it, and the slender silken ankles and slim tan-shod feet below. He remembered that her eyes were blue, and that they met him through long lashes, in a languidly alluring glance; that she was fair; and that her mouth was generous, with lips full but delicate—a face, withal, that clung in his memory, and that he proposed to see again—and soon.

He walked on, so intent on his visual image, he did not notice that the Borden place was behind him now, and he was passing the avenue that led into Clarendon.

"Yass, seh! hyar yo is, marster!—hyar's Clarendon," called the negro, hastening up behind him with his bag.

Croyden turned into the walk—the black followed.

"Cun'l Duval's done been daid dis many a day, seh," he said. "Folks sez ez how it's owned by some city fellah, now. Mebbe yo knows 'im, seh?"

Croyden did not answer, he was looking at the place—and the negro, with an inquisitively curious eye, relapsed into silence.

The house was very similar to the Bordens'—unpretentious, except for the respectability that goes with apparent age, vine clad and tree shaded. It was of generous proportions, without being large—with a central hall, and rooms on either side, that rose to two stories, and was topped by a pitch-roof. There were no piazzas at front or side, just a small stoop at the doorway, from which paths branched around to the rear.

"I done 'speck, seh, yo go roun' to de back," said the negro, as Croyden put his foot on the step. "Ole Mose 'im live dyar. I'll bring 'im heah, ef yo wait, seh."

"Who is old Mose—the caretaker?" said Croyden.

The place was looked after by a real estate man of the village, and neither his father nor he had bothered to do more than meet the accounts for funds. The former had preferred to let it remain unoccupied, so as to have it ready for instant use, if he so wished, and Croyden had done the same.

"He! Mose he's Cun'l Duval's body-survent, seh. Him an' Jos'phine— Jos'phine he wif', seh—dey looks arfter de place sence de ole Cun'l died."

Croyden nodded. "I'll go back."

They followed the right hand path, which seemed to be more used than its fellow. The servants' quarters were disclosed at the far end of the lot.

Before the tidiest of them, an old negro was sitting on a stool, dreaming in the sun. At Croyden's appearance, he got up hastily, and came forward—gray-haired, and bent.

"Survent, seh!" he said, with the remains of what once must have been a wonderfully graceful bow, and taking in the stranger's attire with a single glance. "I'se ole Mose. Cun'l Duval's boy—seh, an' I looks arfter de place, now. De Cun'l he's daid, yo knows, seh. What can I do fur yo, seh?"

"I'm Mr. Croyden," said Geoffrey.

"Yass, seh! yass, seh!" the darky answered, inquiringly.

It was evident the name conveyed no meaning to him.

"I'm the new owner, you know—since Colonel Duval died," Croyden explained.

"Hi! yo is!" old Mose exclaimed, with another bow. "Well, praise de Lawd! I sees yo befo' I dies. So yo's de new marster, is yo? I'm pow'ful glad yo's come, seh! pow'ful glad. What mout yo name be, seh?"

"Croyden!" replied Geoffrey. "Now, Moses, will you open the house and let me in?"

"Yo seen Marster Dick?" asked the darky.

"You mean the agent? No! Why do you ask?"

"Coz why, seh—I'm beggin' yo pa'den, seh, but Marster Dick sez, sez he, 'Don' nuvver lets no buddy in de house, widout a writin' from me.' I ain' doubtin' yo, seh, 'deed I ain', but I ruther hed de writin'."

"You're perfectly right," Croyden answered. "Here, boy!—do you know Mr. Dick? Well, go down and tell him that Mr. Croyden is at Clarendon, and ask him to come out at once. Or, stay, I'll give you a note to him."

He took a card from his pocketbook, wrote a few lines on it, and gave it to the negro.

"Yass, seh! Yass, seh!" said the porter, and, dropping the grip where he stood, he vanished.

Old Mose dusted the stool with his sleeve, and proffered it.

"Set down, seh!" with another bow. "Josh won' be long."

Croyden shook his head.

"I'll lie here," he answered, stretching himself out on the grass. "You were Colonel Duval's body-servant, you say."

"Yass, seh! from de time I wuz so 'igh. I don' 'member when I warn' he body-survent. I follows 'im all th'oo de war, seh, an' I wus wid 'im when he died." Tears were in the darky's eyes. "Hit's purty nigh time ole Mose gwine too."

"And when he died, you stayed and looked after the old place. That was the right thing to do," said Croyden. "Didn't Colonel Duval have any children?"

"No, seh. De Cun'l nuvver married, cuz Miss Penelope——"

He caught himself. "I toles yo 'bout hit some time, seh, mebbe!" he ended cautiously—talking about family matters with strangers was not to be considered.

"I should like to hear some time," said Croyden, not seeming to notice the darky's reticence. "When did the Colonel die?"

"Eight years ago cum corn plantin' time, seh. He jes' wen' right off quick like, when de mis'ry hit 'im in de chist—numonya, de doctors call'd it. De Cun'l guv de place to a No'thern gent'man, whar was he 'ticular frien', and I done stay on an' look arfter hit. He nuvver been heah. Hi! listen to dis nigger! yo's de gent'mans, mebbe."

"I am his son," said Croyden, amused.

"An' yo owns Cla'endon, now, seh? What yo goin' to do wid it?"

"I'm going to live here. Don't you want to look after me?"

"Goin' to live heah!—yo means it, seh?" the darky asked, in great amazement.

Croyden nodded. "Provided you will stay with me—and if you can find me a cook. Who cooks your meals?"

"Lawd, seh! find yo a cook. Didn' Jos'phine cook fur de Cun'l all he life—Jos'phine, she my wife, seh—she jest gone nex' do', 'bout some'n." He got up—"I calls her, seh."

Croyden stopped him.

"Never mind," he said; "she will be back, presently, and there is ample time. Any one live in these other cabins?"

"No, seh! we's all wha' left. De udder niggers done gone 'way, sence de Cun'l died, coz deah war nothin' fur dem to do no mo', an' no buddy to pays dem. —Dyar is Jos'phine, now, sir, she be hear torectly. An' heah comes Marster Dick, hisself."

Croyden arose and went toward the front of the house to meet him.

The agent was an elderly man; he wore a black broadcloth suit, shiny at the elbows and shoulder blades, a stiff white shirt, a wide roomy collar, bound around by a black string tie, and a broad-brimmed drab-felt hat. His greeting was as to one he had known all his life.

"How do you do, Mr. Croyden!" he exclaimed. "I'm delighted to make your acquaintance, sir." He drew out a key and opened the front door. "Welcome to Clarendon, sir, welcome! Let us hope you will like it enough to spend a little time here, occasionally."

"I'm sure I too hope so," returned Croyden; "for I am thinking of making it my home."

"Good! Good! It's an ideal place!" exclaimed the agent. "It's convenient to Baltimore; and Philadelphia, and New York, and Washington aren't very far away. Exactly what the city people who can afford it, are doing now,—making their homes in the country. Hampton's a town, but it's country to you, sir, when compared to Northumberland—open the shutters, Mose, so we can see…. This is the library, with the dining-room behind it, sir—and on the other side of the hall is the drawing-room. Open it, Mose, we will be over there presently. You see, sir, it is just as Colonel Duval left it. Your father gave instructions that nothing should be changed. He was a great friend of the Colonel, was he not, sir?"

"I believe he was," said Croyden. "They met at the White Sulphur, where both spent their summers—many years before the Colonel died."

"There, hangs the Colonel's sword—he carried it through the war, sir—and his pistols—and his silk-sash, and here, in the corner, is one of his regimental guidons—and here his portrait in uniform—handsome man, wasn't he? And as gallant and good as he was handsome. Maryland lost a brave son, when he died, sir."

"He looks the soldier," Croyden remarked.

"And he was one, sir—none better rode behind Jeb Stuart—and never far behind, sir, never far behind!"

"He was in the cavalry?"

"Yes, sir. Seventh Maryland Cavalry—he commanded it during the last two years of the war—went in a lieutenant and came out its colonel. A fine record, sir, a fine record! Pity it is, he had none to leave it to!—he was the last of his line, you know, the last of the line—not even a distant cousin to inherit."

Croyden looked up at the tall, slender man in Confederate gray, with clean-cut aristocratic features, wavy hair, and long, drooping mustache. What a figure he must have been at the head of his command, or leading a charge across the level, while the guns of the Federals belched smoke, and flame and leaden death.

"They offered him a brigade," the agent was saying, "but he declined it, preferring to remain with his regiment."

"What did he do when the war was over?" Croyden asked.

"Came home, sir, and resumed his law practice. Like his great leader, he accepted the decision as final. He didn't spend the balance of his life living in the past."

"And why did he never marry? Surely, such a man" (with a wave of his hand toward the portrait) "could have picked almost where he chose!"

"No one ever just knew, sir—it had to do with Miss Borden,—the sister of Major Borden, sir, who lives on the next place. They were sweethearts once, but something or somebody came between them—and thereafter, the Colonel never seemed to think of love. Perhaps, old Mose knows it, and if he comes to like you, sir, he may tell you the story. You understand, sir, that Colonel Duval is Mose's old master, and that every one stands or falls, in his opinion, according as they measure up to him. I hope you intend to keep him, sir—he has been a faithful caretaker, and there is still good service in him—and his wife was the Colonel's cook, so she must have been competent. She would never cook for anyone, after he died. She thought she belonged to Clarendon, sort of went with the place, you understand. Just stayed and helped Mose take care of it. She doubtless will resume charge of the kitchen again, without a word. It's the way of the old negroes, sir. The young ones are pretty worthless —they've got impudent, and independent and won't work, except when they're out of money. Excuse me, I ramble on——"

"I'm much interested," said Croyden; "as I expect to live here, I must learn the ways of the people."

"Well, let Mose boss the niggers for you, at first; he understands them, he'll make them stand around. Come over to the drawing-room, sir, I want you to see the furniture, and the family portraits.... There, sir, is a set of twelve genuine Hepplewhite chairs—no doubt about it, for the invoice is among the Colonel's papers. I don't know much about such things, but a man was through here, about a year ago, and, would you believe it, when he saw the original invoice and looked at the chairs, he offered me two thousand dollars for them. Of course, as I had been directed by your father to keep everything as the Colonel had it, I just laughed at him. You see, sir, they have the three feathers, and are beautifully carved, otherwise. And, here, is a lowboy, with the shell and the fluted columns, and the cabriole legs, carved on the knees, and the claw and ball feet. He offered two hundred dollars for it. And this sofa, with the lion's claw and the eagle's wing, he wanted to buy it, too. In fact, sir, he wanted to buy about everything in the house—including the portraits. There are two by Peale and one by Stuart—here are the Peales, sir— the lady in white, and the young officer in Continental uniform; and this is the Stuart—the gentleman in knee breeches and velvet coat. I think he is the same as the one in uniform, only later in life. They are the Colonel's grandparents, sir: Major Daniel Duval, of the Tenth Maryland Line, and his wife; she was a Miss Paca—you know the family, of course, sir. The Major's commission, sir, hangs in the hall, between the Colonel's own and his father's—he was an officer in the Mexican war, sir. It was a fighting family, sir, a fighting family —and a gentle one as well. 'The bravest are the tenderest, the loving are the daring.'"

There was enough of the South Carolinian of the Lowlands in Croyden, to appreciate the Past and to honor it. He might not know much concerning Hepplewhite nor the beauty of his lines and carving, and he might be wofully ignorant of his own ancestors, having been bred in a State far removed from their nativity, for he had never given a thought to the old things, whether of furniture or of forebears—they were of the inanimate; his world had to do only with the living and what was incidental to it. The Eternal Now was the Fetich and the God of Northumberland, all it knew and all it lived for—and he, with every one else, had worshipped at its shrine.

It was different here, it seemed! and the spirit of his long dead mother, with her heritage of aristocratic lineage, called to him, stirring him strangely, and his appreciation, that was sleeping and not dead, came slowly back to life. The men in buff-and-blue, in small-clothes, in gray, the old commissions, the savour of the past that clung around them, were working their due. For no man of culture and refinement—nay, indeed, if he have but their veneer—can stand in the presence of an honorable past, of ancestors distinguished and respected, whether they be his or another's, and be unmoved.

"And you say there are none to inherit all these things?" Croyden exclaimed. "Didn't the original Duval leave children?"

The agent shook his head. "There was but one son to each generation, sir— and with the Colonel there was none."

"Then, having succeeded to them by right of purchase, and with no better right outstanding, it falls to me to see that they are not shamed by the new owner. Their portraits shall remain undisturbed either by collectors or by myself. Moreover, I'll look up my own ancestors. I've got some, down in South Carolina and up in Massachusetts, and if their portraits be in existence, I'll add reproductions to keep the Duvals company. Ancestors by inheritance and ancestors by purchase. The two of them ought to keep me straight, don't you think?" he said, with a smile.

IV

Croyden, with Dick as guide and old Mose as forerunner and shutter-opener, went through the house, even unto the garret.

As in the downstairs, he found it immaculate. Josephine had kept everything as though the Colonel himself were in presence. The bed linen, the coverlids, the quilts, the blankets were packed in trunks, the table-linen and china in drawers and closets. None of them was new—practically the entire furnishing antedated 1830, and much of them 1800—except that, here and there, a few old rugs of oriental weaves, relieved the bareness of the hardwood floors.

The one concession to modernism was a bath-room, but its tin tub and painted iron wash-stand, with the plumbing concealed by wainscoting, proclaimed it, alas, of relatively ancient date. And, for a moment, Croyden contrasted it with the shower, the porcelain, and the tile, of his Northumberland quarters, and shivered, ever so slightly. It would be the hardest to get used to, he thought. As yet, he did not know the isolation of the long, interminably long, winter evenings, with absolutely nothing to do and no place to go—and no one who could understand.

At length, when they were ready to retrace their steps to the lower floor, old Mose had disappeared.

"Gone to tell his wife that the new master has come," said Dick. "Let us go out to the kitchen."

And there they found her—bustling around, making the fire, her head tied up in a bandana, her sleeves rolled to the shoulders. She turned, as they entered, and dropped them an old-fashioned curtsy.

"Josephine!" said Dick, "here is Mr. Croyden, the new master. Can you cook for him, as well as you did for Colonel Duval?"

"Survent, marster," she said to Croyden, with another curtsy—then, to the agent, "Kin I cooks, Marster Dick! Kin I cooks? Sut'n'y, I kin. Don' yo t'inks dis nigger's forgot—jest yo waits, Marster Croyden, I shows yo, seh, sho' nuf —jest gives me a little time to get my han' in, seh."

"You won't need much time," Dick commented. "The Colonel considered her very satisfactory, sir, very satisfactory, indeed. And he was a competent judge, sir, a very competent judge."

"Oh, we'll get along," said Croyden, with a smile at Josephine. "If you could please Colonel Duval, you will more than please me."

"Thankee, seh!" she replied, bobbing down again. "I sho' tries, seh."

"Have you had any experience with negro servants?" Dick asked, as they returned to the library.

"No," Croyden responded: "I have always lived at a Club."

"Well, Mose and his wife are of the old times—you can trust them, thoroughly, but there is one thing you'll have to remember, sir: they are nothing but overgrown children, and you'll have to discipline them accordingly. They don't know what it is to be impertinent, sir; they have their faults, but they are always respectful."

"Can I rely on them to do the buying?"

"I think so, sir, the Colonel did, I know. If you wish, I'll send you a list of the various stores, and all you need do is to pay the bills. Is there anything else I can do now, sir?"

"Nothing," said Croyden. "And thank you very much for all you have done."

"How about your baggage—can I send it out? No trouble, sir, I assure you, no trouble. I'll just give your checks to the drayman, as I pass. By the way, sir, you'll want the telephone in, of course. I'll notify the Company at once. And you needn't fear to speak to your neighbors; they will take it as it's meant, sir. The next on the left is Major Borden's, and this, on the right, is Captain Tilghman's, and across the way is Captain Lashiel's, and Captain Carrington's, and the house yonder, with the huge oaks in front, is Major Markoe's."

"Sort of a military settlement," smiled Croyden.

"Yes, sir—some of them earned their title in the war, and some of them in the militia and some just inherited it from their pas. Sort of handed down in the family, sir. The men will call on you, promptly, too. I shouldn't wonder some of them will be over this evening."

Croyden thought instantly of the girl he had seen coming out of the Borden place, and who had directed him to Clarendon.

"Would it be safe to speak to the good-looking girls, too—those who are my neighbors?" he asked, with a sly smile.

"Certainly, sir; if you tell them your name—and don't try to flirt with them," Dick added, with a laugh. "Yonder is one, now—Miss Carrington," nodding toward the far side of the street.

Croyden turned.—It was she! the girl of the blue-black hair and slender silken ankles.

"She's Captain Carrington's granddaughter," Dick went on with the Southerner's love for the definite in genealogy. "Her father and mother both died when she was a little tot, sir, and they—that is, the grandparents, sir— raised her. That's the Carrington place she's turning in at. Ah——"

The girl glanced across and, recognizing Dick (and, it must be admitted, her Clarendon inquirer as well), nodded.

Both men took off their hats. But Croyden noticed that the older man could teach him much in the way it should be done. He did it shortly, sharply, in the city way; Dick, slowly, deferentially, as though it were an especial privilege to uncover to her.

"Miss Carrington is a beauty!" Croyden exclaimed, looking after her. "Are there more like her, in Hampton?"

"I'm too old, sir, to be a competent judge," returned Dick, "but I should say we have several who trot in the same class. I mean, sir——"

"I understand!" laughed Croyden. "It's no disrespect in a Marylander, I take it, when he compares the ladies with his race-horses."

"It's not, sir! At least, that's the way we of the older generation feel; our ladies and our horses run pretty close together. But that spirit is fast disappearing, sir! The younger ones are becoming—commercialized, if you please. It's dollars first, and *then* the ladies, with them—and the horses nowhere. Though I don't say it's not wise. Horses and the war have almost broken us, sir. We lost the dollars, or forgot about them and they lost themselves, whichever way it was, sir. It's right that our sons should start on a new track and run the course in their own way—Yes, sir," suddenly recollecting himself, "Miss Carrington's a pretty girl, and so's Miss Tayloe and Miss Lashiel and a heap more. Indeed, sir, Hampton is famed on the Eastern Sho' for her women. I'll attend to your baggage, and the telephone, sir, and if there is anything else I can do, pray command me. Drop in and see me when you get up town. Good day, sir, good day." And removing his hat with a bow just a little less deferential than the one he had given to Miss Carrington, he proceeded up the street, leisurely and deliberately, as though the world were waiting for him.

"And he is a real estate agent!" reflected Croyden. "The man who, according to our way of thinking, is the acme of hustle and bustle and business, and schemes to trap the unwary. Truly, the Eastern Shore has much to learn—or we have much to unlearn! Well, I have tried the one—and failed. Now, I'm going to try the other. It seems to promise a quiet life, at least."

He turned, to find Moses in the doorway, waiting.

"Marster Croyden," he said, "shall I puts yo satchel an' things in de Cun'l's room, seh?"

Croyden nodded. He did not know which was the Colonel's room, but it was likely to be the best in the house, and, moreover, it was well to follow him wherever he could.

"And see that my luggage is taken there, when the man brings it," he directed —"and tell Josephine to have luncheon at one and dinner at seven."

The darky hesitated.

"De Cun'l hed dinner in de middle o' de day, seh," he said, as though Croyden had inadvertently erred.

And Croyden appreciating the situation, answered:

"Well, you see, Moses, I've been used to the other way and I reckon you will have to change to suit me."

"Yass, seh! yass, seh! I tell Jose. Lunch is de same as supper, I s'pose, seh?"

Croyden had to think a moment.

"Yes," he said, "that will answer—like a light supper."

"There may be an objection, after all, to taking over Colonel Duval's old servants," he reflected. "It may be difficult to persuade them that he is no longer the master. I run the chance of being ruled by a dead man."

Presently his luggage arrived, and he went upstairs to unpack. Moses looked, in wonder, at the wardrobe trunk, with every suit on a separate hanger, the drawers for shirts and linen, the apartments for hats, and collars, and neckties, and the shoes standing neatly in a row below.

"Whar's de use atak'in de things out t'al, Marster Croyden!" he exclaimed.

"So as to put the trunk away."

"Sho'! I mo'nt a kno'd hit. Hit's mons'us strange, seh, whar yo mon't a' kno'd ef yo'd only stop to t'ink. F' instance, I mon't a kno'd yo'd cum back to Clarendon, seh, some day, cuz yo spends yo money on hit. Heh!"

Then a bell tinkled softly from below.

"Dyar's dinner—I means lunch, seh," said Moses. "'Scuse me, seh."

"And I'm ready for it," said Croyden, as he went to the iron wash-stand, and then slowly down stairs to the dining-room.

From some place, Moses had resurrected a white coat, yellow with its ten years' rest, and was waiting to receive him. He drew out Croyden's chair, as only a family servant of the olden times can do it, and bowed him into his place.

The table was set exactly as in Colonel Duval's day, and very prettily set, Croyden thought, with napery spotless, and china that was thin and fine. The latter, if he had but known it, was Lowestoft and had served the Duvals, on that very table, for much more than a hundred years.

There was cold ham, and cold chicken, lettuce with mayonnaise, deviled eggs, preserves, with hot corn bread and tea. When Croyden had about finished a leisurely meal, it suddenly occurred to him that however completely stocked Clarendon was with things of the Past, they did not apply to the larder, and *these* victuals were undoubtedly fresh and particularly good.

"By the way! Moses," he said, "I'm glad you were thoughtful enough to send out and purchase these things," with an indicating motion to the table. "They are very satisfactory."

"Pu'chase!" said the darky, in surprise. "Dese things not pu'chased. No, seh! Dey's borro'd, seh, from Majah Bo'den's, yass, seh!"

"Good God!" Croyden exclaimed. "You don't mean you borrowed my luncheon!"

"Yass, seh! Why not, seh? Jose jes' went ovah an' sez to Cassie—she's de cook, at de Majah's, seh—sez she, Marster Croyden don' cum and warns some'n to eat. An' she got hit, yass, seh!"

"Is it the usual thing, here, to borrow an entire meal from the neighbor's?" asked Croyden.

"Sut'n'y, seh! We borrows anything we needs from the neighbors, an' they does de same wid us."

"Well, I don't want any borrowing by *us*, Moses, please remember," said Croyden, emphatically. "The neighbors can borrow anything we have, and welcome, but we won't claim the favor from them, you understand?"

"Yass, seh!" said the old darky, wonderingly.

Such a situation as one kitchen not borrowing from another was incomprehensible. It had been done by the servants from time immemorial— and, though Croyden might forbid, yet Josephine would continue to do it, just the same—only, less openly.

"And see that everything is returned not later than to-morrow," Croyden continued.

"Yass, seh! I tote's dem back dis minut, seh!——"

"What?"

"Dese things, heah, whar yo didn' eat, seh——"

"Do you mean—Oh, Lord!" exclaimed Croyden.

"Never mind, Moses. I will return them another way. Just forget it."

"Sut'n'y, seh," returned the darky. "Dat's what I wuz gwine do in de fust place."

Croyden laughed. It was pretty hopeless, he saw. The ways they had, were the ways that would hold them. He might protest, and order otherwise, until doomsday, but it would not avail. For them, it was sufficient if Colonel Duval permitted it, or if it were the custom.

"I think I shall let the servants manage me," he thought. "They know the ways, down here, and, besides, it's the line of least resistance."

He went into the library, and, settling himself in a comfortable chair, lit a cigarette…. It was the world turned upside down. Less than twenty-four hours ago it was money and madness, bankruptcy and divorce courts, the automobile pace—the devil's own. Now, it was quiet and gentility, easy-living and refinement. Had he been in Hampton a little longer, he would have added: gossip and tittle-tattle, small-mindedness and silly vanity.

He smoked cigarette after cigarette and dreamed. He wondered what Elaine Cavendish had done last evening—if she had dined at the Club-house, and what gown she had worn, if she had played golf in the afternoon, or tennis, and with whom; he wondered what she would do this evening—wondered if she thought of him more than casually. He shook it off for a moment. Then he wondered again: who had his old quarters at the Heights? He knew a number who would be jumping for them—who had his old table for breakfast? it, too, would be eagerly sought—who would take his place on the tennis and the golf teams?—what Macloud was doing? Fine chap was Macloud! the only man in Northumberland he would trust, the only man in Northumberland, likely, who would care a rap whether he came back or whether he didn't, or who would ever give him a second thought. He wondered if Gaspard, his particular waiter, missed him? yes, he would miss the tips, at least; yes, and the boy who brushed his clothes and drew his bath would miss him, and his caddie, as well. Every one whom he *paid*, would miss him….

He threw away his cigarette and sat up sharply. It was not pleasant thinking.

An old mahogany slant-top escritoire, in the corner by the window, caught his eye. It had a shell, inlaid in maple, in the front, and the parquetry, also, ran around the edges of the drawers and up the sides.

There was one like it in the Cavendish library, he remembered. He went over to it, and, the key being in the lock, drew out pulls and turned back the top. Inside, there was the usual lot of pigeon holes and small drawers, with compartments for deeds and larger papers. All were empty. Either Colonel Duval, in anticipation of death, had cleaned it out, or Moses and Josephine, for their better preservation, had packed the contents away. He was glad of it; he could use it, at least, without ejecting the Colonel.

He closed the lid and had turned away, when the secret drawer, which, sometimes, was in these old desks, occurred to him. He went back and began to search for it.... And, presently, he found it. Under the middle drawer was a sliding panel that rolled back, when he pressed on a carved lion's head ornamentation, and which concealed a hidden recess. In this recess lay a paper.

It was yellow with age, and, when Croyden took it in his fingers, he caught the faint odor of sandal wood. It was brittle in the creases, and threatened to fall apart. So, opening it gently, he spread it on the desk before him. Here is what he read:

"Annapolis, 10 May, 1738.

"Honoured Sir:

"I fear that I am about to Clear for my Last Voyage—the old wounds trouble me, more and more, especially those in my head and chest. I am confined to my bed, and though Doctor Waldron does not say it, I know he thinks I am bound for Davy Jones' locker. So be it—I've lived to a reasonable Age, and had a fair Time in the living. I've done that which isn't according to Laws, either of Man or God—but for the Former, I was not Caught, and for the Latter, I'm willing to chance him in death. When you were last in Annapolis, I intended to mention a Matter to you, but something prevented, I know not what, and you got Away ere I was aware of it. Now, fearing lest I Die before you come again, I will Write it, though it is against the Doctor's orders— which, however, I obey only when it pleases me.

"You are familiar with certain Episodes in my Early Life, spent under the Jolly Roger on the Spanish Main, and you have maintained Silence—for which I shall always be your debtor. You have, moreover, always been my Friend, and for that, I am more than your debtor. It is, therefore, but Mete that you should be my Heir—and I have this day Executed my last Will and Testament, bequeathing to you all my Property and effects. It is left with Mr. Dulany, the Attorney, who wrote it, to be probated in due Season.

31

"But there still remains a goodly portion which, for obvious reasons, may not be so disposed of. I mean my buried Treasure. I buried it in September, 1720, shortly after I came to Annapolis, trusting not to keep so great an Amount in my House. It amounts to about half my Fortune, and Approximates near to Fifty Thousand Pounds, though that may be but a crude Estimate at best, for I am not skilled in the judging of Precious Stones. Where I obtained this wealth, I need not mention, though you can likely guess. And as there is nothing by which it can be identified, you can use it without Hesitation. Subject, however, to one Restriction: As it was not honestly come by (according to the World's estimate, because, forsooth, I only risked my Life in the gathering, instead of pilfering it from my Fellow man in Business, which is the accepted fashion) I ask you not to use it except in an Extremity of Need. If that need does not arise in your Life, you, in turn, may pass this letter on to your heir, and he, in turn, to his heir, and so on, until such Time as the Need may come, and the Restriction be lifted. And now to find the Treasure:—

"Seven hundred and fifty feet—and at right angles to the water line—from the extreme tip of Greenberry Point, below Annapolis, where the Severn runs into the Chesapeake, are four large Beech trees, standing as of the corners of a Square, though not equidistant. Bisect this Square, by two lines drawn from the Corners. At a Point three hundred and thirty feet, North-by-North-East, from where these two lines intersect and at a depth of Six feet, you will come upon an Iron Box. It contains the Treasure. And I wish you (or whoever recovers it) Joy of it!—as much joy with it as I had in the Gathering.

"Lest I die before you come again to Annapolis, I shall leave this letter with Mr. Dulany, to be delivered to you on the First Occasion. I judge him as one who will respect a Dead man's seal. If I see you not again, Farewell. I am, sir, with great respect,

"Y'r humb'l & obed't Serv'nt

"Robert Parmenter.

"To Marmaduke Duval, Esq'r."

Below was written, by another hand:

"The Extremity of Need has not arisen, I pass it on to my son.

"M.D."

And below that, by still another hand:

"Neither has the Need come to me. I pass it to my son.

"D.D."

And below that, by still another hand:

"Nor to me. I pass it to my son.

"M.D."

And below that:

"The Extremity of Need brushed by me so close I heard the rustling of its gown, but I did not dig. I have sufficient for me, and I am the last of my line. I pass it, therefore, to my good friend Hugh Croyden (and, in the event that he predecease me, to his son Geoffrey Croyden), to whom Clarendon will go upon my demise.

"D.D."

Croyden read the last endorsement again; then he smiled, and the smile broadened into an audible laugh.

The heir of a pirate! Well, at least, it promised something to engage him, if time hung heavily on his hands. The Duvals seem to have taken the bequest seriously—so, why not he? And, though the extremity of need seems never to have reached them, it was peculiar that none of the family had inspected the locality and satisfied himself of the accuracy of the description. The extreme tip of Greenberry Point had shifted, a dozen times, likely, in a hundred and ninety years, and the four beech trees had long since disappeared, but there was no note of these facts to aid the search. He must start just where Robert Parmenter had left off: with the letter.

He found an old history of Maryland in the book-case. It contained a map. Annapolis was somewhere on the Western Shore, he knew. He ran his eyes down the Chesapeake. Yes, here it was—with Greenberry Point just across the Severn. So much of the letter was accurate, at least. The rest would bear investigation. Some time soon he would go across, and take a look over the ground. Greenberry Point, for all he knew, might be built up with houses, or blown half a mile inland, or turned into a fort, or anything. It was not likely to have remained the same, as in Parmenter's day; and, yet, if it had changed, why should not the Duvals have remarked it, in making their endorsements.

He put the letter back in the secret compartment, where it had rested for so many years. Evidently, Colonel Duval had forgotten it, in his last brief illness. And Fortune had helped him in the finding. Would it help him to the treasure as well? For with him, the restriction was lifted—the extremity of need was come. Moreover, it was time that the letter should be put to the test.

V

Croyden was sitting before the house, later in the afternoon, when an elderly gentleman, returning leisurely from town, turned in at the Clarendon gates.

"My first caller," thought Croyden, and immediately he arose and went forward to meet him.

"Permit me to present myself, sir," said the newcomer. "I am Charles Carrington."

"I am very glad to meet you, Captain Carrington," said Croyden, taking the proffered hand.

"This is your first visit to Hampton, I believe, sir," the Captain remarked, when they were seated under the trees. "It is not Northumberland, sir; we haven't the push, and the bustle, and the smoke, but we have a pleasant little town, sir, and we're glad to welcome you here. I think you will like it. It's a long time since Clarendon had a tenant, sir. Colonel Duval's been dead nearly ten years now. Your father and he were particular friends, I believe."

Croyden assured him that such was the case.

"Yes, sir, the Colonel often spoke of him to me with great affection. I can't say I was surprised to know that he had made him his heir. He was the last of the Duvals—not even a collateral in the family—there was only one child to a generation, sir."

Manifestly, it was not known in Hampton how Hugh Croyden came to be the Colonel's heir, and, indeed, friendship had prompted the money-loan, without security other than the promise of the ultimate transfer of Clarendon and its contents. And Croyden, respecting the Colonel's wish, evident now, though unexpressed either to his father or himself, resolved to treat the place as a gift, and to suppress the fact that there had been an ample and adequate consideration.

After a short visit, Captain Carrington arose to go.

"Come over and take supper with us, this evening, sir," said he. "I want you to meet Mrs. Carrington and my granddaughter."

"I'll come with pleasure," Croyden answered, thinking of the girl with the blue-black hair and slender ankles.

"It's the house yonder, with the white pillars—at half-after-six, then, sir."

As Croyden approached the Carrington house, he encountered Miss Carrington on the walk.

"We have met before," she said, as he bowed over her hand. "I was your original guide to Clarendon. Have you forgot?"

"Have I forgot?" said Croyden. "Do you think it possible?" looking her in the eyes.

"No, I don't."

"But you wanted to hear me say it?"

"I wanted to know if you could say it," she answered, gayly.

"And how have I succeeded?"

"Admirably!"

"Sufficiently well to pass muster?"

"Muster—for what?" she asked, with a sly smile.

"For enrollment among your victims."

"Shall I put your name on the list—at the foot?" she laughed.

"Why at the foot?"

"The last comer—you have to work your way up by merit, you know."

"Which consists in?"

"*That* you will have to discover."

"I shall try," he said. "Is it so very difficult of discovery?"

"No, it should not be so difficult—for you," she answered, with a flash of her violet eyes. "Mother!" as they reached the piazza—"let me present Mr. Croyden."

Mrs. Carrington arose to greet him—a tall, slender woman, whose age was sixty, at least, but who appeared not a day over forty-five, despite the dark gown and little lace cap she was wearing. She seemed what the girl had called her—the mother, rather than the grandmother. And when she smiled!

"Miss Carrington two generations hence. Lord! how do they do it?" thought Croyden.

"You play Bridge, of course, Mr. Croyden," said Miss Carrington, when the dessert was being served.

"I like it very much," he answered.

"I was sure you did—so sure, indeed, I asked a few friends in later—for a rubber or two—and to meet you."

"So it's well for me I play," he smiled.

"It is indeed!" laughed Mrs. Carrington—"that is, if you care aught for Davila's good opinion. If one can't play Bridge one would better not be born."

"When you know Mother a little better, Mr. Croyden, you will recognize that she is inclined to exaggerate at times," said Miss Carrington. "I admit that I am fond of the game, that I like to play with people who know how, and who, at the critical moment, are not always throwing the wrong card—you understand?"

"In other words, you haven't any patience with stupidity," said Croyden. "Nor have I—but we sometimes forget that a card player is born, not made. All the drilling and teaching one can do won't give card sense to one who hasn't any."

"Precisely!" Miss Carrington exclaimed, "and life is too short to bother with such people. They may be very charming otherwise, but not across the Bridge table."

"Yet ought you not to forgive them their misplays, just because they are charming?" Mrs. Carrington asked. "If you were given your choice between a poor player who is charming, and a good player who is disagreeable, which would you choose, Mr. Croyden?—Come, now be honest."

"It would depend upon the size of the game," Croyden responded. "If it were half a cent a point, I should choose the charming partner, but if it were five cents or better, I am inclined to think I should prefer the good player."

"I'll remember that," said Miss Carrington. "As we don't play, here, for money stakes, you won't care if your partner isn't very expert."

"Not exactly," he laughed. "The stipulation is that she shall be charming. I should be willing to take *you* for a partner though you trumped my ace and forgot my lead."

"*Merci, Monsieur,*" she answered. "Though you know I should do neither."

"Ever play poker?" Captain Carrington asked, suddenly.

"Occasionally," smiled Croyden.

"Good! We'll go down to the Club, some evening. We old fellows aren't much on Bridge, but we can handle a pair or three of-a-kind, pretty good. Have some sherry, won't you?"

"You must not let the Captain beguile you," interposed Mrs. Carrington. "The men all play poker with us,—it is a heritage of the old days—though the youngsters are breaking away from it."

"And taking up Bridge!" the Captain ejaculated. "And it is just as well—we have sense enough to stop before we're broke, but they haven't."

"To hear father talk, you would think that the present generation is no earthly good!" smiled Miss Carrington. "Yet I suppose, when he was young, his elders held the same opinion of him."

"I dare say!" laughed the Captain. "The old ones always think the young ones have a lot to learn—and they have, sir, they have! But it's of another sort than we can teach them, I reckon." He pushed back his chair. "We'll smoke on the piazza, sir—the ladies don't object."

As they passed out, a visitor was just ascending the steps. Miss Carrington gave a smothered exclamation and went forward.

"How do you do, Miss Erskine!" she said.

"How do you do, my dear!" returned Miss Erskine, "and Mrs. Carrington—and the dear Captain, too.—I'm charmed to find you all at home."

She spoke with an affected drawl that would have been amusing in a handsome woman, but was absurdly ridiculous in one with her figure and unattractive face.

She turned expectantly toward Croyden, and Miss Carrington presented him.

"So this is the new owner of Clarendon," she gurgled with an 'a' so broad it impeded her speech. "You have kept us waiting a long time, Mr. Croyden. We began to think you a myth."

"I'm afraid you will find me a very husky myth," Croyden answered.

"'Husky' is scarcely the correct word, Mr. Croyden; *animated* would be better, I think. We scholars, you know, do not like to hear a word used in a perverted sense."

She waddled to a chair and settled into it. Croyden shot an amused glance toward Miss Carrington, and received one in reply.

"No, I suppose not," he said, amiably. "But, then, you know, I am not a scholar."

Miss Erskine smiled in a superior sort of way.

"Very few of us are properly careful of our mode of speech," she answered. "And, oh! Mr. Croyden, I hope you intend to open Clarendon, so as to afford those of us who care for such things, the pleasure of studying the pictures, and the china, and the furniture. I am told it contains a Stuart and a Peale—and they should not be hidden from those who can appreciate them."

"I assume you're talking of pictures," said Croyden.

"I am, sir,—most assuredly!" the dame answered.

"Well, I must confess ignorance, again," he replied. "I wouldn't know a Stuart from a—chromo."

Miss Erskine gave a little shriek of horror.

"I do not believe it, Mr. Croyden!—you're playing on my credulity. I shall have to give you some instructions. I will lecture on Stuart and Peale, and the painters of their period, for your especial delectation—and soon, very soon!"

"I'm afraid it would all be wasted," said Croyden. "I'm not fond of art, I confess—except on the commercial side; and if I've any pictures, at Clarendon, worth money, I'll be for selling them."

"Oh! Mrs. Carrington! Will you listen—did you ever hear such heresy?" she exclaimed. "I can't believe it of you, Mr. Croyden. Let me lend you an article on Stuart to read. I shall bring it out to Clarendon to-morrow morning—and you can let me look at all the dear treasures, while you peruse it."

"Mr. Croyden has an appointment with me to-morrow, Amelia," said Carrington, quickly—and Croyden gave him a look of gratitude.

"It will be but a pleasure deferred, then, Mr. Croyden," said Miss Erskine, impenetrable in her self conceit. "The next morning will do, quite as well—I shall come at ten o'clock—What a lovely evening this is, Mrs. Carrington!" preparing to patronize her hostess.

The Captain snorted with sudden anger, and, abruptly excusing himself, disappeared in the library. Miss Carrington stayed a moment, then, with a word to Croyden, that she would show him the article now, before the others came, if Miss Erskine would excuse them a moment, bore him off.

"What do you think of her?" she demanded.

"Pompous and stupid—an irritating nuisance, I should call her."

"She's more!—she is the most arrogant, self-opinionated, self-complacent, vapid piece of humanity in this town or any other town. She irritates me to the point of impoliteness. She never sees that people don't want her. She's as dense as asphalt."

"It is very amusing!" Croyden interjected.

"At first, yes—pretty soon you will be throwing things at her—or wanting to."

"She's art crazy," he said. "Dilettanteism gone mad."

"It isn't only Art. She thinks she's qualified to speak on every subject under the sun, Literature—Bridge—Teaching—Music. Oh, she is intolerable!"

"What fits her for assuming universal knowledge?" asked Croyden.

"Heaven only knows! She went away to some preparatory school, and finished off with another that teaches pedagogy. Straightway she became an adept in the art of instruction, though, when she tried it, she had the whole academy by the ears in two weeks, and the faculty asked her to resign. Next, she got some one to take her to Europe—spent six weeks in looking at a lot of the famous paintings, with the aid of a guide book and a catalogue, and came home prepared to lecture on Art—and, what's more, she has the effrontery to do it—for the benefit of Charity, she takes four-fifths of the proceeds, and Charity gets the balance.

"Music came next. She read the lives of Chopin and Wagner and some of the other composers, went to a half dozen symphony concerts, looked up theory, voice culture, and the like, in the encyclopædias, and now she's a critic! Literature she imbibed from the bottle, I suppose—it came easy to *her*! And she passes judgment upon it with the utmost ease and final authority. And as for Bridge! She doesn't hesitate to arraign Elwell, and we, of the village, are the very dirt beneath her feet. I hear she's thinking of taking up Civic Improvement. I hope it is true—she'll likely run up against somebody who won't hesitate to tell her what an idiot she is."

"Why do you tolerate her?" Croyden asked. "Why don't you throw her out of society, metaphorically speaking."

"We can't: she belongs—which is final with us, you know. Moreover, she has imposed on some, with her assumption of superiority, and they kowtow to her in a way that is positively disgusting."

"Why don't you, and the rest who dislike her, snub her?"

"Snub *her*! You can't snub her—she never takes a snub to herself. If you were to hit her in the face, she would think it a mistake and meant for some one else."

"Then, why not do the next best thing—have fun with her?"

"We do—but even that grows monotonous, with such a mountain of Egotism —she will stay for the Bridge this evening, see if she doesn't—and never imagine she's not wanted." Then she laughed: "I think if she does I'll give her to you!"

"Very good!" said he. "I'd rather enjoy it. If she is any more cantankerous than some of the women at the Heights, she'll be an interesting study. Yes, I'll be glad to play a rubber with her."

"If you start, you'll play the entire evening with her—we don't change partners, here."

"And what will *you* do?" he asked.

"Look on—at the *other* table. She will have my place. I was going to play with you."

"Then the greater the sacrifice I'm making, the greater the credit I should receive."

"It depends—on how you acquit yourself," she said gayly. "There are the others, now—come along."

There were six of them. Miss Tilghman, Miss Lashiel and Miss Tayloe, Mr. Dangerfield, Mr. Leigh, and Mr. Byrd. They all had heard of Croyden's arrival, in Hampton, and greeted him as they would one of themselves. And it impressed him, as possibly nothing else could have done—for it was distinctly new to him, after the manners of chilliness and aloofness which were the ways of Northumberland.

"We are going to play Bridge, Miss Erskine, will you stay and join us?" asked Miss Carrington.

"I shall be charmed! charmed!" was the answer. "This is an ideal evening for Bridge, don't you think so, Mr. Croyden?"

"Yes, that's what we *thought!*" said Miss Tilghman, dryly.

"And who is to play with me, dear Davila?" Miss Erskine inquired.

"I'm going to put Mr. Croyden with you."

"How nice of you! But I warn you, Mr. Croyden, I am a very exacting partner. I may find fault with you, if you violate rules—just draw your attention to it, you know, so you will not let it occur again. I cannot abide blunders, Mr. Croyden—there is no excuse for them, except stupidity, and stupidity should put one out of the game."

"I'll try to do my very best," said Croyden humbly.

"I do not doubt that you will," she replied easily, her manner plainly implying further that she would soon see how much that "best" was.

As they went in to the drawing-room, where the tables were arranged, Miss

Erskine leading, with a feeling of divine right and an appearance of a Teddy bear, Byrd leaned over to Croyden and said:

"She's the limit!"

"No!" said Leigh, "she's past the limit; she's the sublimated It!"

"Which is another way of saying, she's a superlative d—— fool!" Dangerfield ended.

"I think I understand!" Croyden laughed. "Before you came, she tackled me on Art, and, when I confessed to only the commercial side, and an intention to sell the Stuart and Peale, which, it seems, are at Clarendon, the pitying contempt was almost too much for me."

"My Lord! why weren't we here!" exclaimed Byrd.

"She's coming out to inspect my 'treasures,' on Thursday morning."

"Self invited?"

"I rather think so."

"And you?"

"I shall turn her over to Moses, and decamp before she gets there."

"Gentlemen, we are waiting!" came Miss Erskine's voice.

"Oh, Lord! the old dragoon!" said Leigh. "I trust I'm not at her table."

And he was not—Miss Tilghman and Dangerfield were designated.

"Come over and help to keep me straight," Croyden whispered to Miss Carrington.

She shook her head at him with a roguish smile.

"You'll find your partner amply able to keep you straight," she answered.

The game began. Miss Tilghman won the cut and made it a Royal Spade.

"They no longer play Royal Spades in New York," said MissErskine.

"Don't know about New York," returned Miss Tilghman, placidly, "but *we're* playing them here, this evening. Your lead, Miss Amelia."

The latter shut her thick lips tightly, an instant.

"Oh, well, I suppose we must be provincial a little longer," she said, sarcastically. "Of course, you do not still play Royal Spades in Northumberland, Mr. Croyden."

"Yes, indeed! Play anything to keep the game moving," Croydenanswered.

"Oh, to be sure! I forgot, for the instant, that Northumberland *is* a rapid town. —I call that card, Edith—the King of Hearts!" as Miss Tilghman inadvertently exposed it.

A moment later, Miss Tilghman, through anger, also committed a revoke, which her play on the succeeding trick disclosed.

That it was a game for pure pleasure, without stakes, made no difference to Miss Erskine. Technically it was a revoke, and she was within her rights when she exclaimed it.

"Three tricks!" she said exultantly, "and you cannot make game this hand."

"I'm very sorry, partner," Miss Tilghman apologized.

"It's entirely excusable under the circumstances," said Dangerfield, with deliberate accent. "You may do it again!"

"How courteous Mr. Dangerfield is," Miss Erskine smiled. "To my mind, nothing excuses a revoke except sudden blindness."

"And you would claim it even then, I suppose?" Dangerfield retorted.

"I said, sudden blindness was the only excuse, Mr. Dangerfield. Had you observed my language more closely, you doubtless would have understood.— It is your lead, partner."

Dangerfield, with a wink at Croyden, subsided, and the hand was finished, as was the next, when Croyden was dummy, without further jangling. But midway in the succeeding hand, Miss Erskine began.

"My dear Mr. Croyden," she said, "when you have the Ace, King, and *no more* in a suit, you should lead the Ace and then the King, to show that you have no more—give the down-and-out signal. We would have made an extra trick, if you had done so—I could have given you a diamond to trump. As it was, you led the King and then the Ace, and I supposed, of course, you had at least four in suit."

"I'm very sorry; I'll try to remember in future," said Croyden with affected contrition.

But, at the end of the hand, he was in disgrace again.

"If your original lead had been from your fourth best, partner, I could have understood you," she said. "As it was, you misinformed me. Under the rule of eleven, I had but the nine to beat, I played the ten and Mr. Dangerfield covered with the Knave, which by the rule you should have held. We lost another trick by it, you see."

"It's too bad—too bad!" Croyden answered; "that's two tricks we've lost by my stupid playing. I'm afraid I'm pretty ignorant, Miss Erskine, for I don't know what is meant by the rule of eleven."

Miss Erskine's manner of cutting the cards was somewhat indicative of her contempt—lingeringly, softly, putting them down as though she scorned to touch them except with the tips of her fingers.

"The rule of eleven is usually one of the first things learned by a beginner at Bridge," she said, witheringly. "I do not always agree with Mr. Elwell, some of whose reasoning and inferences, in my opinion, are much forced, but his definition of this rule is very fair. I give it in his exact words, which are: 'Deduct the size of the card led from eleven, and the difference will show how many cards, higher than the one led, are held outside the leader's hand.' For example: if you lead a seven then there are four higher than the seven in the other three hands."

"I see!" Croyden exclaimed. "What a bully rule!—It's very informing, isn't it?"

"Yes, it's very informing—in more ways than one," she answered.

Whereat Miss Tilghman laughed outright, and Dangerfield had to retrieve a card from the floor, to hide his merriment.

"What's the hilarity?" asked Miss Carrington, coming over to their table. "You people seem to be enjoying the game."

Which sent Miss Tilghman into a gale of laughter, in which Dangerfield joined.

Miss Erskine frowned in disapproval and astonishment.

"Don't mind them, Mr. Croyden," she said. "They really know better, but this is the silly season, I suppose. They have much to learn, too—much to learn, indeed." She turned to Miss Carrington. "I was explaining a few things about the game to Mr. Croyden, Davila, the rule of eleven and the Ace-King lead, and, for some reason, it seemed to move them to jollity."

"I'm astonished!" exclaimed Miss Carrington, her violet eyes gleaming with suppressed mirth.

"I hope Mr. Croyden does not think we were laughing at *him!*" cried Miss Tilghman.

"Of course not!" returned Croyden solemnly, "and, if you were, my stupidity quite justified it, I'm sure. If Miss Erskine will only bear with me, I'll try to learn—Bully thing, that rule of eleven!"

It was now Croyden's deal and the score, games all—Miss Erskine having made thirty-six on hers, and Dangerfield having added enough to Miss Tilghman's twenty-eight to, also, give them game.

"How cleverly you deal the cards," Miss Erskine remarked. "You're particularly nimble in the fingers."

"I acquired it dealing faro," Croyden returned, innocently.

"Faro!" exclaimed Miss Carrington, choking back a laugh. "What is faro?"

"A game about which you should know nothing, my dear," Miss Erskine interposed. "Faro is played only in gambling hells and mining camps."

"And in some of the Clubs *in New York*," Croyden added—at which Miss Tilghman's mirth burst out afresh. "That's where I learned to copper the ace or to play it open.—I'll make it no trumps."

"I'll double!" said Miss Tilghman.

"I'll go back!"

"Content."

"Somebody will win the rubber, this hand," Miss Erskine platitudinized,— with the way such persons have of announcing a self evident fact—as she spread out her hand. "It is fair support, partner."

Croyden nodded. Then proceeded with much apparent thought and deliberation, to play the hand like the veriest tyro.

Miss Erskine fidgeted in her seat, gave half smothered exclamations, looked at him appealingly at every misplay. All with no effect. Croyden was wrapped in the game—utterly oblivious to anything but the cards—leading the wrong one, throwing the wrong one, matching pasteboards, that was all.

Miss Erskine was frantic. And when, at the last, holding only a thirteener and a fork in Clubs, he led the losing card of the latter, she could endure the agony no longer.

"That is five tricks you have lost, Mr. Croyden, to say nothing of the rubber!" she snapped. "I must go, now—a delightful game! thank you, my dear Davila. So much obliged to you all, don't you know. Ah, Captain Carrington, will you see me as far as the front gate?—I won't disturb the game. Davila can take my place."

"Yes, I'll take her to the gate!" muttered the Captain aside to Croyden, who was the very picture of contrition. "But if she only were a man! Are you ready, Amelia?" and he bowed her out.

"You awful man!" cried Miss Carrington. "How could you do it!"

"I think it was lovely—perfectly lovely!" exclaimed Miss Tilghman.—"Oh! that last hand was too funny for words.—If only you could have seen her face, Mr. Croyden."

LEADING THE WRONG ONE, THROWING THE WRONG ONE, MATCHING PASTEBOARDS, THAT WAS ALL

"I didn't dare!" laughed he. "One look, and I'd have given the whole thing away."

"She never suspected.—I tell you, she is as dense as asphalt," said Miss Carrington. "Come, now we'll have some Bridge."

"And I'll try to observe the rule of eleven!" said Croyden.

He lingered a moment, after the game was ended and the others had gone. When he came to say good-night, he held Miss Carrington's slender fingers a second longer than the occasion justified.

"And may I come again soon?" he asked.

"As often as you wish," she answered. "You have the advantage of proximity, at least."

VI

CONFIDENCE AND SCRUPLES

The next month, to Croyden, went pleasantly enough. He was occupied with getting the household machinery to run according to his ideas—and still retain Moses and Josephine, who, he early discovered, were invaluable to him; in meeting the people worth knowing in the town and vicinity, and in being entertained, and entertaining—all very quietly and without ostentation.

He had dined, or supped, or played Bridge at all the houses, had given a few small things himself, and ended by paying off all scores with a garden party at Clarendon, which Mrs. Carrington had managed for him with exquisite taste (and, to him, amazing frugality)—and, more wonderful still, with an entire effacement of *self*. It was Croyden's party throughout, though her hand was at the helm, her brain directed—and Hampton never knew.

And the place *had* looked attractive; with the house set in its wide sweep of velvety lawn amid great trees and old-fashioned flowers and hedges. With the furniture cleaned and polished, the old china scattered in cupboard and on table, the portraits and commissions freshly dusted, the swords glistening as of yore.

And in that month, Croyden had come to like Hampton immensely. The absence, in its society, of all attempts at show, to make-believe, to impress, to hoodwink, was refreshingly novel to him, who, hitherto, had known it only as a great sham, a huge affectation, with every one striving to outdo everyone else, and all as hollow as a rotten gourd.

He had not got used, however, to the individual espionage of the country town —the habit of watching one's every movement, and telling it, and drawing inferences therefrom—inferences tinctured according to the personal feelings of the inferer.

He learned that, in three weeks, they had him "taken" with every eligible girl in town, engaged to four and undecided as to two more. They busied themselves with his food,—they nosed into his drinks, his cigars, his cigarettes, his pipes,—they bothered themselves about his meal hours,—they even inspected his wash when it hung on the line! Some of them, that is. The rest were totally different; they let every one alone. They did not intrude nor obtrude—they went their way, and permitted every one to go his.

So much had been the way of Northumberland, so much he had been used to always. But—and here was the difference from Northumberland, the vital difference, indeed—they were interested in you, if *you* wished them to be—and it was genuine interest, not pretense. This, and the way they had treated him as one of them, because Colonel Duval had been his father's friend, made Croyden feel very much at home.

At intervals, he had taken old Parmenter's letter from its secret drawer, and studied it, but he had been so much occupied with getting acquainted, that he had done nothing else. Moreover, there was no pressing need for haste. If the treasure had kept on Greenberry Point for one hundred and ninety years, it would keep a few months longer. Besides, he was a bit uncertain whether or not he should confide in someone, Captain Carrington or Major Borden. He would doubtless need another man to help him, even if the location should be easily determined, which, however, was most unlikely. For him, alone, to go prying about on Greenberry Point, would surely occasion comment and arouse suspicion—which would not be so likely if there were two of them, and especially if one were a well-known resident of Maryland.

He finally determined, however, to go across to Annapolis and look over the ground, before he disclosed the secret to any one. Which was the reasonable decision.

When he came to look up the matter of transportation, however, he was surprised to find that no boat ran between Annapolis and Hampton—or any other port on the Eastern Shore. He either had to go by water to Baltimore (which was available on only three days a week) and thence finish his journey by rail or transfer to another boat, or else he had to go by steam cars north to Wilmington, and then directly south again to Annapolis. In either case, a day's journey between two towns that were almost within seeing distance of each other, across the Bay. Of the two, he chose to go by boat to Baltimore.

Then, the afternoon of the day before it sailed, he received a wire—delivered two hours and more after its receipt, in the leisurely fashion of the Eastern Shore. It was from Macloud, and dated Philadelphia.

"Can I come down to-night? Answer to Bellevue-Stratford."

His reply brought Macloud in the morning train.

Croyden met him at the station. Moses took his bag, and they walked out to Clarendon.

"Sorry I haven't a car!" said Croyden—then he laughed. "The truth is, Colin, they're not popular down here. The old families won't have them—they're innovations—the saddle horse and the family carriage are still to the fore with them. Only the butcher, and the baker and the candlestick maker have motors. There's one, now—he's the candlestick maker, I think. This town is nothing if not conservative. It reminds me of the one down South, where they wouldn't have electric cars. Finally all the street car horses died. Then rather than commit the awful sin of letting *new* horses come into the city, they accepted the trolley. The fashion suits my pocketbook, however, so I've no kick coming."

"What do you want with a car here, anyway?" Macloud asked. "It looks as if you could walk from one end of the town to the other in fifteen minutes."

"You can, easily."

"And the baker et cetera have theirs only for show, I suppose?"

"Yes, that's about it—the roads, hereabout, are sandy and poor."

"Then, I'm with your old families. They may be conservative, at times a trifle too much so, but, in the main, their judgment's pretty reliable, according to conditions. What sort of place did you find—I mean the house?"

"Very fair!"

"And the society?"

"Much better than Northumberland."

"Hum—I see—the aristocracy of birth, not dollars."

"Exactly!—How do you do, Mr. Fitzhugh," as they passed a policeman in uniform.

"Good morning, Mr. Croyden!" was the answer.

"There! that illustrates," said Croyden. "You meet Fitzhugh every place when he is off duty. He *belongs*. His occupation does not figure, in the least."

"So you like it—Hampton, I mean?" said Macloud.

"I've been here a month—and that month I've enjoyed—thoroughly enjoyed. However, I do miss the Clubs and their life."

"I can understand," Macloud interjected.

"And the ability to get, instantly, anything you want——"

"Much of which you don't want—and wouldn't get, if you had to write for it, or even to walk down town for it—which makes for economy," observed Macloud sententiously.

"But, more than either, I miss the personal isolation which one can have in a big town, when he wishes it—and has always, in some degree."

"And *that* gets on your nerves!" laughed Macloud. "Well, you won't mind it after a while, I think. You'll get used to it, and be quite oblivious. Is that all your objections?"

"I've been here only a short time, remember. Come back in six months, say, and I may have kicks in plenty."

"You may find it a bit dreary in winter—who the deuce is that girl yonder, Geoffrey?" he broke off.

They were opposite Carrington's, and down the walk toward the gate was coming the maid of the blue-black hair, and slender ankles. She wore a blue linen gown, a black hat, and her face was framed by a white silk parasol.

"That is Miss Carrington," said Croyden.

"Hum!—Your house near here?" "Yes—

pretty near."

Macloud looked at him with a grin.

"She has nothing to do with your liking the town, I suppose?" he said, knowingly.

"Well, she's not exactly a deterrent—and there are half a dozen more of the same sort. Oh, on that score, Hampton's not half bad, my friend!" he laughed.

"You mean there are half a dozen of *that* sort," with a slight jerk of his head toward Miss Carrington, "who are unmarried?"

Croyden nodded—then looked across; and both men raised their hats and bowed.

"And how many married?" Macloud queried.

"Several—but you let them *alone*—it's not fashionable here, as yet, for a pretty married woman to have an affair. She loves her husband, or acts it, at least. They're neither prudes nor prigs, but they are not *that*."

"So far as you know!" laughed Macloud. "But my experience has been that the pretty married woman who won't flirt, if occasion offers where there is no danger of being compromised, is a pretty scarce article. However, Hampton may be an exception."

"You're too cynical," said Croyden. "We turn in here—this is Clarendon."

"Why! you beggar!" Macloud exclaimed. "I've been sympathizing with you, because I thought you were living in a shack-of-a-place—and, behold!"

"Yes, it is not bad," said Croyden. "I've no ground for complaint, on that head. I can, at least, be comfortable here. It's not bad inside, either."

That evening, after dinner, when the two men were sitting in the library while a short-lived thunder storm raged outside, Macloud, after a long break in the conversation—which is the surest sign of camaraderie among men— observed, apropos of nothing except the talk of the morning:

"Lord! man, you've got no kick coming!"

"Who said I had?" Croyden demanded.

"You did, by damning it with faint praise."

"Damning what?"

"Your present environment—and yet, look you! A comfortable house, fine grounds, beautiful old furnishings, delicious victuals, and two negro servants, who are devoted to you, or the place—no matter which, for it assures their permanence; the one a marvelous cook, the other a competent man; and, by way of society, a lot of fine, old antebellum families, with daughters like the Symphony in Blue, we saw this morning. God! you're hard to please."

"And that is not all," said Croyden, laughing and pointing to the portraits. "I've got ancestors—by purchase."

"And you have come by them clean-handed, which is rare.—Moreover, I fancy you are one who has them by inheritance, as well."

Croyden nodded. "I'm glad to say I have—ancestors are distinctly fashionable down here. But *that's* not all I've got."

"There is only one thing more—money," said Macloud. "You haven't found any of it down here, have you?"

"That is just what I don't know," Croyden replied, tossing away his cigarette, and crossing to the desk by the window. "It depends—on this." He handed the Parmenter letter to Macloud. "Read it through—the endorsements last, in their order—and then tell me what you think of it."...

"These endorsements, I take it," said Macloud, "though without date and signed only with initials, were made by the original addressee, Marmaduke Duval, his son, who was presumably Daniel Duval, and Daniel Duval's son, Marmaduke; the rest, of course, is plain."

"That is correct," Croyden answered. "I have made inquiries—Colonel Duval's father was Marmaduke, whose son was Daniel, whose son was Marmaduke, the addressee."

"Then why isn't it true?" Macloud demanded.

"My dear fellow, I'm not denying it! I simply want your opinion—what to do?"

"Have you shown this letter to anyone else?"

"No one."

"Well, you're a fool to show it even to me. What assurance have you that, when I leave here, I won't go straight to Annapolis and steal your treasure?"

"No assurance, except a lamblike trust in your friendship," said Croyden, with an amused smile.

"Your recent experience with Royster & Axtell and the Heights should beget confidences of this kind?" he said sarcastically, tapping the letter the while. "You trust too much in friendship, Croyden. Tests of half a million dollars aren't human!" Then he grinned. "I always thought there was something God-like about me. So, maybe, you're safe. But it was a fearful risk, man, a fearful risk!" He looked at the letter again. "Sure, it's true! The man to whom it was addressed believed it—else why did he endorse it to his son? And we can assume that Daniel Duval knew his father's writing, and accepted it.—Oh, it's genuine enough. But to prove it, did you identify Marmaduke Duval's writing —any papers or old letters in the house?"

"I don't know," returned Croyden. "I'll ask Moses to-morrow."

"Better not arouse his curiosity—darkies are most inquisitive, you know— where did you find the letter?"

Croyden showed him the secret drawer.

"Another proof of its genuineness," said Macloud. "Have you made any effort to identify this man Parmenter—from the records at Annapolis."

"No—I've done nothing but look at the letter—except to trace the Duval descent," Croyden replied.

"He speaks, here, of his last will and testament being left with Mr. Dulany. If it were probated, that will establish Parmenter, especially if Marmaduke Duval is the legatee. What do you know of Annapolis?"

"Nothing! I never was there—I looked it up on the map I found, here, and Greenberry Point is as the letter says—across the Severn River from it."

Macloud laughed, in good-natured raillery.

"You seem to have been in a devil of a hurry!" he said. "At the same rate of progression, you will go to Annapolis some time next spring, and get over to Greenberry Point about autumn."

"On the contrary, it's your coming that delayed me," Croyden smiled. "But for your wire, I would have started this morning—now, if you will accompany me, we'll go day-after-to-morrow."

"Why delay?" said Macloud. "Why not go to-night?"

"It's a long journey around the Bay by rail—I'd rather cross to Baltimore by boat; from there it's only an hour's ride to Annapolis by electric cars. And there isn't any boat sailing until day-after-to-morrow."

"Where's the map?" said Macloud. "Let me see where we are, and where Annapolis is.... Hum! we're almost opposite! Can't we get a boat in the morning to take us across direct—charter it, I mean? The Chesapeake isn't wide at this point—a sailing vessel ought to make it in a few hours."

"I'll go you!" exclaimed Croyden. He went to the telephone and called up Dick. "This is Geoffrey Croyden!" he said.—"I've a friend who wants to go across the Bay to Annapolis, in the morning. Where can I find out if there is a sailing vessel, or a motor boat, obtainable?... what's that you say?... Miles Casey?—on Fleet Street, near the wharf?... Thank you!—He says," turning to Macloud, "Casey will likely take us—he has a fishing schooner and it is in port. He lives on Fleet Street—we will walk down, presently, and see him."

Macloud nodded assent, and fell to studying the directions again. Croyden returned to his chair and smoked in silence, waiting for his friend to conclude. At length, the latter folded the letter and looked up.

"It oughtn't to be hard to find," he observed.

"Not if the trees are still standing, and the Point is in the same place," said Croyden. "But we're going to find the Point shifted about ninety degrees, and God knows how many feet, while the trees will have long since disappeared."

"Or the whole Point may be built over with houses!" Macloud responded. "Why not go the whole throw-down at once—make it impossible to recover rather than only difficult to locate!" He made a gesture of disbelief. "Do you fancy that the Duvals didn't keep an eye on Greenberry Point?—that they wouldn't have noted, in their endorsements, any change in the ground? So it's clear, in my mind, that, when Colonel Duval transferred this letter to you, the Parmenter treasure could readily be located."

"I'm sure I shan't object, in the least, if we walk directly to the spot, and hit the box on the third dig of the pick!" laughed Croyden. "But let us forget the old pirate, until to-morrow; tell me about Northumberland—it seems a year since I left! When one goes away for good and all, it's different, you know, from going away for the summer."

"And you think you have left it for good and all?" asked Macloud, blowing a smoke-ring and watching him with contemplative eyes—"Well, the place is the same—only more so. A good many people have come back. The Heights is more lively than when you left, teas, and dinners, and tournaments and such like.—In town, the Northumberland's resuming its regulars—the theatres are open, and the Club has taken the bald-headed row on Monday nights as usual. Billy Cain has turned up engaged, also as usual—this time, it's a Richmond girl, 'regular screamer,' he says. It will last the allotted time, of course—six weeks was the limit for the last two, you'll remember. Smythe put it all over Little in the tennis tournament, and 'Pud' Lester won the golf championship. Terry's horse, *Peach Blossom*, fell and broke its neck in the high jump, at the Horse Show; Terry came out easier—he broke only his collar-bone. Mattison is the little bounder he always was—a month hasn't changed him—except for the worse. Hungerford is a bit sillier. Colloden is the same bully fellow; he is disconsolate, now, because he is beginning to take on flesh." Whereat both laughed. "Danridge is back from the North Cape, via Paris, with a new drink he calls *The Spasmodic*—it's made of gin, whiskey, brandy, and absinthe, all in a pint of sarsaparilla. He says it's great—I've not sampled it, but judging from those who have he is drawing it mild.... Betty Whitridge and Nancy Wellesly have organized a Sinners Class, prerequisites for membership in which are that you play Bridge on Sundays and have abstained from church for at least six months. It's limited to twenty. They filled it the first morning, and have a waiting list of something over seventy-five.... That is about all I can think of that's new."

"Has any one inquired about me?" Croyden asked—with the lingering desire one has not to be forgot.

Macloud shot a questioning glance at him.

"Beyond the fact that the bankruptcy schedules show you were pretty hard hit, I've heard no one comment," he said. "They think you're in Europe. Elaine Cavendish is sponsor for that report—she says you told her you were called, suddenly, abroad."

Croyden nodded. Then, after a pause:

"Any one inclined to play the devoted, there?" he asked.

"Plenty inclined—plenty anxious," replied Macloud. "I'm looking a bit that way myself—I may get into the running, since you are out of it," he added.

Croyden made as though to speak, then bit off the words.

"Yes, I'm out of it," he said shortly.

"But you're not out of it—if you find the pirate's treasure."

"Wait until I find it—at present, I'm only an 'also ran.'"

"Who had the field, however, until withdrawn," said Macloud.

"Maybe!" Croyden laughed. "But things have changed with me, Macloud;

I've had time for thought and meditation. I'm not sure I should go back to Northumberland, even if the Parmenter jewels are real. Had I stayed there I suppose I should have taken my chance with the rest, but I'm becoming doubtful, recently, of giving such hostages to fortune. It's all right for a woman to marry a rich man, but it is a totally different proposition for a poor man to marry a rich woman. Even with the Parmenter treasure, I'd be poor in comparison with Elaine Cavendish and her millions—and I'm afraid the sweet bells would soon be jangling out of tune."

"Would you condemn the girl to spinsterhood, because there are few men in Northumberland, or elsewhere, who can match her in wealth?"

"Not at all! I mean, only, that the man should be able to support her according to her condition in life.—In other words, pay all the bills, without drawing on her fortune."

"Those views will never make you the leader of a popular propaganda!" said Macloud, with an amused smile. "In fact, you're alone in the woods."

"Possibly! But the views are not irrevocable—I may change, you know. In the meantime, let us go down to Fleet Street and interview Casey. And then, if you're good, I'll take you to call on Miss Carrington."

"The Symphony in Blue!" exclaimed Macloud. "Come along, man, come along!"

VII

There was no trouble with Casey—he had been mighty glad to take them. And, at about noon of the following day, they drew in to the ancient capital, having made a quick and easy run from Hampton.

It was clear, bright October weather, when late summer seems to linger for very joy of staying, and all nature is in accord. The State House, where Washington resigned his commission—with its chaste lines and dignified white dome, when viewed from the Bay (where the monstrosity of recent years that has been hung on behind, is not visible) stood out clearly in the sunlight, standing high above the town, which slumbers, in dignified ease, within its shadow. A few old mansions, up the Spa, seen before they landed, with the promise of others concealed among the trees, higher up, told their story of a Past departed—a finished city.

"Where is Greenberry Point?" demanded Macloud, suddenly.

"Yonder, sir, on the far side of the Severn—the strip of land which juts out into the Bay."

"First hypothesis, dead as a musket!" looking at Croyden. "There isn't a house in sight—except the light-house, and it's a bug-light."

"No houses—but where are the trees?" Croyden returned. "It seems pretty low," he said, to the skipper; "is it ever covered with water?"

"I think not, sir—the water's just eating it slowly away."

Croyden nodded, and faced townward.

"What is the enormous white stone building, yonder?" he asked.

"The Naval Academy—that's only one of the buildings, sir, Bancroft Hall. The whole Academy occupies a great stretch of land along the Severn."

They landed at the dock, at the foot of Market Place and inquired the way to Carvel Hall—that being the hotel advised by Dick. They were directed up Wayman's alley—one of the numerous three foot thoroughfares between streets, in which the town abounds—to Prince George Street, and turning northward on it for a block, past the once splendid Brice house, now going slowly to decay, they arrived at the hotel:—the central house of English brick with the wings on either side, and a modern hotel building tacked on the rear.

"Rather attractive!" was Macloud's comment, as they ascended the steps to the brick terrace and, thence, into the hotel. "Isn't this an old residence?" he inquired of the clerk, behind the desk.

"Yes, sir! It's the William Paca (the Signer) mansion, but it served as the home of Dorothy Manners in *Richard Carvel*, and hence the name, sir: Carvel Hall. We've many fine houses here: the Chase House—he also was a Signer; the Harwood House, said to be one of the most perfect specimens of Colonial architecture in America; the Scott House, on the Spa; the Brice House, next door; McDowell Hall, older than any of them, was gutted by fire last year, but has been restored; the Ogle mansion—he was Governor in the 1740's, I think. Oh! this was the Paris of America before and during the Revolution. Why, sir, the tonnage of the Port of Annapolis, in 1770, was greater than the tonnage of the Port of Baltimore, to-day."

"Very interesting!" said Macloud. "Very interesting, indeed. What's happened to it since 1770?"

"Nothing, sir—that's the trouble, it's progressed backward—and Baltimore has taken its place."

"I see!" said Macloud, laughing. "What time is luncheon?"

"It's being served now, sir—twelve-thirty to two."

"Order a pair of saddle horses, and have them around at one-thirty, please."

"There is no livery connected with the hotel, sir, but I'll do what I can. There isn't any saddlers for hire, but we will get you a pair of 'Cheney's Best,' sir— they're sometimes ridden. However, you had better drive, if you will permit me to suggest, sir."

Croyden glanced at Macloud. "No!—

we will try the horses," he said.

It had been determined that they should ride for the reasons, as urged by Macloud, that they could go on horseback where they could not in a conveyance, and they would be less likely to occasion comment. The former of which appealed to Croyden, though the latter did not.

Macloud had borrowed an extra pair of riding breeches and puttees, from his friend, and, at the time appointed, the two men passed through the office.

"The horses are waiting, sir!" the clerk informed them.

Two negro lads were holding a pair of rawboned nags, that resembled saddlers about as much as a cigar-store Indian does a sonata. Croyden looked them over in undisguised disgust.

"If these are Cheney's Best," he commented, "what in Heaven's name are his worst?"

"Come on!" said Macloud, adjusting the stirrups. "Get aboard and leave the kicking to the horses, they may be better than they look. Where does one cross the Severn?" he asked a man who was passing.

"Straight up to the College green," he replied, pointing; "then one square to the right to King George Street, and on out it, across College Creek, to the Marine Barracks. The road forks there; you turn to the right; and the bridge is at the foot of the hill."

They thanked him, and rode away.

"He ought to write a guide book," said Croyden.

"How do you know he hasn't?" Macloud retorted. "Well paved streets,—but a trifle hard for riding."

"And more than a trifle dirty," Croyden added. "My horse isn't so bad— how's yours?"

"He'll do!—This must be the Naval Academy," as they passed along a high brick wall—"Yonder, are the Barracks—the Marines are drilling in front."

They clattered over the creek, rounded the quarters of the "Hermaphrodites," and saw below them the wide bridge, almost a half a mile long, which spans the Severn. The draw was open, to let a motor boat pass through, but it closed before they reached it.

"This is exceptionally pretty!" Macloud exclaimed, drawing rein, midway. "Look at the high bluff, on the farther shore, with the view up the river, on one side, and down the Bay, and clear across on the other.... Now," as they wound up on the hill, "for the first road to the right."

"This doesn't look promising!" laughed Croyden, as the road swung abruptly westward and directly away from Greenberry Point.

"Let us go a little farther," said Macloud. "There must be a way—a bridle path, if nothing better—and, if we must, we can push straight through the timber; there doesn't seem to be any fences. You see, it was rational to ride."

"You're a wise old owl!" Croyden retorted.

"Ah!—there's our road!" as one unexpectedly took off to the right, among the trees, and bore almost immediately eastward. "Come along, my friend!"

Presently they were startled by a series of explosions, a short distance ahead.

"What are we getting into?" Macloud exclaimed, drawing up sharply.

"Parmenter's defending his treasure!" said Croyden, with mock seriousness.

"He is warning us off."

"A long way off, then! We must be a mile and more from the Point. It's some one blasting, I think."

"It wasn't sufficiently muffled," Croyden answered.

They waited a few moments: hearing no further noises, they proceeded—a trifle cautiously, however. A little further on, they came upon a wood cutter.

"He doesn't appear at all alarmed," Croyden observed. "What were the explosions, a minute ago?" he called.

"They weren't nothing," said the man, leaning on his axe. "The Navy's got a 'speriment house over here. They're trying things. Yer don't need be skeered. If yer goin' to the station, it's just a little ways, now," he added, with the country-man's curiosity—which they did not satisfy.

They passed the buildings of the Experiment Station and continued on, amid pine and dogwood, elms and beeches. They were travelling parallel with the Severn, and not very distant, as occasional glimpses of blue water, through the trees, revealed. Gradually, the timber thinned. The river became plainly visible with the Bay itself shimmering to the fore. Then the trees ended abruptly, and they came out on Greenberry Point: a long, flat, triangular-shaped piece of ground, possibly two hundred yards across the base, and three hundred from base to point.

The two men halted, and looked around.

"Somewhere near here, possibly just where your horse is standing, is the treasure," said Macloud. "Can't you feel its presence?"

"No, I can't!" laughed Croyden, "and that appears to be my only chance, for I can't see a trace of the trees which formed the square."

"Be not cast down!" Macloud admonished. "Remember, you didn't expect to find things marked off for you."

"No, *I* didn't! but I thought *you* did."

"That was only to stir you up. I anticipated even more adverse conditions. It's amazingly easier than I dared to hope."

"Thunder! man! we can't dig six feet deep over all of forty acres. We shall have the whole of Annapolis over to help us before we've done a square of forty feet."

"You're too liberal!" laughed Macloud. "Twenty feet would be ample." Then he sobered. "The instructions say: seven hundred and fifty feet back, from the extreme tip of Greenberry Point, is the quadrangle of trees. That was in 1720, one hundred and ninety years ago. They must have been of good size then—hence, they would be of the greater size, now, or else have disappeared entirely. There isn't a single tree which could correspond with Parmenter's, closer than four hundred yards, and, as the point would have been receding rather than gaining, we can assume, with tolerable certainty, that the beeches have vanished—either from decay or from wind storms, which must be very severe over in this exposed land. Hence, must not our first quest be for some trace of the trees?"

"That sounds reasonable," said Croyden, "and, if the Point has receded, which is altogether likely, then we are pretty near the place."

"Yes!—if the Point has simply receded, but if it has shifted laterally, as well, the problem is not so simple."

"Let us go out to the Point, and look at the ruins of the light-house. If we can get near enough to ascertain when it was built, it may help us. Evidently there was none erected here, in Parmenter's time, else he would not have chosen this place to hide his treasure."

But the light-house was a barren yield. It was a crumbling mass of ruins, lying out in water, possibly fifty feet—the real house was a bug-light farther out in the Bay.

"Well, there's no one to see us, so why shouldn't we make a search for the trees?" said Croyden.

"Hold my horse!" said Macloud, dismounting.

He went out on the extreme edge, faced about, and taking a line at right angles to it, stepped two hundred and fifty paces. He ended in sand—and, for another fifty paces, sand—sand unrelieved by aught save some low bushes sparsely scattered here and there.

"Somewhere hereabout, according to present conditions, the trees should be," he said.

"Not very promising," was Croyden's comment.

"Let us assume that the diagonal lines drawn between the trees intersect at this point," Macloud continued, producing a compass. "Then, one hundred and ten paces North-by-North-East is the place we seek."

He stepped the distance carefully—Croyden following with the horses—and sunk his heel into the sand beside a clump of wire grass.

"Here is the old buccaneer's hoard!" he exclaimed, dramatically.

"Shall we dig, immediately?" Croyden laughed.

HE WENT OUT ON THE EXTREME EDGE, FACED ABOUT, AND STEPPED TWO HUNDRED AND FIFTY PACES

"You dig—I'll hold the horses; your hands are tougher than mine."

"I wonder who owns this land?" said Croyden, suddenly.

"We can ascertain very readily. You mean, you would try to purchase it?"

"Yes, as a site for a house, ostensibly. I might buy a lot beginning, say one hundred and fifty yards back from the Point, and running, at an even width of two hundred yards, from the Severn to the Bay. That would surely include the treasure."

"A fine idea!" Macloud agreed.

"If the present owner will sell," appended Croyden—"and if his price isn't out of all reason. I can't go much expense, you know."

"Never mind the expense—that can be arranged. If he will sell, the rest is easy. I'll advance it gladly to you."

"And we will share equally, then," said Croyden.

"Bosh!" Macloud answered. "I've got more money than I want, let me have some fun with the excess, Croyden. And this promises more fun than I've had for a year—hunting a buried treasure, within sight of Maryland's capital. Moreover, it won't likely be out of reach of your own pocketbook, this can't be very valuable land." He remounted his horse. "Let us ride around over the intended site, and prospect—we may discover something."

But, though, they searched for an hour, they were utterly unsuccessful. The four beech trees had disappeared as completely as though they never were.

"I'm perfectly confident, however," Macloud remarked as they turned away toward town, "that somewhere, within the lines of your proposed lot, lie the Parmenter jewels. Now, for the lot. Once you have title to it, you may plow up the whole thing to any depth you please, and no one may gainsay you."

"I'm not so sure," replied Croyden. "My knowing that the treasure was on it when purchased, may make me liable to my grantor for an accounting."

"But you don't *know*!" objected Macloud.

"Yet, I have every reason to believe—the letter is most specific."

"Suppose, after you've paid a big price for the land, you don't find the treasure, could you make him take it back and refund the purchase money?"

"No, most assuredly, no," smiled Croyden.

"Mighty queer doctrine! You must account for what you find—if you don't find it, you must keep the land, anyway. The other fellow wins whatever happens."

"It's predicated on the proposition that I have knowingly deceived him into selling something for nothing. However, I'm not at all clear about it; and we will buy if we can—and take the chances. But we won't go to work with a brass band, old man."

At the top of the hill, beyond the Severn, there was a road which took off to the left.

"This parallels the road by the Marine Barracks, suppose we turn in here," Macloud said. "It probably goes through the Academy grounds."

A little way on, they passed what was evidently a fine hospital, with the United States flag flying over it. Just beyond, occupying the point of land where College Creek empties into the Severn, was the Naval Cemetery.

"Very fitting!" Croyden laughed. "They have the place of interment exceedingly handy to the hospital. What in thunder's that?" he asked, indicating a huge dome, hideously ornate with gold and white, that projected above the trees, some distance ahead.

"Give it up!" said Macloud. "Unless it's a custard-and-cream pudding for the Midshipmen's supper. Awful looking thing, isn't it! Oh! I recollect now: the Government has spent millions in erecting new Academy buildings; and someone in the Navy remarked, 'If a certain chap *had* to kill somebody, he couldn't see why he hadn't selected the fellow who was responsible for them —his work at Annapolis would have been ample justification.' Judging from the atrocity to our fore, the officer didn't overdraw it."

They took the road along the officers' quarters on Upshur Row, and came out the upper gate into King George Street, thereby missing the Chapel (of the custard-and-cream dome) and all the other Smith buildings.

"We can see them again!" said Croyden. "The real estate agent is more important now."

It was the quiet hour when they got back to the hotel, and the clerk was standing in the doorway, sunning himself.

"Enjoy your ride, sirs?" he asked.

"It wasn't bad," returned Croyden. Then he stopped. "Can you tell me who owns Greenberry Point?"

"Yes, sir! The Government owns it—they bought it for the Rifle Range."

"The whole of it?"

"Yes, sir!—from the Point clear up to the Experiment Station."

Croyden thanked him and passed on.

"That's the end of the purchase idea!" he said. "I thought it was 'most too good to last."

"It got punctured very early," Macloud agreed.

"And the question is, what to do, now? Might the clerk be wrong?"

Macloud shook his head. "There isn't a chance of it. Titles in a small town are known, particularly, when they're in the United States. However, it's easy to verify—we'll hunt up a real estate office—they'll know."

But when they had dressed, and sought a real estate office, the last doubt vanished: it confirmed the clerk.

"If you haven't anything particularly pressing," said Macloud, "I suggest that we remain here for a few days and consider what is best to do."

"My most pressing business is to find the treasure!" Croyden laughed.

"Good! then we're on the job until it's found—if it takes a year or longer." And when Croyden looked his surprise: "I've nothing to do, old chap, and one doesn't have the opportunity to go treasure hunting more than once in a lifetime. Picture our satisfaction when we hear the pick strike the iron box, and see the lid turned back, and the jewels coruscating before us."

"But what if there isn't any coruscating—that's a good word, old man—nor any iron box?"

"Don't be so pessimistic—*think* we're going to find it, it will help a lot."

"How about if we *don't* find it?"

"Then, at least, we'll have had a good time in hunting, and have done our best to succeed."

"It's a new thing to hear old cynical Macloud preaching optimism!" laughed Croyden—"our last talk, in Northumberland, wasn't particularly in that line, you'll remember."

"Our talk in Northumberland had to do with other people and conditions. This is an adventure, and has to do solely with ourselves. Some difference, my dear Croyden, some difference! What do you say to an early breakfast to-morrow, and then a walk over to the Point. It's something like your Eastern Shore to get to, however,—just across the river by water, but three miles around by the Severn bridge. We can have the whole day for prospecting."

"I'm under your orders," said Croyden. "You're in charge of this expedition."

They had been passing numerous naval officers in uniform, some well set-up, some slouchy.

"The uniform surely does show up the man for what he is," said Macloud. "Look at these two for instance—from the stripes on the sleeves, a Lieutenant-Commander and a Senior Lieutenant. Did you ever see a real Bowery tough?—they are in that class, with just enough veneer to deceive, for an instant. There, are two others, opposite. They look like soldiers. Observe the dignity, the snappy walk, the inherent air of command."

"Isn't it the fault of the system?" asked Croyden. "Every Congressman holds a competitive examination in his district; and the appointment goes to the applicant who wins—be he what he may. For that reason, I dare say, the Brigade of Midshipmen contains muckers as well as gentlemen—and officers are but midshipmen of a larger growth."

"Just so! and it's wrong—all wrong! To be a commissioned officer, in either Army or Navy, ought to attest one's gentle birth."

"It raises a presumption in their favor, at least."

"Presumption! do you think the two who passed us could hide behind that presumption longer than the fraction of an instant?"

"Don't get excited, old man! I was accounting for it, not defending it. It's a pity, of course, but that's one of the misfortunes of a Republic where all men are equal."

"Rot! damn rot!" Macloud exclaimed. "Men aren't equal!—they're born to different social scales, different intellectualities, different conditions otherwise. For the purpose of suffrage they may, in the theory of our government, be equal—but we haven't yet demonstrated it. We exclude the Japanese and Chinese. We have included the negro, only within the living generation—and it's entirely evident, now, we made a monstrous mistake by doing it. Equal! Equal! Never in this world!"

"How about the next world?" asked Croyden.

"I don't know!" laughed Macloud, as they ascended the steps of the hotel. "For my part, I'm for the Moslem's Paradise and the Houris who attend the Faithful. And, speaking of houris!—see who's here!"

Croyden glanced up—to see Elaine Cavendish and Charlotte Brundage standing in the doorway.

VIII

"This is, truly, a surprise!" Miss Cavendish exclaimed. "Who would ever have thought of meeting you two in this out-of-the-way place."

"Here, too!" replied Macloud.

"When did you return, Geoffrey?" she inquired.

"From abroad?—I haven't gone," said Croyden. "The business still holds me."

She looked at him steadily a moment—Macloud was talking to Miss Brundage.

"How much longer will it hold you?" she asked.

He shrugged his shoulders. "I don't know—it's difficult of adjustment.— What brings you here, may I inquire?"

"We were in Washington and came over with the Westons to the Officers' Hop to-night—given for the Secretary of something. He's one of the Cabinet. We return in the morning."

"Oh, I see," he answered; the relief in his voice would have missed a less acute ear. "Where are you going now?"

"To a tea at the Superintendent's, when the Westons join us. Come along!"

"I haven't acquired the Washington habit,—yet!" he laughed. "A man at a tea fight! Oh, no!"

"Then go to the dance with us—Colin! you'll go, won't you?"

"Sure!" said Macloud. "I'll follow your voice any place. Where shall it be?"

"To the Hop, to-night."

"We're not invited—if that cuts any figure."

"You'll go in our party. Ah! Mrs. Weston, I've presumed to ask Mr. Macloud and Mr. Croyden to join our party to-night."

"The Admiral and I shall be delighted to have them," Mrs. Weston answered —"Will they also go with us to the tea? No? Well, then, to-night."

Macloud and Croyden accompanied them to the Academy gates, and then returned to the hotel.

In the narrow passage between the news-desk and the office, they bumped, inadvertently, into two men. There were mutual excuses, and the men went on.

An hour or so later, Macloud, having changed into his evening clothes, came into Croyden's room and found him down on his knees looking under the bureau, and swearing vigorously.

"Whee!" he said; "you *are* a true pirate's heir! Old Parmenter, himself, couldn't do it better. What's the matter—lose something?"

"No, I didn't lose anything!" said Croyden sarcastically. "I'm saying my prayers."

"And incidentally searching for this, I suppose?" picking up a pearl stud from under the bed.

Croyden took it without a word.

"And when you've sufficiently recovered your equanimity," Macloud went on, "you might let me see the aforesaid Parmenter's letter. I want to cogitate over it."

"It's in my wallet!" grinding in the stud—"my coat's on the chair, yonder."

"I don't find it!" said Macloud, searching. "What pocket is it in?"

"The inside breast pocket!" exclaimed Croyden, ramming the last stud home. "Where would you think it is—in the small change pocket?"

"Then suppose you find it for me."

"I'll do it with——" He stopped. "Do you mean it isn't there?" he exclaimed.

"It isn't there!" said Macloud, holding up the coat.

Croyden's fingers flew to the breast pocket—empty! to the other pockets—no wallet! He seized his trousers; then his waistcoat—no wallet.

"My God! I've lost it!" he cried.

"Maybe you left it in Hampton?" said Macloud.

Croyden shook his head. "I had it when we left the Weston party—I felt it in my pocket, as I bent to tie Miss Cavendish's shoe."

"Then, it oughtn't to be difficult to find—it's lost between the Sampson Gate and the hotel. I'm going out to search, possibly in the fading light it has not been noticed. You telephone the office—and then join me, as quickly as you can get into your clothes."

He dashed out and down the stairs into the Exchange, passing midway, with the barest nod, the Weston party, nor pausing to answer the question Miss Cavendish flung after him.

Once on the rear piazza, however, he went slowly down the broad white steps to the broad brick walk—the electric lights were on, and he noted, with keen regret, how bright they made it—and thence to the Sampson Gate. It was vain! He inquired of the guard stationed there, and that, too, proving unavailing, left directions for its return, if found.

"What a misfortune!" he muttered, as he renewed the search. "What a misfortune! If any one reads that letter, the jig is up for us…. Here! boys," to a crowd of noisy urchins, sitting on the coping along the street, "do you want to make a dollar?"

The enthusiasm of the response, not to mention its unanimity, threatened dire disaster to Macloud's toilet.

"Hold on!" he said. "Don't pull me apart. You all can have a chance for it. I've lost a wallet—a pocketbook—between the gate yonder and the hotel. A dollar to the boy who finds it."

With a shout, they set to work. A moment later Croyden came down the walk.

"I haven't got it," Macloud said, answering his look. "I've been over to the gate and back, and now I've put these gamins to work. They will find it, if it's to be found. Did you telephone the office?"

"Nothing doing there!" Croyden answered. "And what's more, there won't be anything doing here—we shall never find the letter, Macloud."

"That's my fear," Macloud admitted. "Somebody's already found it."

"Somebody's *stolen* it," Croyden answered.

"What?"

"Precisely!—do you recall our being jostled by two men in the narrow corridor of the hotel? Well, then is when I lost my wallet. I am sure of it. I wasn't in a position to drop it from my pocket."

Macloud's hand sought his own breast pocket and stopped.

"I forgot to change, when I dressed. Maybe the other fellow made off with mine. I'll go and investigate—you keep an eye on the boys."

Presently he returned.

"You're right!" he said. "Mine is missing, too. We'll call off the boys."

He flung them some small coins, thereby precipitating a scramble and a fight, and they went slowly in.

"There is just one chance," he continued. "Pickpockets usually abstract the money, instantly, and throw the book and papers away. They want no tell-tale evidence. It may be the case here—they, likely, didn't examine the letter, just saw it *was* a letter and went no further."

"That won't help us much," said Croyden. "It will be found—it's only a question of the pickpockets or some one else."

"But the some one else may be honest. Your card is in the wallet?"

"With Hampton on it."

"The finder may advertise—may look you up at the hotel—may——"

"May bring it back on a gold salver!" Croyden interjected. "No! No! Colin. Our only hope is that the thief threw away the letter, and that no one finds it until after we have the treasure. The man isn't born who, under the circumstances, will renounce the opportunity for a half million dollars."

"Well, at the worst, we have an even chance! Thank Heaven! We know the directions without the letter. Don't be discouraged, old man—we'll win out, yet."

"I'm not discouraged!" laughed Croyden. "I have never anticipated success. It was sport—an adventure and a problem to work out, nothing more. Now, if we have some one else to combat, so much greater the adventure, and more intricate the problem."

"Shall we notify the police?" Macloud asked. "Or isn't it well to get them into it?"

"I'll confess I don't know. If we could jug the thieves quickly, and recover the plunder, it might be well. On the other hand, they might disclose the letter to the police or to some pal, or try even to treat with us, on the threat of publicity. On the whole, I'm inclined to secrecy—and, if the thieves show up on the Point, to have it out with them. There are only two, so we shall not be overmatched. Moreover, we can be sure they will keep it strictly to themselves, if we don't force their hands by trying to arrest them."

Macloud considered a moment. "I incline to your opinion. We will simply advertise for the wallets to-morrow, as a bluff—and go to work in earnest to find the treasure."

They had entered the hotel again; in the Exchange, the rocking chair brigade and the knocker's club were gathered.

"The usual thing!" Croyden remarked. "Why can't a hotel ever be free of them?"

"Because it's a hotel!" laughed Macloud. "Let's go in to dinner—I'm hungry."

The tall head-waiter received them like a host himself, and conducted them down the room to a small table. A moment later, the Weston party came in, with Montecute Mattison in tow, and were shown to one nearby, with Harvey's most impressive manner.

An Admiral is some pumpkins in Annapolis, when he is on the *active* list.

Mrs. Weston and the young ladies looked over and nodded; Croyden and Macloud arose and bowed. They saw Miss Cavendish lean toward the Admiral and say a word. He glanced across.

"We would be glad to have you join us," said he, with a man's fine indifference to the fact that their table was, already, scarcely large enough for five.

"I am afraid we should crowd you, sir. Thank you!—we'll join you later, if we may," replied Macloud.

A little time after, they heard Mattison's irritating voice, pitched loud enough to reach them:

"I wonder what Croyden's doing here with Macloud?" he remarked. "I thought you said, Elaine, that he had skipped for foreign parts, after the Royster smash, last September."

"I did say, Mr. Mattison, I *thought* he had gone abroad, but I most assuredly did not say, nor infer, that he had *skipped*, nor connect his going with Royster's failure!" Miss Cavendish responded. "If you must say unjust and unkind things, don't make other people responsible for them, please. Shoulder them yourself."

"Good girl!" muttered Macloud. "Hand him another!" Then he shot a look at his friend.

"I don't mind," said Croyden. "They may think what they please—and Mattison's venom is sprinkled so indiscriminately it doesn't hurt. Everyone comes in for a dose."

They dallied through dinner, and finished at the same time as the Westons. Croyden walked out with Miss Cavendish.

"I couldn't help overhearing that remark of Mattison's—the beggar intended that I should," said he—"and I want to thank you, Elaine, for your 'come back' at him."

"I'm sorry I didn't come back harder," said she.

"And if you prefer me not to go with you to the Hop to-night don't hesitate to say so—I'll understand, perfectly. The Westons may have got a wrong impression——"

"The Westons haven't ridden in the same motor, from Washington to Annapolis, with Montecute for nothing; but I'll set you straight, never fear. We are going over in the car—there is room for you both, and Mrs. Weston expects you. We will be down at nine. It's the fashion to go early, here, it seems."

Zimmerman was swinging his red-coated military band through a dreamy, sensuous waltz, as they entered the gymnasium, where the Hops, at the Naval Academy, are held. The bareness of the huge room was gone entirely— concealed by flags and bunting, which hung in brilliant festoons from the galleries and the roof. Myriads of variegated lights flashed back the glitter of epaulet and the gleam of white shoulders, with, here and there, the black of the civilian looking strangely incongruous amid the throng that danced itself into a very kaleidoscope of color.

The Secretary was a very ordinary man, who had a place in the Cabinet as a reward for political deeds done, and to be done. He represented a State machine, nothing more. Quality, temperament, fitness, poise had nothing to do with his selection. His wife was his equivalent, though, superficially, she appeared to better advantage, thanks to a Parisian modiste with exquisite taste, and her fond husband's bottomless bank account.

Having passed the receiving line, the Westons held a small reception of their own. The Admiral was still upon the active list, with four years of service ahead of him. He was to be the next Aide on Personnel, the knowing ones said, and the orders were being looked for every day. Therefore he was decidedly a personage to tie to—more important even than the Secretary, himself, who was a mere figurehead in the Department. And the officers— and their wives, too, if they were married—crowded around the Westons, fairly walking over one another in their efforts to be noticed.

"What's the meaning of it?" Croyden asked Miss Cavendish as they joined the dancing throng. "Are the Westons so amazingly popular?"

"Not at all! they're hailing the rising sun," she said—and explained: "They would do the same if he were a mummy or had small-pox. 'Grease,' they call it."

(The watchword, in the Navy, is "grease." From the moment you enter the Academy, as a plebe, until you have joined the lost souls on the retired list, you are diligently engaged in greasing every one who ranks you and in being greased by every one whom you rank. And the more assiduous and adroit you are at the greasing business, the more pleasant the life you lead. The man who ranks you can, when placed over you, make life a burden or a pleasure as his fancy and his disposition dictate. Consequently the "grease," and the higher the rank the greater the "grease," and the number of "greasers.")

"Well-named!—dirty, smeary, contaminating business," said Croyden. "And the best 'greasers' have the best places, I reckon. I prefer the unadorned garb of the civilian—and independence. I'll permit those fellows to fight the battles and draw the rewards—they can do both very well."

He did not get another dance with her until well toward the end—and would not then, if the lieutenant to whom it belonged had not been a second late— late enough to lose her.

"We are going back to Washington, in the morning," she said. "Can't you come along?"

"Impossible!" he answered. "Much as I'd like to do it."

She looked up at him, quickly.

"Are you sure you would like to do it?" she asked.

"What a question!" he exclaimed.

"Geoffrey!—what is this business which keeps you here—in the East?"

"Business!" he replied, smiling.

"Which means, I must not ask, I suppose."

He did not answer.

"Will you tell me one thing—just one?" she persisted. "Has Royster & Axtell's failure anything to do with it?"

"Yes—it has!" he said, after a moment's hesitation.

"And is it true that you are seriously embarrassed—have lost most of your fortune?"

"It was to be just one question!" he smiled.

"I'm a woman," she explained.

They danced half the length of the room before he replied. He would tell her. She, alone, deserved to know—and, if she cared, would understand.

"I have lost most of my fortune!" he admitted. "I am not, however, in the least embarrassed—I have no debts."

"And is it 'business,' which keeps you?—will you ever come back to

Northumberland?"

"Yes, it is business that keeps me—important business. Whether or not I shall return to Northumberland, depends on the outcome of that business."

"Why did you leave without a word of farewell to your friends?" she persisted.

"Was that unusual?" said Croyden. "Has any of my friends cared—sincerely cared? Has any one so much as inquired for me?"

She looked away.

"They thought you were called to Europe, suddenly," she replied.

"For which thinking you were responsible, Elaine."

"Why I?" she demanded.

"You were the only one I told."

Her eyes sought his, then fell.

"It was because of the failure," she said. "You were the largest creditor—you disappeared—there were queries and rumors—and I thought it best to tell. I hope I did no harm."

"On the contrary," he said, "I am very, very grateful to know that some one thought of me."

The music stopped. It was just in time. Another moment, and he might have said what he knew was folly. Her body close to his, his arm around her, the splendor of her bared shoulders, the perfume of her hair, the glory of her face, were overcoming him, were intoxicating his senses, were drugging him into non-resistance. The spell was broken not an instant too soon. He shook himself—like a man rousing from dead sleep—and took her back to their party.

The next instant, as she was whirled away by another, she shot him an alluringly fascinating smile, of intimate camaraderie, of understanding, which well-nigh put him to sleep again.

"I would that I might get such a smile," sighed Macloud.

"You go to the devil!" said Croyden. "She has the same smile for all her friends, so don't be silly."

"And don't be blind!" Macloud laughed.

"Moreover, if it's a different smile, the field is open. I'm scratched, you know."

"Can a man be scratched *after* he has won?" asked Macloud.

"More silliness!" Croyden retorted, as he turned away to search for his partner.

When the Hop was over, they said good-night at the foot of the stairs, in the Exchange.

"We shall see you in the morning, of course—we leave about ten o'clock," said Miss Cavendish.

"We shall be gone long before you are awake," answered Croyden. And, when she looked at him inquiringly, he added: "It's an appointment that may not be broken."

"Well, till Northumberland, then!" Miss Brundage remarked.

But Elaine Cavendish's only reply was a meaning nod and another fascinating smile. She wished him success.

As they entered their own rooms, a little later, Macloud, in the lead, switched on the lights—and stopped!

"Hello!—our wallets, by all that's good!" he exclaimed.

"Hurrah!" cried Croyden, springing in, and stumbling over Macloud in his eagerness.

He seized his wallet!—A touch, and the story was told. No need to investigate —it was as empty as the day it came from the shop, save for a few visiting cards, and some trifling memoranda. The letter and the money were gone.

"Damn!" said Croyden.

Macloud laughed.

"You didn't fancy you would find it?" he said.

"No, I didn't, but damn! anyway—who wouldn't?"

"Oh, you're strictly orthodox!" Macloud laughed. "But the pity is that won't help us. They've got old Parmenter's letter—and our ready cash as well; but the cash does not count."

"It counts with me," said Croyden. "I'm out something over a hundred—and that's considerable to me now. Anything to show where they were recovered?"

Macloud was nearest the telephone. He took down the receiver. After a time he was answered.

"What do you know about our wallets?" he asked.... "Thank you!—The office says, they were found by one of the bell-boys in a garbage can on King George Street."

"Very good," said Croyden. "If they mean fight, I reckon we can accommodate them. Greenberry Point early in the morning."

IX

"I've been thinking," said Croyden, as they footed it across the Severn bridge, "that, if we knew the year in which the light-house was erected, we could get the average encroachment of the sea every year, and, by a little figuring, arrive at where the point was in 1720. It would be approximate, of course, but it would give us a start—something more definite than we have now. For all we know Parmenter's treasure may be a hundred yards out in the Bay."

Macloud nodded. "And if we don't find the date, here," he added, "we can go to Washington and get it from the Navy Department. An inquiry from Senator Rickrose will bring what we want, instantly."

"At the same time, why shouldn't we get permission to camp on the Point for a few weeks?" Croyden suggested. "It would make it easy for us to dig and investigate, and fish and measure, in fact, do whatever we wished. Having a permit from the Department, would remove all suspicion."

"Bully! We're fond of the open—with a town convenient!" Macloud laughed. "I know Rickrose well, we can go down this afternoon and see him. He will be so astonished that we are not seeking a political favor, he will go to the Secretary himself and make ours a personal request. Then we will get the necessary camp stuff, and be right on the job."

They had passed the Experiment Station and the Rifle Range, and were rounding the shoal onto the Point, when the trotting of a rapidly approaching horse came to them from the rear.

"Suppose we conceal ourselves, and take a look," suggested Macloud. "Here is a fine place."

He pointed to some rocks and bushes that lined the roadway. The next instant, they had disappeared behind them.

A moment more, and the horse and buggy came into view. In it were two men —of medium size, dressed quietly, with nothing about them to attract attention, save that the driver had a hook-nose, and the other was bald, as the removal of his hat, an instant, showed.

"The thieves!" whispered Croyden.

"Yes—I'll bet a hundred on it!" Macloud answered.

"Greenberry Point seems far off," said the driver—"I wonder if we can have taken the wrong road?"

"This is the only one we could take," the other answered, "so we must be right. I wonder what that jay's doing?" he added, with a laugh.

"Cussing himself for——" The rest was lost in the noise of the team.

"Right, you are!" said Croyden, lifting himself from a bed of stones and vines. "Right, you are, my friend! And if I had a gun, I'd give the Coroner a job with both of you."

Macloud looked thoughtful.

"It would be most effective," he said. "But could we carry it off cleanly? The law is embarrassing if we're detected, you know."

"You're not serious?" said Croyden.

"I never was more so," the other answered. "I'd shoot those scoundrels down without a second's hesitation, if I could do it and not be caught."

"A trifle unconventional!" commented Croyden. "However, your idea isn't half bad; they wouldn't hesitate to do the same to us."

"Exactly! They won't hesitate—and, what's more, they have the nerve to take the chance. That is the difference between us and them."

They waited until they could no longer hear the horse's hoof-falls nor the rumble of the wheels. Then they started forward, keeping off the road and taking a course that afforded the protection of the trees and undergrowth. Presently, they caught sight of the two men—out in the open, their heads together, poring over a paper, presumably the Parmenter letter.

"It is not as easy finding the treasure, as it was to pick my pocket!" chuckled Croyden. "There's the letter—and there are the men who stole it. And we are helpless to interfere, and they know it. It's about as aggravating as——" He stopped, for want of a suitable comparison.

Macloud only nodded in acquiescence.

The men finished with the letter. Hook-nose went on to the Point, and stood looking at the ruins of the light-house out in the Bay; the other turned and viewed the trees that were nearest.

"Much comfort you'll get from either," muttered Croyden.

Hook-nose returned, and the two held a prolonged conversation, each of them gesticulating, now toward the water, and again toward the timber. Finally, one went down to the extreme point and stepped off two hundred and fifty paces inland. He marked this point with a stone.

Bald-head pointed to the trees, a hundred yards away, and shook his head. More talk followed. Then they produced a compass, and ran the additional distance to the North-east.

"Dig! damn you, dig!" exclaimed Macloud. "The treasure's not there."

"You'll have to work your brain a bit," Croyden added. "The letter's not all that's needed, thank Heaven! You've stolen the one, but you can't steal the other."

The men, after consulting together, went to the buggy, took out two picks and shovels, and, returning to the place, fell to work.

"Did you ever see such fools?" said Macloud. "Dig! damn you, dig!"

After a short while, Bald-head threw down his pick and hoisted himself out of the hole. An animated discussion followed.

"He's got a glimmer of intelligence, at last," Croyden muttered.

The discussion grew more animated, they waved their arms toward the Bay, and toward the Severn, and toward the land. Hook-nose slammed his pick up and down to emphasize his argument. Bald-head did likewise.

"They'll be doing the war dance, next!" laughed Macloud.

"'When thieves fall out, honest men come by their own,'" Croyden quoted.

"*More* honest men, you mean—the comparative degree."

"Life is made up of comparatives," said Croyden. "What's the matter now?" as Bald-head faced about and stalked back to the buggy. "Has he quit work so soon?"

"He has simply quit digging a hole at random," Macloud said. "My Lord, he's taking a drink!"

Bald-head, however, did not return to his companion. Instead, he went out to the Bay and stood looking across the water toward the bug-light. Then he turned and looked back toward the timber.

He was thinking, as they had. The land had been driving inward by the encroachment of the Bay—the beeches had, long since, disappeared, the victims of the gales which swept the Point. There was no place from which to start the measurements. Beyond the fact that, somewhere near by, old Parmenter had buried his treasure, one hundred and ninety years before, the letter was of no definite use to anyone.

From the Point, he retraced his steps leisurely to his companion, who had continued digging, said something—to which Hook-nose seemingly made no reply, save by a shovel of sand—and continued directly toward the timber.

"Has he seen us?" said Croyden.

"I think not—these bushes are ample protection. Lie low…. He's not coming this way—he's going to inspect the big trees, on our left…. They won't help you, my light-fingered friend; they're not the right sort."

After a time, Bald-head abandoned the search and went back to his friend. Throwing himself on the ground, he talked vigorously, and, apparently, to some effect, for, presently, the digging ceased and Hook-nose began to listen. At length, he tossed the pick and shovel aside, and lifted himself out of the hole. After a few more gesticulations, they picked up the tools and returned to the buggy.

"Have they decided to abandon it?" said Croyden, as they drove away.

The thieves, themselves, answered the question. At the first heavy undergrowth, they stopped the horse and proceeded carefully to conceal the tools. This accomplished, they drove off toward the town.

"Hum!" said Macloud. "So you're coming back are you? I wonder what you intend to do?"

"I wish we knew," Croyden returned. "It might help us—for quite between ourselves, Macloud, I think we're stumped."

"Our first business is to move on Washington and get the permit," Macloud returned. "Hook-nose and his friend may have the Point, for to-day; they're not likely to injure it. Come along!"

They were passing the Marine Barracks when Croyden, who had been pondering over the matter, suddenly broke out:

"We've got to get rid of those two fellows, Colin!"

"Granted!" said Macloud. "But how are we to manage it?"

"We agree that we dare not have them arrested—they would blow everything to the police. And the police would either graft us for all the jewels are worth, or inform the Government."

"Yes, but we may have to take the risk—or else divide up with the thieves. Which do you prefer to do?"

"Neither!" said Croyden. "There is another way—except killing them, which, of course, would be the most effective. Why shouldn't we imprison them—be our own jailers?"

Macloud threw away his cigarette and lit another before he replied, then he shook his head.

"Too much risk to ourselves," he said. "Somebody would likely be killed in the operation, with the chances strongly favoring ourselves. I'd rather shoot them down from ambush, at once."

"That may require an explanation to a judge and jury, which would be a trifle inconvenient. I'd prefer to risk my life in a fight. Then, if it came to court, our reputation is good, while theirs is in the rogues' gallery."

"Where would you imprison them?" asked Macloud, dubiously.

"That is the difficulty, I admit. Think over it, while we're going to Washington and back; see if you can't find a way out. Either we must jug them, securely, for a week or two, or we must arrest them. On the whole, it might be wiser to let them go free—let them make a try for the treasure, unmolested. When they fail and retire, we can begin."

"Your last alternative doesn't sound particularly attractive to me—or to you, either, I fancy."

"This isn't going to be a particularly attractive quest, if we want to succeed," said Croyden. "Pirate's gold breeds pirate's ways, I reckon—blood and violence and sudden death. We'll try to play it without death, however, if our opponents will permit. Such title, as exists to Parmenter's hoard, is in me, and I am not minded to relinquish it without a struggle. I wasn't especially keen at the start, but I'm keen enough, now—and I don't propose to be blocked by two rogues, if there is a way out."

"And the way out, according to your notion, is to be our own jailers, think you?" said Macloud. "Well, we can chew on it—the manner of procedure is apt to keep us occupied a few hours."

They took the next train, on the Electric Line, to Washington, Macloud having telephoned ahead and made an appointment with Senator Rickrose—whom, luckily, they found at the Capital—to meet them at the Metropolitan Club for luncheon. At Fourteenth Street, they changed to a Connecticut Avenue car, and, dismounting at Seventeenth and dodging a couple of automobiles, entered the Pompeian brick and granite building, the home of the Club which has the most representative membership in the country.

Macloud was on the non-resident list, and the door-man, with the memory for faces which comes from long practice, greeted him, instantly, by name, though he had not seen him for months.

"Yes, Mr. Macloud, Senator Rickrose just came in," he said.

They met the Senator in the Red Room. He was very tall, with a tendency to corpulency, which, however, was lost in his great height; very dignified, and, for one of his service, very young—of immense influence in the councils of his party, and the absolute dictator in his own State. Inheriting a superb machine from a "matchless leader,"—who died in the harness—he had developed it into a well nigh perfect organization for political control. All power was in his hands, from the lowest to the highest, he ruled with a sway as absolute as a despot. His word was the ultimate law—from it an appeal did not lie.

"How are you, old fellow?" he said to Macloud, dropping a hand on his shoulder. "I haven't seen you for a long time—and, Mr. Croyden, I think I have met you in Northumberland. I'm glad, indeed, to see you both." He touched a bell. "Take the orders!" he said, to the boy.

"Senator!" said Macloud, a little later, when they had finished luncheon. "I want to ask a slight favor—not political however—so it won't have to be endorsed by the organization."

The Senator laughed. "In that event, it is granted before you ask. What is it I can do?"

"Have the Secretary of the Navy issue us a permit to camp on Greenberry Point."

"Where the devil is Greenberry Point?" said Rickrose.

"Across the Severn River from Annapolis."

Rickrose turned in his chair and glanced over the dining-room. Then he raised his hand to the head waiter.

"Has the Secretary of the Navy had luncheon?" he asked.

"Yes, sir—before you came in."

The Senator nodded.

"We would better go over to the Department, at once, or we shall miss him," he said. "Chevy Chase is the drawing card, in the afternoon."

The reception hour was long passed, but the Secretary was in and would see Senator Rickrose. He came forward to meet him—a tall, middle-aged, well-groomed man, with sandy hair, whose principal recommendation for the post he filled was the fact that he was the largest contributor to the campaign fund in his State, and his senior senator needed him in his business, and had refrigerated him into the Cabinet for safe keeping—that being the only job which insured him from being a candidate for the Senator's own seat. It is a great game, is politics!

"Mr. Secretary!" said Rickrose, "my friends want a permit to camp for two weeks on Greenberry Point."

"Greenbury Point!" said the Secretary, vaguely—"that's somewhere out in San Francisco harbor?"

"Not the Greenberry Point they mean," the Senator replied. "It's down at Annapolis—across the Severn from the Naval Academy, and forms part of that command, I presume. It is waste land, unfortified and wind swept."

"Oh! to be sure. I know it. Why wouldn't the Superintendent give you a permit?" turning to Macloud. "It is within his jurisdiction."

"We didn't think to ask him," said Macloud. "We supposed it was necessary to apply direct to you."

"They are not familiar with the customs of the service," explained Rickrose, "and, as I may run down to see them, just issue the permit to me and party. The Chairman of the Naval Affairs Committee is inspecting the Point, if you need an excuse."

"Oh, no! none whatever—however, a duplicate will be forwarded to the Superintendent. If it should prove incompatible with the interests of the service," smiling, "he will inform the Department, and we shall have to revoke it."

He rang for his stenographer and dictated the permit. When it came in, he signed it and passed it over to Rickrose.

"Anything else I can do for you, Senator?" he asked.

"Not to-day, thank you, Mr. Secretary," Rickrose answered.

"Do you actually intend to come down?" asked Macloud, when they were in the corridor. "That will be bully."

He shot a look at Croyden. His face was a study. Hunting the Parmenter treasure, with the Chairman of the Naval Affairs Committee as a disinterested spectator, was rather startling, to say the least. The Senator's reply reassured them.

"Impossible!" he said. "The campaign opens next week, and I'm drawn as a spell-binder in the Pacific States. That figurehead was ruffling his feathers on you, just to show himself, so I thought I'd comb him down a bit. You'll experience no difficulty, I fancy. If you do, wire me, and I'll get busy. I've got to go over to the State Department now, so I'll say good-bye—anything else you want let me know."

"Next for a sporting goods shop," said Macloud as they went down the steps into Pennsylvania Avenue; "for a supply of small arms and ammunition—and, incidentally, a couple of tents. We can get a few cooking utensils in Annapolis, but we will take our meals at Carvel Hall. I think neither of us is quite ready to turn cook."

"I am sure, I'm content!" laughed Croyden. "We can hire a horse and buggy by the week, and keep them handy—better get a small tent for the horse, while we're about it."

They went to a shop on F Street, where they purchased three tents of suitable size, two Winchester rifles, and a pair of Colt's military revolvers with six-and-a-half inch barrels, and the necessary ammunition. These they directed should be sent to Annapolis immediately. Cots and blankets could be procured there, with whatever else was necessary.

They were bound up F Street, toward the Electric Station, when Macloud broke out.

"If we had another man with us, your imprisonment idea would not be so difficult—we could bag our game much more easily, and guard them more securely when we had them. As it is, it's mighty puzzling to arrange."

"True enough!" said Croyden, "but where is the man who is trustworthy—not to mention willing to take the risk, of being killed or tried for murder, for someone else's benefit? They're not many like you, Colin."

A man, who was looking listlessly in a window just ahead, turned away. He bore an air of dejection, and his clothes, while well cut, were beginning to show hard usage and carelessness.

"Axtell!" Macloud observed—"and on his uppers!"

"There's our man!" exclaimed Croyden. "He is down hard, a little money with a small divide, if successful, will get him. What do you say?"

"Nothing!" replied Macloud. "It's up to you."

Axtell saw them; he hesitated, whether to speak or to go on. Croyden solved the question.

"Hello! Axtell, what are you doing here?" he said, extending his hand.

Axtell grasped it, as a drowning man a straw.

"You're kind to ask, Mr. Croyden! Mighty kind in one who lost so much through us."

"You were not to blame—Royster's responsible, and he's gone——"

"To hell!" Axtell interrupted, bitterly. "May he burn forever!"

"Amen to that wish!" Croyden smiled. "Meanwhile, can I do anything for you? You're having a run of hard luck, aren't you?"

For a moment, Axtell did not answer—he was gulping down his thoughts.

"I am," he said. "I've just ten dollars to my name. I came here thinking the Congressmen, who made piles through our office, would get me something, but they gave me the marble stare. I was good enough to tip them off and do favors for them, but they're not remembering me now. Do you know where I can get a job?"

"Yes—I'll give you fifty dollars and board, if you will come with us for two weeks. Will you take it?"

"Will I take it?—Well, rather!"

"What you're to do, with Mr. Macloud and myself, we will disclose later. If, then, you don't care to aid us, we must ask you to keep silence about it."

"I don't want to know anything!" said Axtell. "I'll do my part, and ask no questions—and thank you for trusting me. You're the first man since our failure, who hasn't hit me in the face—don't you think I appreciate it?"

"Very good!" said Croyden. "Have you any other baggage?" nodding toward a small bag, which Axtell had in his hand.

"No."

"Then, come along—we're bound for Annapolis, and the car leaves in ten minutes."

X

That evening, in the seclusion of their apartment at Carvel Hall, they took Axtell into their confidence—to a certain extent (though, again, he protested his willingness simply to obey orders). They told him, in a general way, of Parmenter's bequest, and how Croyden came to be the legatee—saying nothing of its great value, however—its location, the loss of the letter the previous evening, the episode of the thieves on the Point, that morning, and their evident intention to return to the quest.

"Now, what we want to know is: are you ready to help us—unaided by the law—to seize these men and hold them prisoners, while we search for the treasure?" Croyden asked. "We may be killed in the attempt, or we may kill one or both of them, and have to stand trial if detected. If you don't want to take the risk, you have only to decline—and hold your tongue."

"My dear Mr. Croyden!" said Axtell, "I don't want you to pay me a cent—just give me my board and lodging and I'll gladly aid you as long as necessary. It's a very little thing to do for one who has lost so much through us. You provide for our defense, if we're apprehended by the law, and *that*" (snapping his fingers) "for the risk."

Croyden held out his hand.

"We'll shake hands on that, Axtell, if you please," he said; "and, if we recover what Parmenter buried, you'll not regret it."

The following morning saw them down at the Point with the equipage and other paraphernalia. The men, whom they had brought from Annapolis for the purpose, pitched the tents under the trees, ditched them, received their pay, climbed into the wagons and rumbled away to town—puzzled that anyone should want to camp on Greenberry Point when they had the price of a hotel, and three square meals a day.

"It looks pretty good," said Croyden, when the canvases were up and everything arranged—"and we shan't lack for the beautiful in nature. This is about the prettiest spot I've ever seen, the Chesapeake and the broad river—the old town and the Academy buildings—the warships at anchor—the *tout ensemble!* We may not find the treasure, but, at least, we've got a fine camp—though, I reckon, it is a bit breezy when the wind is from the Bay."

"I wonder if we should have paid our respects to the Superintendent before poaching on his preserves?" said Macloud.

"Hum—hadn't thought of that!" Croyden answered. "Better go in and show ourselves to him, this afternoon. He seems to be something of a personage down here, and we don't want to offend him. These naval officers, I'm told, are sticklers for dignity and the prerogatives due their rank."

"Hold on!" exclaimed Macloud. "On that score, we've got some rank ourselves to uphold."

"What!" said Croyden.

"Certainly! the Chairman of the Committee on Naval Affairs, of the United States Senate, is with us. According to the regulations, is it his duty to call *first* on the Superintendent?—that's the point."

"Give it up!" laughed Croyden. "However, the Superintendent has a copy of the letter, and he will know the ropes. We will wait a day, then, if he's quiescent, it's up to us."

"Great head!" laughed Macloud. "You should have been a diplomat, Croyden —nothing less than an Ambassadorship for you, my boy!"

Croyden smiled.

"A motor boat would be mighty convenient to go back and forth to Annapolis," he said. "Look at the one cutting through the water there, midway across!"

It came nearer, halted a little way off in deep water, and an officer in uniform swept the tents and them with a glass. Then the boat put about and went chugging upstream.

"We didn't seem to please him," remarked Macloud, gazing after the boat. Suddenly it turned in toward shore and made the landing at the Experiment Station.

"We are about to be welcomed or else ordered off—I'll take a bet either way," said Macloud.

"Welcomed!" Croyden responded. "Otherwise, they wouldn't have despatched an officer—it would have been a file of marines instead. You haven't lost the permit, Macloud!"

"You don't seem very sure!" Macloud laughed.

Presently, the officer appeared, walking rapidly down the roadway. As soon as he sighted the tents, he swung over toward them. Macloud went a few steps forward to meet him.

"Is this Senator Rickrose?" the Lieutenant inquired.

"No," said Macloud. "Senator Rickrose isn't coming until later. I am one of his friends, Colin Macloud, and this is Mr. Croyden and Mr. Axtell."

"Very glad to meet you, gentlemen!" said the Lieutenant. "The Superintendent presents his compliments and desires to place himself and the Academy at your disposal." (He was instructed to add, that Captain Boswick would pay his respects to-morrow, having been called to Washington to-day by an unexpected wire, but the absence of the Chairman of the Naval Affairs Committee rendered it unnecessary.)

"Thank Captain Boswick, for Senator Rickrose and us, and tell him we appreciate his kindness exceedingly," Macloud answered. "We're camping here for a week or so, to try sleeping in the open, under sea air. We're not likely to prove troublesome!" he added.

Then they took several drinks, and the aide departed.

"So far, we're making delightful progress," said Croyden; "but there are breakers ahead when Hook-nose and his partner get in the game. Suppose we inspect the premises and see if they have been here in our absence."

They went first to the place where they had seen them conceal the tools— these were gone; proof that the thieves had paid a second visit to the Point. But, search as they might, no evidence of work was disclosed.

"What does it mean?" said Croyden. "Have they abandoned the quest?"

"Not very likely," replied Macloud, "with half a million at stake. They probably are seeking information; when they have it, we shall see them back again."

"Suppose they bring four or five others to help them?"

"They won't—never fear!—they're not sharing the treasure with any one else. Rather, they will knife each other for it. Honor among thieves is like the Phœnix—it doesn't exist."

"If the knifing business were to occur before the finding, it would help some!" laughed Croyden. "Meantime, I'm going to look at the ruins of the light-house. I discovered in an almanac I found in the hotel last night, that the original light-house was erected on Greenberry Point in 1818. This fact may help us a lot."

They went out to the extreme edge, and stood gazing across the shoals toward the ruins.

"What do you make the distance from the land?" Croyden asked.

"About one hundred yards—but it's very difficult to estimate over water. It may be two hundred for all I can tell."

"It is exactly three hundred and twenty-two feet from the Point to the near side of the ruins," said Croyden.

"Why not three hundred and twenty-two and a half feet!" scoffed Macloud.

"I measured it this morning while you were dawdling over your breakfast," answered Croyden.

"Hitched a line to the land and waded out, I suppose."

"Not exactly; I measured it on the Government map of the Harbor. It gives the distance as three hundred and twenty-two feet, in plain figures."

"I said you had a great head!" Macloud exclaimed. "Now, what's the rest of the figures—or haven't you worked it out?"

Croyden drew out a paper. "The calculation is of value only on the assumption—which, however, is altogether reasonable—that the light-house, when erected, stood on the tip of the Point. It is now three hundred and twenty-two feet in water. Therefore, dividing ninety-two—the number of years since erection—into three hundred and twenty-two, gives the average yearly encroachment of the Bay as three and a half feet. Parmenter buried the casket in 1720, just a hundred and ninety years ago; so, multiplying a hundred and ninety by three and a half feet gives six hundred and sixty-five feet. In other words, the Point, in 1720, projected six hundred and sixty-five feet further out in the Bay than it does to-day."

"Then, with the point moved in six hundred and sixty-five feet Parmenter's beeches should be only eighty-five feet from the shore line, instead of seven hundred and fifty!" Macloud reflected.

"Just so!" said Croyden.

"But where are the beeches?" asked Axtell.

"Disappeared!" Croyden replied. "As the Point from year to year slipped into the Bay, the fierce gales, which sweep up the Chesapeake, gradually ate into the timber. It is seventy years, at least, since Parmenter's beeches went down."

"Why shouldn't the Duvals have noticed the encroachment of the Bay, and made a note of it on the letter?" Macloud asked.

"Probably, because it was so gradual they did not observe it. They, likely, came to Annapolis only occasionally, and Greenberry Point seemed unchanged—always the same narrow stretch of sand, with large trees to landward."

Macloud nodded. "I reckon that's reasonable."

"Next let us measure back eighty-five feet," said Croyden, producing a tape-line.... "There! this is where the beech tree should stand. But where were the other trees, and where did the two lines drawn from them intersect?"...

"Yes, now you have it!" said Macloud—"where were the trees, and where did the lines intersect? I reckon you're stumped."

"Let us try some more assuming. You had a compass yesterday, still got it?"

Macloud drew it out and tossed it over.

"I took the trouble to make a number of diagrams last night, and they disclosed a peculiar thing. With the location of the first tree fixed, it matters little where the others were, in determining the direction of the treasure. It is practically the same. The *objective point* will change as you change the position of the trees, but the *direction* will vary scarcely at all. It is self-evident, of course, to those who understand such things, but it was a valuable find for me. Now, if we are correct in our assumption, thus far, the treasure is buried——"

He opened the compass, and having brought North under the needle, ran his eye North-by-North-east. A queer look passed over his face, then he glanced at Macloud and smiled.

"The treasure is buried," he repeated—"the treasure is buried—*out in the Bay.*"

Macloud laughed!

"Looks as if wading would be a bit difficult," he said dryly.

Croyden produced the tape-line again, and they measured to the low bluff at the water's edge.

"Two hundred and eighty-two feet to here," he said, "and Parmenter buried the treasure at three hundred and thirty feet—therefore, it's forty-eight feet out in the Bay."

"Then your supposition is that, since Parmenter's time, the Bay has not only encroached on the Point, but also has eaten in on the sides."

"It would seem so."

"It's hard to dig in water," Macloud remarked. "It's apt to fill in the hole, you know."

"Don't be sarcastic," Croyden retorted. "I'm not responsible for the Bay, nor the Point, nor Parmenter, nor anything else connected with the fool quest, please remember."

"Except the present measurements and the theory on which they're based," Macloud replied. "And as the former seem to be accurate, and the latter more than reasonable, we'd best act on them."

"At least, I am satisfied that the treasure lies either in the Bay, or close on shore; if so, we have relieved ourselves from digging up the entire Point."

"You have given us a mighty plausible start," said Macloud.

"Land or water?" Croyden laughed. "Hello, whom have we here?" as a buggy emerged from among the timber, circled around, and halted before the tents.

"It is Hook-nose back again," said Macloud. "Come to pay a social call, I suppose! Anything about for them to steal?"

"Nothing but the shooting-irons."

"They're safe—I put them under the blankets."

"What the devil do they want?"

"Come to treat with us—to share the treasure."

"Hum! they've got their nerve!" exclaimed Croyden.

By this time, they had been observed by the men in the buggy who, immediately, came toward them.

"Let us get away from this place!" said Croyden, and they sauntered along landward.

"And make them stop us—don't give the least indication that we know them," added Macloud.

As the buggy neared, Macloud and Croyden glanced carelessly at the occupants, and were about to pass on, when Hook-nose calmly drew the horse over in front of them.

"Which of you men is named Croyden?" he asked.

"I am," said Geoffrey.

"Well, you're the man we're lookin' for. Geoffrey is the rest of your handle, isn't it?"

"You have the advantage of me," Croyden assured him.

"Yes, I think I have, in more ways than your name. Where can we have a little private talk?"

"We can't!" said Croyden, stepping quickly around the horse and continuing on his way—Macloud and Axtell following.

"If you'd rather have it before your friends, I'm perfectly ready to accommodate you," said the fellow. "I thought, however, you'd rather keep the little secret. Well, we'll be waiting for you at the tents, all right, my friend!" and he drove ahead.

"Macloud, we are going to bag those fellows right now—and easy, too," said Croyden. "When we get to the tents, I'll take them into one—and give them a chance to talk. When you and Axtell have the revolvers, with one for me, you can join us. They are armed, of course, but only with small pistols, likely, and you should have the drop on them before they can draw. Come, at any time— I'll let down the tent flaps on the plea of secrecy (since they've suggested it), so you can approach with impunity."

"This is where *we* get killed, Axtell!" said Macloud. "I would that I were in my happy home, or any old place but here. But I've enlisted for the war, so here goes! If you think it will do any good to pray, we can just as well wait until you've put up a few. I'm not much in that line, myself."

"Imagine a broker praying!" laughed Axtell.

"I can't," said Macloud. "But there seem to be no rules to the game we're playing, so I wanted to give you the opportunity."

As they approached the tents, Hook-nose passed the reins to Bald-head and got out.

"What's to do now?" asked Macloud. "They're separated."

"Leave it to me, I'll get them together," Croyden answered.... "You wish to see me, privately?" to Hook-nose.

"I wish to see you—it's up to you whether to make it private or not."

"Come along!" said Croyden, leading the way toward the tent, which was pitched a trifle to one side.... "Now, sir, what is it?" as the flaps dropped behind them.

"You've a business way about you, which I like——" began Hook-nose.

"Never mind my ways!" Croyden interrupted. "Come to the point—what do you want?"

"There's no false starts with you, my friend, are there!" laughed the other. "That's the thing—bang! and we are off. Good!—we'll get to business. You lost a letter recently——"

"Not at all," Croyden cut in. "I had a letter *stolen*—you, I suppose, are the thief."

"I, or my pal—it matters not which," the fellow replied easily. "Now, what we want, is to make some arrangement as to the division of the treasure, when you've found it."

"I thought as much!" said Croyden. "Well, let me tell you there won't be any arrangement made with you, alone. You must get your pal here—I don't agree with one. I agree with both or none."

"Oh, very well, I'll have him in, if you wish."

Croyden bowed.

"I do wish," he said.

Hook-nose went to the front of the tent and raised the flap.

"Bill!" he called, "hitch the horse and come in."

And Macloud and Axtell heard and understood.

While Hook-nose was summoning his partner, Croyden very naturally retired to the rear of the tent, thus obliging the rogues to keep their backs to the entrance.

"Mr. Smith, this is Mr. Croyden!" said Hook-nose.

"I'm glad to make your acquaint——" began Smith.

"There is no need for an introduction," Croyden interrupted curtly. "You're thieves, by profession, and blackmailers, in addition. Get down to business, if you please!"

"You're not overly polite, my friend—but we'll pass that by. You're hell for business, and that's our style. You understand, I see, that this treasure hunt has got to be kept quiet. If anyone peaches, the Government's wise and Parmenter's chest is dumped into its strong box—that is, as much as is left after the officials get their own flippers out. Now, my idea is for you people to do the searching, and, when the jewels is found, me and Bill will take half and youn's half. Then we all can knock off work, and live respectable."

"Rather a good bargain for you," said Croyden. "We supply the information, do all the work and give up half the spoils—for what, pray?"

"For our silence, and an equal share in the information. You have doubtless forgot that we have the letter now."

"And what if I refuse?" Croyden asked.

"You're not likely to refuse!" the fellow laughed, impudently. "Better half a big loaf than no loaf at all."

"But *if* I refuse?" Croyden repeated.

"I see what's in your mind, all right. But it won't work, and you know it. You can have us arrested, yes—and lose your plunder. Parmenter's money belongs to the United States because it's buried in United States land. A word to the Treasury Department, with the old pirate's letter, and the jig is up. We'll risk your giving us to the police, my friend!" with a sneering laugh. "If you're one to throw away good money, I miss my guess."

Croyden affected to consider.

"I forgot to say, that as you're fixed so comfortable here, me and Bill might as well stay with you—it will be more convenient, when you uncover the chest, you know; in the excitement, you're liable to forget that we come in for a share."

"Anything else you are moved to exact?" said Croyden. His ears were primed, and they told him that Macloud and Axtell were coming—"Let us have them all, so I can decide—I want no afterthoughts."

"You've got them all—and very reasonable they are!" laughed Hook-nose.

Just then, Macloud and Axtell stepped noiselessly into the tent.

Something in Croyden's face caused Hook-nose's laugh to end abruptly. He swung sharply around—and faced Macloud's leveled revolver—Axtell's covered his pal.

"Hands up! Both of you!"—Croyden cried—"None of that, Hook-nose!— make another motion to draw a gun, and we'll scatter your brains like chickenfeed." His own big revolver was sticking out of Macloud's pocket. He took it. "Now, I'll look after you, while my friends tie up your pal, and the first one to open his head gets a bullet down his throat."

"Hands behind your back, Bald-head," commanded Axtell, briskly. "Be quick about it, Mr. Macloud is wonderfully easy on the trigger. So, that's better! just hold them there a moment."

He produced a pair of nippers, and snapped them on.

"Now, lie down and put your feet together—closer! closer!" Another pair were snapped on them.

"Now, I'll do for you," Axtell remarked, turning toward Hook-nose.

With Croyden's and Macloud's guns both covering him, the fellow was quickly secured.

"With your permission, we will search you," said Croyden. "Macloud, if you will look to Mr. Smith, I'll attend to Hook-nose. We'll give them a taste of their own medicine."

"You think you're damn smart!" exclaimed Hook-nose.

"Shut up!" said Croyden. "I don't care to shoot a prisoner, but I'll do it without hesitation. It's going to be either perfect quiet or permanent sleep—and you may do the choosing."

He slowly went through Hook-nose's clothes—finding a small pistol, several well-filled wallets, and, in his inside waistcoat pocket, the Parmenter letter. Macloud did the same for Bald-head.

"You stole one hundred and seventy-nine dollars from Mr. Macloud and one hundred and eight from me," said Croyden. "You may now have the privilege of returning it, and the letter. If you make no more trouble, lie quiet and take your medicine, you'll receive no further harm. If you're stubborn, we'll either kill you and dump your bodies in the Bay, or give you up to the police. The latter would be less trouble, for, without the letter, you can tell your story to the Department, or whomever else you please—it's your word against ours—and you are thieves!"

"How long are you going to hold us prisoners?" asked Bald-head—"till you find the treasure? Oh, Lord!"

"As long as it suits our convenience."

"And luck is with you," Hook-nose sneered.

"At present, it *is* with us—very much with us, my friend," said Croyden. "You will excuse us, now, we have pressing business, elsewhere."

When they were out of hearing, Macloud said:

"Doesn't our recovery of Parmenter's letter change things very materially?"

"It seems to me it does," Croyden answered. "Indeed, I think we need fear the rogues no longer—we can simply have them arrested for the theft of our wallets, or even release them entirely."

"Arrest is preferable," said Macloud. "It will obviate all danger of our being shot at long range, by the beggars. Let us put them where they're safe, for the time."

"But the arrest must not be made here!" interposed Croyden. "We can't send for the police: if they find them here it would give color to their story of a treasure on Greenberry Point."

"Then Axtell and I will remain on guard, while you go to town and arrange for their apprehension—say, just as they come off the Severn bridge. When you return, we can release them."

"What if they don't cross the Severn—what if they scent our game, and keep straight on to Baltimore? They can abandon their team, and catch a Short Line train at a way station."

"Then the Baltimore police can round them up. I'm for chancing it. They've lost Parmenter's letter; haven't anything to substantiate their story. Furthermore, we have a permit for the Chairman of the Naval Affairs Committee and friends to camp here. I think that, now, we can afford to ignore them—the recovery of the letter was exceedingly lucky."

"Very good!" said Macloud—"you're the one to be satisfied; it's a whole heap easier than running a private prison ourselves."

Croyden looked the other's horse over carefully, so he could describe it accurately, then they hitched up their own team and he drove off to Annapolis.

In due time, he returned.

"It's all right!" he said. "I told the Mayor we had passed two men on the Severn bridge whom we identified as those who picked our pockets, Wednesday evening, in Carvel Hall—and gave him the necessary descriptions. He recognized the team as one of 'Cheney's Best,' and will have the entire police force—which consists of four men—waiting at the bridge on the Annapolis side." He looked at his watch. "They are there, now, so we can turn the prisoners loose."

Croyden and Macloud resumed their revolvers, and returned to the tent—to be greeted with a volley of profanity which, for fluency and vocabulary, was distinctly marvelous. Gradually, it died away—for want of breath and words.

"Choice! Choice!" said Croyden. "In the cuss line, you two are the real thing. Why didn't you open up sooner?—you shouldn't hide such proficiency from an admiring world."

Whereat it flowed forth afresh from Hook-nose. Bald-head, however, remained quiet, and there was a faint twinkle in his eyes, as though he caught the humor of the situation. They were severely cramped, and in considerable pain, but their condition was not likely to be benefited by swearing at their captors.

"Just listen to him!" said Croyden, as Hook-nose took a fresh start. "Did you ever hear his equal!... Now, if you'll be quiet a moment, like your pal, we will tell you something that possibly you'll not be averse to hear.... So, that's better. We're about to release you—let you go free; it's too much bother to keep you prisoners. These little toy guns of yours, however, we shall throw into the Bay, in interest of the public peace. May we trouble you, Mr. Axtell, to remove the bonds?... Thank you! Now, you may arise and shake yourselves—you'll, likely, find the circulation a trifle restricted, for a few minutes."

Hook-nose gave him a malevolent look, but made no reply, Bald-head grinned broadly.

"Now, if you have sufficiently recovered, we will escort you to your carriage! Forward, march!"

And with the two thieves in front, and the three revolvers bringing up the rear, they proceeded to the buggy. The thieves climbed in.

"We wish you a very good day!" said Croyden. "Drive on, please!"

———————————————————

XI

"May we have seen the last of you!" said Macloud, as the buggy disappeared among the trees; "and may the police provide for you in future."

"And while you're about it," said Croyden, "you might pray that we find the treasure—it would be quite as effective." He glanced at his watch. "It's four o'clock. Now, to resume where those rogues interrupted us. We had the jewels located, somewhere, within a radius of fifty feet. They must be, according to our theory, either on the bank or in the Bay. We can't go at the water without a boat. Shall we tackle the land at once? or go to town and procure a boat, and be ready for either in the morning."

"I have an idea," said Macloud.

"Don't let it go to waste, old man, let's have it!" Croyden encouraged.

"If you can give up hearing yourself talk, for a moment, I'll try!" laughed Macloud. "It is conceded, I believe, that digging on the Point by day may, probably will, provoke comment and possibly investigation as well. My idea is this. Do no work by day. Then as soon as dusky Night has drawn her robes about her——"

"Oh, Lord!" ejaculated Croyden, with upraised hands.

"Then, as soon as dusky Night has drawn her robes about her," Macloud repeated, imperturbably, "we set to work, by the light of the silvery moon. We arouse no comment—provoke no investigation. When morning dawns, the sands are undisturbed, and we are sleeping as peacefully as guinea pigs."

"And if there isn't a moon, we will set to work by the light of the silvery lantern, I reckon!" said Croyden.

"And, when we tackle the water, it will be in a silver boat and with silver cuirasses and silver helmets, à la Lohengrin."

"And I suppose, our swan-song will be played on silver flutes!" laughed Croyden.

"There won't be a swan-song—we're going to find Parmenter's treasure," said Macloud.

Leaving Axtell in camp, they drove to town, stopping at the North end of the Severn bridge to hire a row-boat,—a number of which were drawn up on the bank—and to arrange for it to be sent around to the far end of the Point. At the hotel, they found a telephone call from the Mayor's office awaiting them.

The thieves had been duly captured, the Mayor said, and they had been sent to Baltimore. The Chief of Detectives happened to be in the office, when they were brought in, and had instantly recognized them as well-known criminals, wanted in Philadelphia for a particularly atrocious hold-up. He had, thereupon, thought it best to let the Chief take them back with him, thus saving the County the cost of a trial, and the penitentiary expense—as well as sparing Mr. Croyden and his friend much trouble and inconvenience in attending court. He had had them searched, but found nothing which could be identified. He hoped this was satisfactory.

Croyden assured him it was more than satisfactory.

That night they began the hunt. That night, and every night for the next three weeks, they kept at it.

They tested every conceivable hypothesis. They dug up the entire zone of suspicion—it being loose sand and easy to handle. On the plea that a valuable ruby ring had been lost overboard while fishing, they dragged and scraped the bottom of the Bay for a hundred yards around. All without avail. Nothing smiled on them but the weather—it had remained uniformly good until the last two days before. Then there had set in, from the North-east, such a storm of rain as they had never seen. The very Bay seemed to be gathered up and dashed over the Point. They had sought refuge in the hotel, when the first chilly blasts of wind and water came up the Chesapeake. As it grew fiercer,—and a negro sent out for information returned with the news that their tents had been blown away, and all trace of the camp had vanished—it was decided that the quest should be abandoned.

"It's a foolish hunt, anyway!" said Croyden. "We knew from the first it couldn't succeed."

"But we wanted to prove that it couldn't succeed," Macloud observed. "If you hadn't searched, you always would have thought that, maybe, you could have been successful. Now, you've had your try—and you've failed. It will be easier to reconcile yourself to failure, than not to have tried."

"In other words, it's better to have tried and lost, than never to have tried at all," Croyden answered. "Well! it's over and there's no profit in thinking more about it. We have had an enjoyable camp, and the camp is ended. I'll go home and try to forget Parmenter, and the jewel box he buried down on Greenberry Point."

"I think I'll go with you," said Macloud.

"To Hampton!" Croyden exclaimed, incredulously.

"To Hampton—if you can put up with me a little longer."

A knowing smile broke over Croyden's face.

"The Symphony in Blue?" he asked.

"Maybe!—and maybe it is just you. At any rate, I'll come if I may."

"My dear Colin! You know you're more than welcome, always!"

Macloud bowed. "I'll go out to Northumberland to-night, arrange a few matters which are overdue, and come down to Hampton as soon as I can get away."

The next afternoon, as Macloud was entering the wide doorway of the Tuscarora Trust Company, he met Elaine Cavendish coming out.

"Stranger! where have you been these many weeks?" she said, giving him her hand.

"Out of town," he answered. "Did you miss me so much?"

"I did! There isn't a handy dinner man around, with you and Geoffrey both away. Dine with us this evening, will you?—it will be strictly *en famille*, for I want to talk business."

"Wants to talk business!" he thought, as, having accepted, he went on to the coupon department. "It has to do with that beggar Croyden, I reckon."

And when, the dinner over, they were sitting before the open grate fire, in the big living room, she broached the subject without timidity, or false pride.

"You are more familiar with Geoffrey Croyden's affairs than any one else, Colin," she said, crossing her knees, in the reckless fashion women have now-a-days, and exposing a ravishing expanse of blue silk stockings, with an unconscious consciousness that was delightfully naive. "And I want to ask you something—or rather, several things."

Macloud blew a whiff of cigarette smoke into the fire, and waited.

"I, naturally, don't ask you to violate any confidence," she went on, "but I fancy you may tell me this: was the particular business in which Geoffrey was engaged, when I saw him in Annapolis, a success or a failure?"

"Why do you ask!" Macloud said. "Did he tell you anything concerning it?"

"Only that his return to Northumberland would depend very much on the outcome."

"But nothing as to its character?"

"No," she answered.

"Well, it wasn't a success; in fact, it was a complete failure."

"And where is Geoffrey, now?" she asked.

"I do not know," he replied.

She laughed lightly. "I do not mean, where is he this minute, but where is he in general—where would you address a wire, or a letter, and know that it would be received?"

He threw his cigarette into the grate and lit another.

"I am not at liberty to tell," he said.

"Then, it is true—he is concealing himself."

"Not exactly—he is not proclaiming himself——"

"Not proclaiming himself or his whereabouts to his Northumberland friends, you mean?"

"Friends!" said Macloud. "Are there such things as friends, when one has been unfortunate?"

"I can answer only for myself," she replied earnestly.

"I believe you, Elaine——"

"Then tell me this—is he in this country or abroad?"

"In this country," he said, after a pause.

"Is he in want,—I mean, in want for the things he has been used to?"

"He is not in want, I can assure you!—and much that he was used to having, he has no use for, now. Our wants are relative, you know."

"Why did he leave Northumberland so suddenly?" she asked.

"To reduce expenses. He was forced to give up the old life, so he chose wisely, I think—to go where his income was sufficient for his needs."

"But *is* it sufficient?" she demanded.

"He says it is."

She was silent for a while, staring into the blaze. He did not interrupt—thinking it wise to let her own thoughts shape the way.

"You will not tell me where he is?" she said suddenly, bending her blue eyes hard upon his face.

"I may not, Elaine. I ought not to have told you he was not abroad."

"This business which you and he were on, in Annapolis—it failed, you say?"
He nodded.

"And is there no chance that it may succeed, some time?"

"He has abandoned it."

"But may not conditions change—something happen——" she began.

"It is the sort that does not happen. In this case, abandonment spells finis."

"Did he know, when we were in Annapolis?" she asked.

"On the contrary, he was very sanguine—it looked most promising then."

Her eyes went back to the flames. He blew ring after ring of smoke, and waited, patiently. He was the friend, he saw, now. He could never hope to be more. Croyden was the lucky fellow—and would not! Well, he had his warning and it was in time. Since she was baring her soul to him, as friend to friend, it was his duty to help her to the utmost of his power.

Suddenly, she uncrossed her knees and sat up.

"I have bought all the stock, and the remaining bonds of the Virginia Development Company, from the bank that held them as collateral for Royster & Axtell's loan," she said. "Oh, don't be alarmed! I didn't appear in the matter—my broker bought them in *your* name, and paid for them in actual money."

"I am your friend—use me!" he said, simply.

She arose, and bending swiftly over, kissed him on the cheek.

"Don't, Elaine," he said. "I am, also, Geoffrey Croyden's friend, but there are temptations which mortal man cannot resist."

"You think so?" she smiled, leaning over the back of his chair, and putting her head perilously close to his—"but I trust you—though I shan't kiss you again —at least, for the present. Now, you have been so *very* good about the bonds, I want you to be good some more. Will you, Colin?"

He held his hands before him, to put them out of temptation.

"Ask me to crawl in the grate, and see how quickly I do it!" he declared.

"It might prove my power, but I should lose my friend," she whispered.

"And that would be inconvenient!" he laughed. "Come, speak up! it's already granted, that you should know, Elaine."

"You're a very sweet boy," she said, going back to her seat.

"Which needs demonstration. But that you're a very sweet girl, needs no proof—unless——" looking at her with a meaning smile.

"Would that be proof, think you?" with a sidelong glance.

"I should accept it as such," he averred—"whenever you choose to confer it."

"*Confer* smacks of reward for service done," she said. "Will it bide till then?"

"Not if it may come sooner?"

"Wait—If you choose such pay, the——"

"I choose no pay," he interrupted.

"Then, the reward will be in kind," she answered enigmatically. "I want you ——" She put one slender foot on the fender, and gazed at it, meditatively, while the firelight stole covert glances at the silken ankles thus exposed. "I want you to purchase for me, from Geoffrey Croyden, at par, his Virginia Development Company bonds," she said. "You can do it through your broker. I will give you a check, now——"

"Wait!" he said; "wait until he sells——"

"You think he won't sell?" she inquired.

"I think he will have to be satisfied, first, as to the purchaser—in plain words, that it isn't either you or I. We can't give Geoffrey money! The bonds are practically worthless, as he knows only too well."

"I had thought of that," she said, "but, isn't it met by this very plan? Your broker purchases the bonds for your account, but he, naturally, declines to reveal the identity of his customer. You can, truthfully, tell Geoffrey that *you* are not buying them—for you're not. And *I*—if he will only give me the chance—will assure him that I am *not* buying them from him—and you might confirm it, if he asked."

"Hum! It's juggling with the facts—though true on the face," said Macloud, "but it's pretty thin ice we're skating on."

"You are assuming he suspects or questions. He may take the two hundred thousand and ask no question."

"You don't for a moment believe that!" he laughed.

"It *is* doubtful," she admitted.

"And you wouldn't think the same of him, if he did."

"I admit it!" she said.

"So, we are back to the thin ice. I'll do what I can; but, you forgot, I am not at liberty to give his address to my brokers. I shall have to take their written offer to buy, and forward it to him, which, in itself will oblige me, at the same time, to tell him that *I* am not the purchaser."

"I leave it entirely to you—manage it any way you see fit. All I ask, is that you get him to sell. It's horrible to think of Geoffrey being reduced to the bare necessities of life—for that's what it means, when he goes 'where his income is sufficient for his needs.'"

"It's unfortunate, certainly: it would be vastly worse for a woman—to go from luxury to frugality, from everything to relatively nothing is positively pathetic. However, Croyden is not suffering—he has an attractive house filled with old things, good victuals, a more than competent cook, and plenty of society. He has cut out all the non-essentials, and does the essentials economically."

"You have been there?" she demanded. "You speak of your own knowledge, not from his inferences?"

"I have been there!" he answered.

"And the society—what of it?" she asked quickly.

"Better than our own!" he said, instantly.

"Indeed!" she replied with lifted eye-brows. "Our own in the aggregate or differentiated?"

"In the aggregate!" he laughed; "but quite the equal of our own differentiated. If Croyden were a marrying man—with sufficient income for two—I should give him about six months, at the outside."

"And how much would you give one with sufficient for two—*yourself*, for instance?"

"Just long enough to choose the girl—and convince her of the propriety of the choice."

"And do you expect to join Geoffrey, soon?" meaningly.

"As soon as I can get through here,—probably in a day or two."

"Then, we may look for the new Mrs. Macloud in time for the holidays, I presume.—Sort of a Christmas gift?"

"About then—if I can pick among so many, and she ratifies the pick."

"You haven't, yet, chosen?"

"No!—there are so many I didn't have time to more than look them over. When I go back, I'll round them up, cut out the most likely, and try to tie and brand her."

"Colin!" cried Miss Cavendish. "One would think, from your talk, that Geoffrey was in a cowboy camp, with waitresses for society."

He grinned, and lighted a fresh cigarette.

She tossed him an alluring look.

"And nothing can induce you to tell me the location of the camp?" she implored.

He smoked, a bit, in silence. Should he or should he not?...

"No!—not now!" he said, slowly. "Let us try the bond matter, first. If he sells, I think he will return; if not, I'll then consider telling."

"You're a good fellow, Colin, dear!" she whispered, leaning over and giving his hand an affectionate little pat. "You're so nice and comfortable to have around—you never misunderstand, nor draw inferences that you shouldn't."

"Which means, I'm not to draw inferences now?" he said.

"Nor at any other time," she remarked.

"And the reward?"

"Will be forthcoming," with an alluring smile.

"I've a mind to take part payment now," said he, intercepting the hand before she could withdraw it.

"If you can, sir!" whisking it loose, and darting around a table.

"A challenge, is it? Oh, very well!" and he sprang after.

With a swift movement, she swept up her skirts and fled—around chairs, and tables, across rugs, over sofas and couches—always manœuvring to gain the doorway, yet always finding him barring the way;—until, at last, she was forced to refuge behind a huge davenport, standing with one end against the wall.

"Now, will you surrender?" he demanded, coming slowly toward her in the cul de sac.

She shook her head, smiling the while.

"I'll be merciful," he said. "It is five steps, until I reach you—One!—Will you yield?"

"No!"

"Two!—will you yield?"

"No!"

"Three!—will you yield?"

"No!"

"Four——"

Quick as thought, she dropped one hand on the back of the davenport; there was a flash of slippers, lingerie and silk, and she was across and racing for the door, now fair before her, leaving him only the echo of a mocking laugh.

"Five!" she counted, tauntingly, from the hall. "Why don't you continue, sir?"

"I stop with four," he said. "I'll be good for to-night, Elaine—you need have no further fear."

She tossed her head ever so slightly, while a bantering look came into her eyes.

"I'm not much afraid of you, now—nor any time," she answered. "But you have more courage than I would have thought, Colin—decidedly more!"

———————

XII

ONE LEARNED IN THE LAW

It was evening, when Croyden returned to Hampton—an evening which contained no suggestion of the Autumn he had left behind him on the Eastern Shore. It was raw, and damp, and chill, with the presage of winter in its cold; the leaves were almost gone from the trees, the blackening hand of frost was on flower and shrubbery. As he passed up the dreary, deserted street, the wind was whistling through the branches over head, and moaning around the houses like spirits of the damned.

He turned in at Clarendon—shivering a little at the prospect. He was beginning to appreciate what a winter spent under such conditions meant, where one's enjoyments and recreations are circumscribed by the bounds of comparatively few houses and few people—people, he suspected, who could not understand what he missed, of the hurly-burly of life and amusement, even if they tried. Their ways were sufficient for them; they were eminently satisfied with what they had; they could not comprehend dissatisfaction in another, and would have no patience with it.

He could imagine the dismalness of Hampton, when contrasted with the brightness of Northumberland. The theatres, the clubs, the constant dinners, the evening affairs, the social whirl with all that it comprehended, compared with an occasional dinner, a rare party, interminable evenings spent, by his own fireside, alone! Alone! Alone!

To be sure, Miss Carrington, and Miss Borden, and Miss Lashiel, and Miss Tilghman, would be available, when they were home. But the winter was when they went visiting, he remembered, from late November until early April, and, at that period, the town saw them but little. There was the Hampton Club, of course, but it was worse than nothing—an opportunity to get mellow and to gamble, innocent enough to those who were habituated to it, but dangerous to one who had fallen, by adversity, from better things....

However, Macloud would be there, shortly, thank God! And the dear girls were not going for a week or so, he hoped. And, when the worst came, he could retire to the peacefulness of his library and try to eke out a four months' existence, with the books, and magazines and papers.

Moses held open the door, with a bow and a flourish, and the lights leaped out to meet him. It was some cheer, at least, to come home to a bright house, a full larder, faithful servants—and supper ready on the table, and tuned to even a Clubman's taste.

"Moses, do you know if Miss Carrington's at home?" he asked, the coffee on and his cigar lit.

"Yass, seh! her am home, seh, I seed she herse'f dis mornin' cum down de parf from de front poach wid de dawg, seh."

Croyden nodded and went across the hall to the telephone.

Miss Carrington, herself, answered his call.—Yes, she intended to be home all evening. She would be delighted to see him and to hear a full account of himself.

He was rather surprised at his own alacrity, in finishing his cigar and changing his clothes—and he wondered whether it was the girl, or the companionship, or the opportunity to be free of himself? A little of all three, he concluded.... But, especially, the *girl*, as she came from the drawing-room to meet him.

"So you have really returned," she said, as he bowed over her slender fingers. "We were beginning to fear you had deserted us."

"You are quite too modest," he replied. "You don't appreciate your own attractions."

The "you" was plainly singular, but she refused to see it.

"Our own attractions require us to be modest," she returned; "with a—man of the world."

"Don't!" he laughed. "Whatever I may have been, I am, now, a man of Hampton."

She shook her head. "You can never be a man of Hampton."

"Why not, if I live among you?"

"If you live here—take on our ways, our beliefs, our mode of thinking, you may, in a score of years, grow like us, outwardly; but, inwardly, where the true like must start, *never!*"

"How do we differ?"

"Ask me something easier! You've been bred differently, used to different things, to doing them in a different way. We do things slowly, leisurely, with a fine disregard of time, you, with the modern rush, and bustle, and hurry. You are a man of the world—I repeat it—up to the minute in everything—never lagging behind, unless you wish. You never put off till to-morrow what you can do to-day. We never do anything to-day that can be put off till to-morrow."

"And which do you prefer, the to-day or the to-morrow?" he asked.

"It depends on my humor, and my location, at the time—though, I must admit, the to-day makes for thrift, and business, and success in acquiring wealth."

"And success also in getting rid of it. It is a return toward the primitive condition—the survival of the fittest. There must be losers as well as acquirers."

"There's the pity of it!" she exclaimed, "that one must lose in order that another may gain."

"But as we are not in Utopia or Altruria," he smiled, "it will continue so to be. Why, even in Baltimore, they——"

"Oh, Baltimore is only an overgrown country town!" she exclaimed.

"Granted!" he replied. "With half a million population, it is as provincial as Hampton, and thanks God for it—the most smug, self-satisfied, self-sufficient municipality in the land, with its cobblestones, its drains-in-the-gutters, its how much-holier-than-thou air about everything."

"But it has excellent railway facilities!" she laughed.

"Because it happens to be on the main line between Washington and the North."

"At least, the people are nice, barring a few mushrooms who are making a great to-do."

"Yes, the people *are* delightful!—And, when it comes to mushrooms, Northumberland has Baltimore beaten to a frazzle. We raise a fresh crop every night."

"Northumberland society must be exceedingly large!" she laughed.

"It is—but it's not overcrowded. About as many die every day, as are born every night; and, at any rate, they don't interfere with those who really belong —except to increase prices, and the cost of living, and clog the avenue with automobiles."

"That is progress!"

"Yes, it's progress! but whither it leads no one knows—to the devil, likely— or a lemon garden."

"'Blessed are the lemons on earth, for they shall be peaches in Heaven!'" she quoted.

"What a glorious peach your Miss Erskine will be," he replied.

"I'm afraid you don't appreciate the great honor the lady did you, in condescending to view the *treasures* of Clarendon, and to talk about them afterward. To hear her, she is the most intimate friend you have in Hampton."

"Good!" he said, "I'm glad you told me. Somehow, I'm always drawing lemons."

"Am I a lemon?" she asked, abruptly.

"You! do you think you are?"

"One can never know."

"Have I drawn *you*?" he inquired.

"Quite immaterial to the question, which is: A lemon or not a lemon?"

"If you could but see yourself at this moment, you would not ask," he said, looking at her with amused scrutiny.

The lovely face, the blue black hair, the fine figure in the simple pink organdie, the slender ankles, the well-shod feet—a lemon!

"But as I can't see myself, and have no mirror handy, your testimony is desired," she insisted. "A lemon or not a lemon?"

"A lemon!" he answered.

"Then you can't have any objection——"

"If you bring Miss Erskine in?" he interrupted. "Nay! Nay! *Nay!* NAY!"

"——if I take you there for a game of Bridge—shall we go this very evening?"

"If you wish," he answered.

She laughed. "I don't wish—and we are growing very silly. Come, tell about your Annapolis trip. You stayed a great while."

"Something more than three weeks!"

"It's a queer old town, Annapolis—they call it the 'Finished City!' It's got plenty of landmarks, and relics, but nothing more. If it were not for the State Capitol and Naval Academy, it would be only a lot of ruins, lost in the sand. In midsummer, it's absolutely dead. No one on the streets, no one in the shops, no one any place.—Deserted—until there's a fire. Then you should see them come out!"

"That is sufficiently expressed!" laughed Croyden. "But, with the autumn and the Academy in session, the town seemed very much alive. We sampled 'Cheney's Best,' Wegard's Cakes, and saw the Custard-and-Cream Chapel."

"You've been to Annapolis, sure!" she replied. "There's only one thing more —did you see Paul Jones?"

He shook his head. "We missed him."

"Which isn't surprising. You can't find him without the aid of a detective or a guide."

"Then, who ever finds him?"

"No one!—and there is the shame. We accepted the vast labors and the money of our Ambassador to France in locating the remains of America's first Naval Hero; we sent an Embassy and a warship to bring them back; we received them with honor, orated over them, fired guns over them. And then, when the spectators had departed—assuming they were to be deposited in the crypt of the Chapel—we calmly chucked them away on a couple of trestles, under a stairway in Bancroft Hall, as we would an old broom or a tin can. That's *our* way of honoring the only Naval Commander we had in the Revolution. It would have been better, much better, had we left him to rest in the quiet seclusion of his grave in France—lost, save in memory, with the halo of the past and privacy of death around him."

"And why didn't we finish the work?" said Croyden. "Why bring him here, with the attendant expense, and then stop, just short of completion? Why didn't we inter him in the Chapel (though, God save me from burial there), or any place, rather than on trestles under a stairway in a midshipmen's dormitory?"

"Because the appropriation was exhausted, or because the Act wasn't worded to include burial, or because the Superintendent didn't want the bother, or because it was a nuisance to have the remains around—or some other absurd reason. At all events, he is there in the cellar, and he is likely to stay there, till Bancroft Hall is swallowed up by the Bay. The junket to France, the parade, the speeches, the spectacular part are over, so, who cares for the entombment, and the respect due the distinguished dead?"

"I don't mean to be disrespectful," he observed, "but it's hard luck to have one's bones disturbed, after more than a hundred years of tranquillity, to be conveyed clear across the Atlantic, to be orated over, and sermonized over, and, then, to be flung aside like old junk and forgot. However, we have troubles of our own—I know I have—more real than Paul Jones! He may be glad he's dead, so he won't have any to worry over. In fact, it's a good thing to be dead—one is saved from a heap of worry."

She looked at him, without replying.

"What's the use?" he said. "A daily struggle to procure fuel sufficient to keep up the fire."

"What's the use of anything! Why not make an end of life, at once?" she asked.

"Sometimes, I'm tempted," he admitted. "It's the leap in the dark, and no returning, that restrains, I reckon—and the fact that we must face it alone. Otherwise——"

She laughed softly. "Otherwise death would have no terrors! You have begged the question, or what amounts to it. But, to return to Annapolis; what else did you see?"

"You have been there?"

"Many times."

"Then you know what I saw," he replied. "I had no wonderful adventures. This isn't the day of the rapier and the mask."

She half closed her eyes and looked at him through the long lashes.

"What were you doing down on Greenberry Point?" she demanded.

"How did you know?" he asked, surprised.

"Oh! very naturally. I was in Annapolis—I saw your name on the register—I inquired—and I had the tale of the camp. No one, however, seemed to think it queer!" laughing.

"Why should they? Camping out is entirely natural," Croyden answered.

"With the Chairman of the Senate Committee on Naval Affairs?"

"We were in his party!"

"A party which until five days ago he had not joined—at least, so the Superintendent told me, when I dined at his house. He happened to mention your name, found I knew you—and we gossiped. Perhaps we shouldn't, but we did."

"What else did he tell you?"

"Nothing! he didn't seem even to wonder at your being there——"

"But *you* did?"

"It's the small town in me, I suppose—to be curious about other people and their business; and it was most suspicious."

"What was most suspicious?" he asked.

"Your actions. First, you hire a boat and cross the Bay direct from Hampton to Annapolis. Second, you procure, through Senator Rickrose, a permit from the Secretary of the Navy to camp on Greenberry Point. Third, you actually do camp, there, for nearly, or quite three weeks. Query:—Why? Why go clear to the Western Shore, and choose a comparatively inaccessible and exposed location on United States property, if the idea were only a camp? Why not camp over on Kent Island, or on this coast? Anywhere, within a few miles of Hampton, there are scores of places better adapted than Greenberry Point."

"You should be a story teller!" he laughed. "Your imagination is marvelous. With a series of premises, you can reach whatever conclusion you wish— you're not bound by the probabilities."

"You're simply obscuring the point," she insisted. "In this instance, my premises are facts which are not controverted. You admit them to be correct. So, why? Why?——" She held up her hand. "Don't answer! I'm not asking for information. I don't want to be told. I'm simply 'chaffing of you,' don't you know!"

"With just a lingering curiosity, however," he added.

"A casual curiosity, rather," she amended.

"Which, some time, I shall gratify. You've trailed me down—we *were* on Greenberry Point for a purpose, but nothing has come of it, yet—and it's likely a failure."

"My dear Mr. Croyden, I don't wish to know. It was a mistake to refer to it. I should simply have forgot what I heard in Annapolis—I'll forget now, if you will permit."

"By no means, Miss Carrington. You can't forget, if you would—and I would not have you, if you could. Moreover, I inherited it along with Clarendon, and, as you were my guide to the place, it's no more than right that you should know. I think I shall confide in you—no use to protest, it's got to come!" he added.

"You are determined?—Very well, then, come over to the couch in the corner, where we can sit close and you can whisper."

He arose, with alacrity. She put out her hand and led him—and he suffered himself to be led.

"Now!" when they were seated, "you may begin. Once upon a time——" and laughed, softly. "I'll take this, if you've no immediate use for it," she said, and released her hand from his.

"For the moment," he said. "I shall want it back, presently, however."

"Do you, by any chance, get all you want?" she inquired.

"Alas! no! Else I would have kept what I already had."

She put her hands behind her, and faced around.

"Begin, sir!" she said. "Begin! and try to be serious."

"Well,—once upon a time——" Then he stopped. "I'll go over to the house and get the letter—it will tell you much better than I can. You will wait here, *right here*, until I return?"

She looked at him, with a tantalizing smile.

"Won't it be enough, if I am here *when* you return?" she asked.

When he came out on the piazza the rain had ceased, the clouds were gone, the temperature had fallen, and the stars were shining brightly in a winter sky.

He strode quickly down the walk to the street and crossed it diagonally to his own gates. As he passed under the light, which hung near the entrance, a man walked from the shadow of the Clarendon grounds and accosted him.

"Mr. Croyden, I believe?" he said.

Croyden halted, abruptly, just out of distance.

"Croyden is my name?" he replied, interrogatingly.

"With your permission, I will accompany you to your house—to which I assume you are bound—for a few moments' private conversation."

"Concerning what?" Croyden demanded.

"Concerning a matter of business."

"My business or yours?"

"Both!" said the man, with a smile.

Croyden eyed him suspiciously. He was about thirty years of age, tall and slender, was well dressed, in dark clothes, a light weight top-coat, and a derby hat. His face was ordinary, however, and Croyden had no recollection of ever having seen it—certainly not in Hampton.

"I'm not in the habit of discussing business with strangers, at night, nor of taking them to my house," he answered, brusquely. "If you have anything to say to me, say it now, and be brief. I've no time to waste."

"Some one may hear us," the man objected.

"Let them—I've no objection."

"Pardon me, but I think, in this matter, you would have objection."

"You'll say it quickly, and here, or not at all," snapped Croyden.

The man shrugged his shoulders.

"It's scarcely a subject to be discussed on the street," he observed, "but, if I must, I must. Did you ever hear of Robert Parmenter? Oh! I see that you have! Well, the business concerns a certain letter—need I be more explicit?"

"If you wish to make your business intelligible."

The fellow shrugged his shoulders again.

"As you wish," he said, "though it only consumes time, and I was under the impression that you were in a hurry. However: To repeat—the business concerns a letter, which has to do with a certain treasure buried long ago, on Greenberry Point, by the said Robert Parmenter. Do I make myself plain, now, sir?"

"Your language is entirely intelligible—though I cannot answer for the facts recited."

The man smiled imperturbably, and went on:

"The letter in question having come into your possession recently, you, with two companions, spent three weeks encamped on Greenberry Point, ostensibly for your health, or the night air, or anything else that would deceive the Naval authorities. During which time, you dug up the entire Point, dragged the waters immediately adjoining—and then departed, very strangely choosing for it a time of storm and change of weather. My language is intelligible, thus far?"

Croyden nodded—rather amused. Evidently, the thieves had managed to communicate with a confederate, and this was a hold-up. They assumed he had been successful.

"Therefore, it is entirely reasonable to suppose that your search was not ineffectual. In plain words, you have recovered the treasure."

The man paused, waiting for an answer.

Croyden only smiled, and waited, too.

"Very good!—we will proceed," said the stranger. "The jewels were found on Government land. It makes no difference whether recovered on the Point or on the Bay—the law covering treasure trove, I am informed, doesn't apply. The Government is entitled to the entire find, it being the owner in fee of the land."

"You talk like a lawyer!" said Croyden.

The stranger bowed. "I have devoted my spare moments to the study of the law——"

"And how to avoid it," Croyden interjected.

The other bowed again.

"And also how to prevent *others* from avoiding it," he replied, suggestively. "Let us take up that phase, if it please you."

"And if it doesn't please?" asked Croyden, suppressing an inclination to laugh.

"Then let us take it up, any way—unless you wish to forfeit your find to the Government."

"Proceed!" said Croyden. "We are arriving, now, at the pith of the matter. What do you offer?"

"We want an equal divide. We will take Parmenter's estimate and multiply it by two, though jewels have appreciated more than that in valuation. Fifty thousand pounds is two hundred and fifty thousand dollars, which will total, according to the calculation, half a million dollars,—one half of which amount you pay us as our share."

"Your share! Why don't you call it properly—blackmail?" Croyden demanded.

"As you wish!" the other replied, airily. "If you prefer blackmail to share, it will not hinder the contract—seeing that it is quite as illegal on your part as on ours. Share merely sounds a little better but either obtains the same end. So, suit yourself. Call it what you will—but *pay*."

"Pay—or what?"

"Pay—or lose everything!" was the answer. "If you are not familiar with the law covering the subject under discussion, let me enlighten you."

"Thunder! how you do roll it out!" laughed Croyden. "Get on! man, get on!"

"I was endeavoring to state the matter succinctly," the stranger replied, refusing to be hurried or flustered. "The Common Law and the practice of the Treasury Department provide, that all treasure found on Government land or within navigable waters, is Government property. If declared by the finder, immediately, he shall be paid such reward as the Secretary may determine. If he does not declare, and is informed on, the informer gets the reward. You will observe that, under the law, you have forfeited the jewels—I fancy I do not need to draw further deductions."

"No!—it's quite unnecessary," Croyden remarked. "Your fellow thieves went into that phase (good word, I like it!) rather fully, down on Greenberry Point. Unluckily, they fell into the hands of the police, almost immediately, and we have not been able to continue the conversation."

"I have the honor to continue the conversation—and, in the interim, you have found the treasure. So, Parmenter's letter won't be essential—the facts, circumstances, your own and Mr. Macloud's testimony, will be sufficient to prove the Government's case. Then, as you are aware, it's pay or go to prison for larceny."

"There is one very material hypothesis, which you assume as a fact, but which is, unfortunately, not a fact," said Croyden. "We did not find the treasure."

The man laughed, good-humoredly.

"Naturally!" he replied. "We don't ask you to acknowledge the finding—just pay over the quarter of a million and we will forget everything."

"My good man, I'm speaking the truth!" Croyden answered. "Maybe it's difficult for you to recognize, but it's the truth, none the less. I only wish I *had* the treasure—I think I'd be quite willing to share it, even with a blackmailer!"

The man laughed, again.

"I trust it will give no offence if I say I don't believe you."

"You can believe what you damn please!" Croyden retorted.

And, without more ado, he turned his back and went up the path to Clarendon.

———————————————

XII

I COULD TELL SOME THINGS

When Croyden had got Parmenter's letter from the secret drawer in the escritoire, he rang the old-fashioned pull-bell for Moses. It was only a little after nine, and, though he did not require the negro to remain in attendance until he retired, he fancied the kitchen fire still held him.

And he was not mistaken. In a moment Moses appeared—his eyes heavy with the sleep from which he had been aroused.

"Survent, marster!" he said, bowing from the doorway.

"Moses, did you ever shoot a pistol?" Croyden asked.

"Fur de Lawd, seh! Hit's bin so long sence I dun hit, I t'ink I'se gun-shy, seh."

"But you have done it?"

"Yass, seh, I has don hit."

"And you could do it again, if necessary?"

"I speck so, seh—leas'wise, I kin try—dough I'se mons'us unsuttin, seh, mons'us unsuttin!"

"Uncertain of what—your shooting or your hitting?"

"My hittin', seh."

"Well, we're all of us somewhat uncertain in that line. At least you know enough not to point the revolver toward yourself."

"Hi!—I sut'n'y does! seh, I sut'n'y does!" said the negro, with a broad grin.

"There is a revolver, yonder, on the table," said Croyden, indicating one of those they used on Greenberry Point. "It's a self-cocker—you simply pull the trigger and the action does the rest. You understand?"

"Yass, seh, I onderstands," said Moses.

"Bring it here," Croyden ordered.

Moses' fingers closed around the butt, a bit timorously, and he carried it to his master.

"I'll show you the action," said Croyden. "Here, is the ejector," throwing the chamber out, "it holds six shots, you see: but you never put a cartridge under the firing-pin, because, if anything strikes the trigger, it's likely to be

117

discharged."

"Yass, seh!"

Croyden loaded it, closed the cylinder, and passed it over to Moses, who took it with a little more assurance. He was harkening back thirty years, and more.

"What do yo warn me to do, seh?" he asked.

"I want you to sit down, here, while I'm away, and if any one tries to get in this house, to-night, you're to shoot him. I'm going over to Captain Carrington's—I'll be back by eleven o'clock. It isn't likely you will be disturbed; if you are, one shot will frighten him off, even if you don't hit him, and I'll hear the shot, and come back at once. You understand?"

"Yass, seh!—I'm to shoot anyone what tries to get in."

"Not exactly!" laughed Croyden. "You're to shoot anyone who tries to *break* in. For Heaven's sake! don't shoot me, when I return, or any one else who comes legitimately. Be sure he is an intruder, then bang away."

"Sut'n'y, seh! I onderstands. I'se dub'us bout hittin', but I kin bang away right nuf. Does yo' spose any one will try to git in, seh?"

"No, I don't!" Croyden smiled—"but you be ready for them, Moses, be ready for them. It's just as well to provide against contingencies."

"Yass, seh!" as Croyden went out and the front door closed behind him, "but dem 'tingencies is monty dang'ous t'ings to fools wid. I don' likes hit, dat's whar I don'."

Croyden found Miss Carrington just where he had left her—a quick return to the sofa having been synchronous with his appearance in the hall.

"I had a mind not to wait here," she said; "you were an inordinately long time, Mr. Croyden."

"I was!" he replied, sitting down beside her. "I was, and I admit it—but it can be explained."

"I'm listening!" she smiled.

"Before you listen to me, listen to Robert Parmenter, deceased!" said he, and gave her the letter.

"Oh, this is the letter—do you mean that I am to read it?"

"If you please!" he answered.

She read it through without a single word of comment—an amazing thing in a woman, who, when her curiosity is aroused, can ask more questions to the minute than can be answered in a month. When she had finished, she turned back and read portions of it again, especially the direction as to finding the treasure, and the postscript bequests by the Duvals.

At last, she dropped the letter in her lap and looked up at Croyden.

"A most remarkable document!" she said. "Most extraordinary in its ordinariness, and most ordinary in its extraordinariness. And you searched, carefully, for three weeks and found—nothing?"

"We did," he replied. "Now, I'll tell you about it."

"First, tell me where you obtained this letter?"

"I found it by accident—in a secret compartment of an escritoire at Clarendon," he answered.

She nodded.

"Now you may tell me about it?" she said, and settled back to listen.

"This is the tale of Parmenter's treasure—and how we did *not* find it!" he laughed.

Then he proceeded to narrate, briefly, the details—from the finding of the letter to the present moment, dwelling particularly on the episode of the theft of their wallets, the first and second coming of the thieves to the Point, their capture and subsequent release, together with the occurrence of this evening, when he was approached, by the well-dressed stranger, at Clarendon's gates.

And, once again, marvelous to relate, Miss Carrington did not interrupt, through the entire course of the narrative. Nor did she break the silence for a time after he had concluded, staring thoughtfully, the while, down into the grate, where a smouldering back log glowed fitfully.

"What do you intend to do, as to the treasure?" she asked, slowly.

"Give it up!" he replied. "What else is there to do?"

"And what about this stranger?"

"He *must* give it up!" laughed Croyden. "He has no recourse. In the words of the game, popular hereabout, he is playing a bobtail!"

"But he doesn't know it's a bobtail. He is convinced you found the treasure," she objected.

"Let him make whatever trouble he can, it won't bother me, in the least."

"He is not acting alone," she persisted. "He has confederates—they may attack Clarendon, in an effort to capture the treasure."

"My dear child! this is the twentieth century, not the seventeenth!" he laughed. "We don't 'stand-by to repel boarders,' these days."

"Pirate's gold breeds pirate's ways!" she answered.

He stared at her, in surprise.

"Rather queer!—I've heard those same words before, in this connection."

"Community of minds."

"Is it a quotation?" he asked.

"Possibly—though I don't recall it. Suppose you are attacked and tortured till you reveal where you've hidden the jewels?" she insisted.

"I cannot suppose them so unreasonable!" he laughed, again. "However, I put Moses on guard—with a big revolver and orders to fire at anyone molesting the house. If we hear a fusillade we'll know it's he shooting up the neighborhood."

"Then the same idea *did* suggest itself to you!"

"Only to the extent of searching for the jewels—I regarded that as vaguely possible, but there isn't the slightest danger of any one being tortured."

"You know best, I suppose," she said—"but you've had your warning—and pirate's gold breeds pirate's ways. You've given up all hope of finding the treasure—abandoned jewels worth—how many dollars?"

"Possibly half a million," he filled in.

"Without a further search? Oh! Mr. Croyden!"

"If you can suggest what to do—anything which hasn't been done, I shall be only too glad to consider it."

"You say you dug up the entire Point for a hundred yards inland?"

"We did."

"And dredged the Bay for a hundred yards?"

"Yes."

She puckered her brows in thought. He regarded her with an amused smile.

"I don't see what you're to do, except to do it all over again," she announced —"Now, don't laugh! It may sound foolish, but many a thing has been found on a second seeking—and this, surely, is worth a second, or a third, or even many seekings."

"If there were any assurance of ultimate success, it would pay to spend a lifetime hunting. The two essentials, however, are wanting: the extreme tip of Greenberry Point in 1720, and the beech-trees. We made the best guess at their location. More than that, the zone of exploration embraced every possible extreme of territory—yet, we failed. It will make nothing for success to try again."

"But it is somewhere!" she reflected.

"Somewhere, in the Bay!—It's shoal water, for three or four hundred feet around the Point, with a rock bottom. The Point itself has been eaten into by the Bay, down to this rock. Parmenter's chest disappeared with the land in which it was buried, and no man will find it now, except by accident."

"It seems such a shame!" she exclaimed. "A fortune gone to waste!"

"Without anyone having the fun of wasting it!" laughed Croyden.

She took up Parmenter's letter again, and glanced over it. Then she handed it back, and shook her head.

"It's too much for my poor brain," she said. "I surrender."

"Precisely where we landed. We gave it rather more than a fair trial, and, then, we gave it up. I'm done. When I go home, to-night, I shall return the letter to the escritoire where I found it, and forget it. There is no profit in speculating further."

"You can return it to its hiding place," she reflected, "but you can't cease wondering. Why didn't Marmaduke Duval get the treasure while the landmarks were there? Why did he leave it for his heirs?"

"Probably on account of old Parmenter's restriction that it be left until the 'extremity of need.'"

She nodded, in acquiescence.

"Probably," she said, "the Duvals would regard it as a matter of honor to observe the exact terms of the bequest. Alas! Alas! that they did so!"

"It's only because they did so, that I got a chance to search!" Croyden laughed.

"You mean that, otherwise, there would be no buried treasure!" she exclaimed. "Of course!—how stupid! And with all that money, the Duvals might have gone away from Hampton—might have experienced other conditions. Colonel Duval might never have met your father—you might have never come to Clarendon.—My goodness! Where does it end?"

"In the realm of pure conjecture," he answered. "It is idle to theorize on the might-have-beens, or what might-have-happened if the what-did-happen hadn't happened. Dismiss it, at least, for this evening. You asked what I was doing for three weeks at Annapolis, and I have consumed a great while in answering—let us talk of something else. What have you been doing in those three weeks?"

"Nothing! A little Bridge, a few riding parties, some sails on the Bay, with an occasional homily by Miss Erskine, when she had me cornered, and I couldn't get away. Then is when I learned what a deep impression you had made!" she laughed.

"We both were learning, it seems," he replied.

She looked at him, inquiringly.

"I don't quite understand," she said.

"You made an impression, also—of course, that's to be expected, but this impression is much more than the ordinary kind!"

"Merci, Monsieur," she scoffed.

"No, it isn't *merci*, it's a fact. And he is a mighty good fellow on whom to make an impression."

"You mean, Mr.—Macloud?"

"Just so! I mean Macloud."

"You're very safe in saying it!"

"Wherefore?"

"He is absent. It's not susceptible of proof."

"You think so?"

"Yes, I think so!"

"I don't!"

She shrugged her shoulders.

"For he's coming back——"

"To Hampton?"

"To Hampton."

"When?" she said, sceptically.

"Very soon!"

"Delightfully indefinite!" she laughed.

"In fact, within a week."

She laughed, again!

"To be accurate, I expect him not later than the day-after-to-morrow."

"I shall believe you, when I see him!" incredulously.

"He is, I think, coming solely on your account."

"But you're not quite sure?—oh! modest man!"

"Naturally, he hasn't confided in me."

"So you're confiding in me—how clever!"

"I could tell some things——"

"Which are fables."

"——but I won't—they might turn your head——"

"Which way—to the right or left?"

"——and make you too confident and too cruel. He saw you but twice——"

"Once!" she corrected.

"Once, on the street; again, when we called in the evening—but he gave you a name, the instant he saw you——"

"How kind of him!"

"He called you: 'The Symphony in Blue.'"

"Was I in blue?" she asked.

"You were—and looking particularly fit."

"Was that the first time you had noticed it?" she questioned blandly.

"Do you think so?" he returned.

"I am asking you, sir."

"Do I impress you as being blind?"

"No, you most assuredly do not!" she laughed.

He looked at her with daring eyes.

"Yes!" she said, "I know you're intrepid—but you *won't*!"

"Why?—why won't I?"

"Because, it would be false to your friend. You have given me to him."

"I have given you to him!" he exclaimed, with denying intonation.

"Yes!—as between you two, you have renounced, in his favor."

"I protest!"

"At least, I so view it," with a teasingly fascinating smile.

"I protest!" he repeated.

"I heard you."

"I protest!" he reiterated.

"Don't you think that you protest over-much?" she inquired sweetly.

"If we were two children, I'd say: 'You think you're smart, don't you?'"

"And I'd retort: 'You got left, didn't you?'"

Then they both laughed.

"Seriously, however—do you really expect Mr. Macloud?" she asked.

"I surely do—probably within two days; and I'm not chaffing when I say that you're the inducement. So, be good to him—he's got more than enough for two, I can assure you."

"Mercenary!" she laughed. "No—

just careful!" he answered.

"And what number am I—the twenty-first, or thereabout?"

"What matters it, if you're *the* one, at present?"

She raised her shoulders in the slightest shrug.

"I'd sooner be the present one than all the has-beens," he insisted.

"Opinions differ," she remarked.

"If it will advantage any——"

"I didn't say so," she interrupted. "——

——I can tell you——"

"Many fables, I don't doubt!" she cut in, again.

"——that we have been rather intimate, for a few years, and I have never before known him to exhibit particular interest in any woman."

"'Why don't you speak for yourself, John,'" she quoted, merrily.

"Because, to be frank, I haven't enough for two," he answered, gayly.

But beneath the gayety, she thought she detected the faintest note of regret. So! there was some one!

And, woman-like, when he had gone, she wondered about her—whether she was dark or fair, tall or small, vivacious or reserved, flirtatious or sedate, rich or poor—and whether they loved each other—or whether it was he, alone, who loved—or whether he had not permitted himself to be carried so far—or whether—then, she dropped asleep.

Croyden went back to Clarendon, keeping a sharp look-out for anyone under the trees around the house. He found Moses in the library, evidently just aroused from slumber by the master's door key.

"No one's bin heah, seh, 'cep de boy wid dis 'spatch," he hastened to say.

Croyden tore open the envelope:—It was a wire from Macloud, that he would be down to-morrow.

"You may go to bed, Moses."

"Yass, seh! yass, seh!—I'se pow'ful glad yo's back, seh. Nothin' I kin git yo befo I goes?"

"Nothing!" said Croyden. "You're a good soldier, Moses, you didn't sleep on guard."

"No, seh! I keps wide awake, Marster Croyden, wide awake all de time, seh. Survent, seh!" and, with a bow, he disappeared.

Croyden finished his cigar, put out the light, and went slowly upstairs—giving not a thought to the Parmenter treasure nor the man he had met outside. His mind was busy with Elaine Cavendish—their last night on the moonlit piazza—the brief farewell—the lingering pressure of her fingers—the light in her eyes—the subdued pleasure, when they met unexpectedly in Annapolis—her little ways to detain him, keep him close to her—her instant defense of him at Mattison's scurrilous insinuation—the officers' hop—the rhythmic throb of the melody—the scented, fluttering body held close in his arms—the lowered head—the veiled eyes—the trembling lashes—his senses steeped in the fragrance of her beauty—the temptation well-nigh irresistible—his resolution almost gone—trembling—trembling——

The vision passed—music ceased—the dance was ended. Sentiment vanished —reason reigned once more.

He was a fool! a fool! to think of her, to dream of the past, even. But it is pleasant, sometimes, to be a fool—where a beautiful woman is concerned, and only one's self to pay the piper.

XIV

Macloud arrived the next day, bringing for his host a great batch of mail, which had accumulated at the Club.

"I thought of it at the last moment—when I was starting for the station, in fact," he remarked. "The clerk said he had no instructions for forwarding, so I just poked it in my bag and brought it along. Stupid of me not to think of it sooner. Why didn't you mention it? I can understand why you didn't leave an address, but not why I shouldn't forward it."

"I didn't care, when I left—and I don't care much, now—but I'm obliged, just the same!" said Croyden. "It's something to do; the most exciting incident of the day, down here, is the arrival of the mail. The people wait for it, with bated breath. I am getting in the way, too, though I don't get much.... I never did have any extensive correspondence, even in Northumberland—so this is just circulars and such trash."

He took the package, which Macloud handed him, and tossed it on the desk.

"What's new?" he asked.

"In Northumberland? Nothing—beyond the usual thing. Everybody is back—everybody is hard up or says he is—everybody is full of lies, as usual, and is turning them loose on anyone who will listen, credulous or sophisticated, it makes no difference. It's the telling, not the believing that's the thing. Oh! the little cad Mattison is engaged—Charlotte Brundage has landed him, and the wedding is set for early next month."

"I don't envy her the job," Croyden remarked.

"It won't bother her!" Macloud laughed. "She'll be privileged to draw on his bank account, and that's the all important thing with her. He will fracture the seventh commandment, and she won't turn a hair. She is a chilly proposition, all right."

"Well, I wish her joy of her bargain," said Croyden. "May she have everything she wants, and see Mattison not at all, after the wedding journey—and but very occasionally, then."

He took up the letters and ran carelessly through them.

"Trash! Trash! Trash!" he commented, as he consigned them, one by one, to the waste-basket.

Macloud watched him, languidly, behind his cigar smoke, and made no comment.

Presently Croyden came to a large, white envelope—darkened on the interior so as to prevent the contents from being read until opened. It bore the name of a firm of prominent brokers in Northumberland.

"Humph! Blaxham & Company!" he grunted. "'We own and offer, subject to prior sale, the following high grade investment bonds.' Oh yes! I'll take the whole bundle." He drew out the letter and looked at it, perfunctorily, before sending it to rest with its fellows.—It wasn't in the usual form.—He opened it, wider.—It was signed by the senior partner.

"My dear Mr. Croyden:

"We have a customer who is interested in the Virginia Development Company. He has purchased the Bonds and the stock of Royster & Axtell, from the bank which held them as collateral. He is willing to pay you par for your Bonds, without any accrued interest, however. If you will consent to sell, the Company can proceed without reorganization but, if you decline, he will foreclose under the terms of the mortgage. We have suggested the propriety and the economy to him—since he owns or controls all the stock—of not purchasing your bonds, and, frankly, have told him it is worse than bad business to do so. But he refuses to be advised, insisting that he must be the sole owner, and that he is willing to submit to the additional expense rather than go through the tedious proceeding for foreclosure and sale. We are prepared to honor a sight-draft with the Bonds attached, or to pay cash on presentation and transfer. We shall be obliged for a prompt reply.

"Yours very truly,

"R. J. Blaxham."

"What the devil!——"

He read it a second time. No, he wasn't asleep—it was all there, typewritten and duly signed. Two hundred thousand dollars!—honor sight draft, or pay cash on presentation and transfer!

"What the devil!" he said, again. Then he passed it across to Macloud. "Read this aloud, will you,—I want to see if I'm quite sane!"

Macloud was at his favorite occupation—blowing smoke rings through one another, and watching them spiral upward toward the ceiling.

"I beg your pardon!" he said, as Croyden's words roused him from his meditation. "I must have been half asleep. What did you say—read it?" taking the letter.

He and Blaxham had spent considerable time on that letter, trying to explain the reason for the purchase, and the foolishly high price they were offering, in such a way as to mislead Croyden.

"Yes,—aloud! I want to hear someone else read it."

Macloud looked at him, curiously.

"It is typewritten, you haven't a chance to get wrong!" he said, wonderingly.

Croyden laughed!

"Read it, please!" he exclaimed.... "So, I wasn't crazy: and either Blaxham is lying or his customer needs a guardian—which is it?"

"I don't see that it need concern you, in the least, which it is," said Macloud. "Be grateful for the offer—and accept by wireless or any other way that's quicker."

"But the bonds aren't worth five cents on the dollar!"

"So much the more reason to hustle the deal through. Sell them! man, sell them! You may have slipped up on the Parmenter treasure, but you have struck it here."

"Too rich," Croyden answered. "There's something queer about that letter."

Macloud smoked his cigar, and smiled.

"There's nothing queer about the letter!"—he said. "Blaxham's customer may have the willies—indeed, he as much as intimates that such is the case—but, thank God! we're not obliged to have a commission-in-lunacy appointed on everybody who makes a silly stock or bond purchase. If we were, we either would have no markets, or the courts would have time for nothing else. No! no! old man! take what the gods have given you and be glad. There's ten thousand a year in it! You can return to Northumberland, resume the old life, and be happy ever after;—or you can live here, and there, and everywhere. You're unattached—not even a light-o'-love to squander your money, and pester you for gowns and hats, and get in a hell of a temper—and be false to you, besides."

"No, I haven't one of them, thank God!" laughed Croyden. "I've got troubles enough of my own. The present, for instance."

"Troubles!" marvelled Macloud. "You haven't any troubles, now. This clears them all away."

"It clears some of them away—if I take it."

"Thunder! man, you're not thinking, seriously, of refusing?"

"It will put me on 'easy street,'" Croyden observed.

"So, why hesitate an instant?"

"And it comes with remarkable timeliness—so timely, indeed, as to be suspicious."

"Suspicious? Why suspicious? It's a bona fide offer."

"It's a bona fide offer—there's no trouble on that score."

"Then, what is the trouble?"

"This," said Croyden: "I'm broke—finally. The Parmenter treasure is moonshine, so far as I'm concerned. I'm down on my uppers, so to speak— my only assets are some worthless bonds. Behold! along comes an offer for them at par—two hundred thousand dollars for nothing! I fancy, old man, there is a friend back of this offer—the only friend I have in the world—and I did not think that even he was kind and self-sacrificing enough to do it.—I'm grateful, Colin, grateful from the heart, believe me, but I can't take your money."

"My money!" exclaimed Macloud—"you do me too much credit, Croyden. I'm ashamed to admit it, but I never thought of the bonds, or of helping you out, in your trouble. It's a way we have in Northumberland. We may feel for misfortune, but it rarely gets as far as our pockets. Don't imagine for a moment that I'm the purchaser. I'm not, though I wish, now, that I was."

"Will you give me your word on that?" Croyden demanded.

"I most assuredly will," Macloud answered.

Croyden nodded. He was satisfied.

"There is no one else!" he mused, "no one else!" He looked at the letter again…. "And, yet, it is very suspicious, very suspicious…. I wonder, could I ascertain the name of the purchaser of the stocks and bonds, from the Trust Company who held them as collateral?"

"They won't know," said Macloud. "Blaxham & Company bought them at the public sale."

"I could try the transfer agent, or the registrar."

"They never tell anything, as you are aware," Macloud replied.

"I could refuse to sell unless Blaxham & Company disclosed their customer."

"Yes, you could—and, likely, lose the sale; they won't disclose. However, that's your business," Macloud observed; "though, it's a pity to tilt at windmills, for a foolish notion."

Croyden creased and uncreased the letter—thinking.

Macloud resumed the smoke rings—and waited. It had proved easier than he had anticipated. Croyden had not once thought of Elaine Cavendish—and his simple word had been sufficient to clear himself....

At length, Croyden put the letter back in its envelope and looked up.

"I'll sell the bonds," he said—"forward them at once with draft attached, if you will witness my signature to the transfer. But it's a queer proceeding, a queer proceeding: paying good money for bad!"

"That's his business—not yours," said Macloud, easily.

Croyden went to the escritoire and took the bonds from one of the drawers.

"You can judge, from the place I keep them, how much I thought them worth!" he laughed.

When they were duly transferred and witnessed, Croyden attached a draft drawn on an ordinary sheet of paper, dated Northumberland, and payable to his account at the Tuscarora Trust Company. He placed them in an envelope, sealed it and, enclosing it in a second envelope, passed it over to Macloud.

"I don't care to inform them as to my whereabouts," he remarked, "so, if you don't mind, I'll trouble you to address this to some one in New York or Philadelphia, with a request that he mail the enclosed envelope for you."

Macloud, when he had done as requested, laid aside the pen and looked inquiringly at Croyden.

"Which, being interpreted," he said, "might mean that you don't intend to return to Northumberland."

"The interpretation does not go quite so far; it means, simply, that I have not decided."

"Don't you want to come back?" Macloud asked.

"It's a question of resolution, not of inclination," Croyden answered. "I don't know whether I've sufficient resolution to go, and sufficient resolution to stay, if I do go. It may be easier not to go, at all—to live here, and wander, elsewhere, when the spirit moves."

And Macloud understood. "I've been thinking over the proposition you recently advanced of the folly of a relatively poor man marrying a rich girl," he said, "and you're all wrong. It's a question of the respective pair, not a theory that can be generalized over. I admit, the man should not be a pauper, but, if he have enough money to support *himself*, and the girl love him and he loves the girl, the fact that she has gobs more money, won't send them on the rocks. It's up to the pair, I repeat."

"Meaning, that it would be up to Elaine Cavendish and me?" answered Croyden.

"If you please, yes!" said Macloud.

"I wish I could be so sure," Croyden reflected. "Sure of the girl, as well as sure of myself."

"What are you doubtful about—yourself?"

Croyden laughed, a trifle self-consciously.

"I fancy I could manage myself," he said.

"Elaine?"

"Yes, Elaine!"

"Try her!—she's worth the try."

"From a monetary standpoint?" smiling.

"Get the miserable money out of your mind a moment, will you?—you're hipped on it!"

"All right, old man, anything for peace! Tell me, did you see her, when you were home?"

"I did—I dined with her."

"Who else was there?"

"You—she talked Croyden at least seven-eighths of the time; I, the other eighth."

"Must have been an interesting conversation. Anything left of the victim, afterward?"

"I refuse to become facetious," Macloud responded. Then he threw his cigar into the grate and arose. "It matters not what was said, nor who said it! If you will permit me the advice, you will take your chance while you have it."

"Have I a—chance?" Croyden asked.

"You have—more than a chance, if you act, now——" He walked across to the window. He would let that sink in.—"How's the Symphony in Blue?" he asked.

"As charming as ever—and prepared for your coming."

"What?"

"As charming as ever, and prepared for your coming."

"Some of your work!" he commented. "Did you propose for me?"

"I left that finality for you—being the person most interested."

"Thanks! you're exceedingly considerate."

"I thought you would appreciate it."

"When did you arrange for me to go over?" asked Macloud.

"Any time—the sooner the quicker. She'll be glad to see you."

"She confided in you, I suppose?"

"Not directly; she let me infer it."

"In other words, you worked your imagination—overtime!" laughed Macloud. "It's a pity you couldn't work it a bit over the Parmenter jewels. You might locate them."

"I'm done with the Parmenter jewels!" said Croyden.

"But they're not done with you, my friend. So long as you live, they'll be present with you. You'll be hunting for them in your dreams."

"Meet me to-night in dream-land!" sang Croyden. "Well, they're not likely to disturb my slumbers—unless—there was a rather queer thing happened, last night, Colin."

"Here?"

"Yes!—I got in to Hampton, in the evening; about nine o'clock, I was returning to Clarendon when, at the gates, I was accosted by a tall, well-dressed stranger. Here is the substance of our talk.... What do you make of it?" he ended.

"It seems to me the fellow made it very plain," Macloud returned, "except on one possible point. He evidently believes we found the treasure."

"He is convinced of it."

"Then, he knows that you came direct from Annapolis to Hampton—I mean, you didn't visit a bank nor other place where you could have deposited the jewels. Ergo, the jewels are still in your possession, according to his theory, and he is going to make a try for them while they are within reach. Informing the Government is a bluff. He hoped, by that means, to induce you to keep the jewels on the premises—not to make evidence against yourself, which could be traced by the United States, by depositing them in any bank."

"Why shouldn't I have taken them to a dealer in precious stones?" said

Croyden.

"Because that would make the best sort of evidence against you. You must remember, he thinks you have the jewels, and that you will try to conceal it, pending a Government investigation."

"You make him a very canny gentleman."

"No—I make him only a clever rogue, which, by your own account, he is."

"And the more clever he is, the more he will have his wits' work for naught. There's some compensation in everything—even in failure!"

"It would be a bit annoying," observed Macloud, "to be visited by burglars, who are obsessed with the idea that you have a fortune concealed on the premises, and are bent on obtaining it."

"Annoying?—not a bit!" smiled Croyden. "I should rather enjoy the sport of putting them to flight."

"Or of being bound, and gagged, and ill-treated."

"Bosh! you've transferred your robber-barons from Northumberland to the Eastern Shore."

"No, I haven't!" laughed Macloud. "The robber-barons were still on the job in Northumberland. These are banditti, disguised as burglars, about to hold you up for ransom."

"I wish I had your fine imagination," scoffed Croyden. "I could make a fortune writing fiction."

"Oh, you're not so bad yourself!" Macloud retorted. Then he smiled. "Apropos of fortunes!" and nodded toward the envelope on the table. "It's bully good to think you're coming back to us!"

At that moment Moses passed along the hall.

"Here, Moses," said Croyden, "take this letter down to the post office—I want it to catch the first mail."

"I fancy you haven't heard of the stranger since last evening?" Macloud asked.

Croyden shook his head.

"And of course you haven't told any one?"

"Yes, I have!" said Croyden.

"A woman?"

"A woman."

"How strange!" commented Macloud, mockingly. "I suppose you even told her the entire story—from the finding of the letter down to date."

"I did!—and showed her the letter besides. Why shouldn't I have done it?"

"No reason in the world, my dear fellow—except that in twenty-four hours the dear public will know it, and we shall be town curiosities."

"We don't have to remain," said Croyden, with affected seriousness—"there are trains out, you know, as well as in."

"I don't want to go away—I came here to visit you."

"We will go together."

"But we can't take the Symphony in Blue!"

"Oh! that's it!" Croyden laughed.

"Certainly, that's it! You don't think I came down here to see only you, after having just spent nearly four weeks with you, in that fool quest on Greenberry Point?" He turned, suddenly, and faced Croyden. "Who was the woman you told?"

"Miss Carrington!" Croyden laughed. "Think she will retail it to the dear public?"

"Oh, go to thunder!"

"Because, if you do, you might mention it to her—there, she goes, now!"

"Where?" said Macloud, whirling around toward the window.

Croyden made no reply. It was not necessary. On the opposite side of the street, Miss Carrington—in a tailored gown of blue broadcloth, close fitting and short in the skirt, with a velvet toque to match—was swinging briskly back from town.

Macloud watched her a moment in silence.

"The old man is done for, at last!" Croyden thought.

"Isn't she a corker!" Macloud broke out. "Look at the poise of the head, and ease of carriage, and the way she puts down her feet!—that's the way to tell a woman. God! Croyden, she's thoroughbred!"

"You better go over," said his friend. "It's about the tea hour, she'll brew you a cup."

"And I'll drink it—as much as she will give me. I despise the stuff, but I'll drink it!"

"She'll put rum in it, if you prefer!" laughed Croyden; "or make you a high ball, or you can have it straight—just as you want."

"Come along!" exclaimed Macloud. "We're wasting time."

"I'll be over, presently," Croyden replied. "*I* don't want any tea, you know."

"Good!" Macloud answered, from the hallway. "Come along, as soon as you wish—but don't come *too soon*."

———————————

XV

Macloud found Miss Carrington plucking a few belated roses, which, somehow, had escaped the frost.

She looked up at his approach, and smiled—the bewilderingly bewitching smile which lighted her whole countenance and seemed to say so much.

"Back again! to Clarendon and its master?" was her greeting.

"And, if I may, to you," he replied.

"Very good! After them, you belong to *me*," she laughed.

"Why after?" he inquired.

"I don't know—it was the order of speech, and the order of acquaintance," with a naive look.

"But not the order of—regard."

"Content!" she exclaimed. "You did it very well for a—novice."

He tapped the gray hair upon his temples.

"A novice?" he inflected.

"You decline to accept it?—Very well, sir, very well!"

"I can't accept, and be honest," he replied.

"And you must be honest! Oh, brave man! Oh, noble gentleman! Perchance, you will accept a reward: a cup of tea—or a high ball!"

"Perchance, I will—the high ball!"

"I thought so! come along."

"You were not going out?"

She looked at him, with a sly smile.

"You know that I have just returned," she said. "I saw you in the window at Clarendon."

"I was there," he admitted.

"And you came over at once—prepared to be surprised that I was here."

"And found you waiting for me—just as I expected."

"Oh!" she cried. "You're horrid! perfectly horrid!"

"*Peccavi! Peccavi!*" he said humbly.

"*Te absolvo!*" she replied, solemnly. "Now, let us make a fresh start—by going for a walk. You can postpone the high ball until we return."

"I can postpone the high ball for ever," he averred.

"Meaning, you could walk forever, or you're not thirsty?" she laughed.

"Meaning, I could walk forever *with you*—on, and on, and on——"

"Until you walked into the Bay—I understand. I'll take the will for the deed —the water's rather chilly at this season of the year."

Macloud held up his hand, in mock despair.

"Let us make a third start—drop the attempt to be clever and talk sense. I think I can do it, if I try."

"Willingly!" she responded.

As they came out on the side walk, Croyden was going down the street. He crossed over and met them.

"I've not forgot your admonition, so don't be uneasy," he observed to Macloud. "I'm going to town now, I'll be back in about half an hour—is that too soon?"

"It's quite soon enough!" was the answer.

Miss Carrington looked at Macloud, quizzically, but made no comment.

"Shall we take the regulation walk?" she asked.

"The what?"

"The regulation walk—to the Cemetery and back."

"I'm glad we're coming back?" he laughed.

"It's the favorite walk, here," she explained—"the most picturesque and the smoothest."

"To say nothing of accustoming the people to their future home," Macloud remarked.

"You're not used to the ways of small towns—the Cemetery is a resort, a place to spend a while, a place to visit."

"Does it make death any easier to hob-nob with it?" he asked.

"I shouldn't think so," she replied. "However, I can see how it would induce morbidity, though there are those who are happiest only when they're miserable."

"Such people ought to live in a morgue," agreed Macloud. "However we're safe enough—we can go to the Cemetery with impunity."

"There are some rather queer old headstones, out there," she said. "Remorse and the inevitable pay-up for earthly transgression seem to be the leading subjects. There is one in the Duval lot—the Duvals from whom Mr. Croyden got Clarendon, you know—and I never have been able to understand just what it means. It is erected to the memory of one Robert Parmenter, and has cut in the slab the legend: 'He feared nor man, nor god, nor devil,' and below it, a man on his knees making supplication to one standing over him. If he feared nor man, nor god, nor devil, why should he be imploring mercy from any one?"

"Do you know who Parmenter was?" said Macloud.

"No—but I presume a connection of the family, from having been buried with them."

"You read his letter only last evening—his letter to Marmaduke Duval."

"His letter to Marmaduke Duval!" she repeated. "I didn't read any——"

"Robert Parmenter is the pirate who buried the treasure on Greenberry Point," he interrupted.

Then, suddenly, a light broke in on her.

"I see!—I didn't look at the name signed to the letter. And the cutting on the tombstone——?"

"Is a victim begging mercy from him," said Macloud. "I like that Marmaduke Duval—there's something fine in a man, in those times, bringing the old buccaneer over from Annapolis and burying him beside the place where he, himself, some day would rest.—That is friendship!"

"And that is like the Duvals!" said she. "It was a sad day in Hampton when the Colonel died."

"He left a good deputy," Macloud replied. "Croyden is well-born and well-bred (the former does not always comprehend the latter, these days), and of Southern blood on his mother's side."

"Which hasn't hurt him with us!" she smiled. "We are a bit clannish, still."

"Delighted to hear you confess it! I've got a little of it myself."

"Southern blood?"

He nodded. "Mine doesn't go so far South, however, as Croyden's—only, to Virginia."

"I knew it! I knew there was some reason for my liking you!" she laughed.

"Can I find any other reason?"

"Than your Southern ancestors?—isn't that enough?"

"Not if there be a means to increase it."

"Southern blood is never satisfied with *some* things—it always wants more!"

"Is the disposition to want more, in Southerners, confined to the male sex?" he laughed.

"In *some things*—yes, unquestionably yes!" she retorted. Then changed the subject. "Has Mr. Croyden told you of his experience, last evening?"

"With the stranger, yes?"

"Do you think he is in danger?"

"What possible danger could there be—the treasure isn't at Clarendon."

"But they think it is—and desperate men sometimes take desperate means, when they feel sure that money is hidden on the premises."

"In a town the size of Hampton, every stranger is known."

"How will that advantage, in the prevention of the crime?" she asked.

"By making it difficult."

"They don't need stay in the town—they can come in an automobile."

"They could also drive, or walk, or come by boat," he added.

"They are not so likely to try it if there are two in the house. Do you intend to remain at Clarendon some time?"

"It depends—on how you treat me."

"I engage to be nice for—two weeks!" she smiled.

"Done!—I'm booked for two weeks, at least."

"And when the two weeks have expired we shall consider whether to extend the period."

"To—life?" smiling down at her.

She flung him a look that was delightfully alluring.

"Do you wish me to—consider that?" she asked, softly.

"If you will," he said, bending down.

She laughed, gayly.

"We are coming on!" she exclaimed. "This pace is getting rather brisk—did you notice it, Mr. Macloud?"

"You're in a fast class, Miss Carrington."

She glanced up quickly.

"Now don't misunderstand me——"

"You were speaking in the language of the race track, I presume."

"I was—you understand?"

"A Southern girl usually loves—horses," with a tantalizing smile.

"It is well for you this is a public street," he said.

"Why?" she asked, with assumed innocence.

"But then if it hadn't been, you would not have ventured to tempt me," he added. "I'm grateful for the temptation, at any rate."

"His first temptation!" she mocked.

"No, not likely—but his first that he has resisted."

"And why did you resist? The fact that we are on a public street would not restrain you. There was absolutely no one within sight—and you knew it."

"How do *you* know it?"

"Because I looked."

"You were afraid?"

"Not at all!—only careful."

"This is rather faster than the former going!" he laughed.

"We would better slow down a bit!" she laughed back. "Any way, here is the Cemetery, and we dare not go faster than a walk in it. Yonder, just within the gates, is the Duval burial place. Come, I'll show you Parmenter's grave?"

They crossed to it—marked by a blue slate slab, which covered it entirely. The inscription, cut in script, was faint in places and blurred by moss, in others.

Macloud stooped and, with his knife, scratched out the latter.

"He died two days after the letter was written: May 12, 1738," said he. "His age is not given. Duval did not know it, I reckon."

"See, here is the picture—it stands out very plainly," said Miss Carrington, indicating with the point of her shoe.

"I'm not given to moralizing, particularly over a grave," observed Macloud, "but it's queer to think that the old pirate, who had so much blood and death on his hands, who buried the treasure, and who wrote the letter, lies at our feet; and we—or rather Croyden is the heir of that treasure, and that we searched and dug all over Greenberry Point, committed violence, were threatened with violence, did things surreptitiously, are threatened, anew, with blackmail and violence——"

"Pirate's gold breeds pirate's ways," she quoted.

"It does seem one cannot get away from its pollution. It was gathered in crime and crime clings to it, still. However, I fancy Croyden would willingly chance the danger, if he could unearth the casket."

"And is there no hope of finding it?" she asked.

"Absolutely none—there's half a million over on Greenberry Point, or in the water close by, and none will ever see it—except by accident."

"What sort of accident?"

"I don't know!" he laughed. "My own idea—and Croyden's (as he has, doubtless, explained to you) is that the place, where Parmenter buried the jewels, is now under water, possibly close to the shore. We dragged every inch of the bottom, which has been washed away to a depth more than sufficient to uncover the iron box, but found nothing. A great storm, such as they say sometimes breaks over the Chesapeake, may wash it on the beach—that, I think, is the only way it will ever be found.... It makes everything seem very real to have stood by Parmenter's grave!" he said, thoughtful, as they turned back toward town.

On nearing the Carrington house, they saw Croyden approaching. They met him at the gates.

"I've been communing with Parmenter," said Macloud.

"I didn't know there was a spiritualistic medium in Hampton! What does the old man look like?" smiled Croyden.

"I didn't see him."

"Well, did he help you to locate his jewel box?"

"He wasn't especially communicative—he was in his grave."

"That isn't surprising—he's been dead something over one hundred and seventy years. Did he confide where he's buried?"

"He's buried with the Duvals in the Cemetery, here."

"He is!" Croyden exclaimed. "Humph! one more circumstance to prove the letter speaks the truth. Everything but the thing itself. We find his will, probated with Marmaduke Duval as executor, we even discover a notice of his death in the *Gazette*, and now, finally, you find his body—or the place of its interment! But, hang it all! what is really worth while, we can't find."

"Come into the house—I'll give you something to soothe your feelings temporarily," said Miss Carrington.

They encountered Miss Erskine just coming from the library on her way to the door.

"My dear Davila, so glad to see you!" she exclaimed. "And Mr. Croyden, we thought you had deserted us, and just when we're trying to make you feel at home. So glad to welcome you back!" holding out her fat hand.

"I'm delighted to be back," said Croyden. "The Carringtons seemed genuinely glad to see me—and, now, if I may include you, I'm quite content to return," and he shook her hand, as though he meant it.

"Of course you may believe it," with an inane giggle. "I'm going to bring my art class over to Clarendon to revel in your treasures, some day, soon. You'll be at home to them, won't you, dear Mr. Croyden?"

"Surely! I shall take pleasure in being at home," Croyden replied, soberly.

Then Macloud, who was talking with the Captain, was called over and presented, that being, Miss Carrington thought, the quickest method of getting rid of her. The evident intention to remain until he was presented, being made entirely obvious by Miss Erskine, who, after she had bubbled a bit more, departed.

"What is her name, I didn't catch it?—and" (observing smiles on Croyden and Miss Carrington's faces) "what is she?"

"I think father can explain, in more appropriate language!" Miss Carrington laughed.

"She's the most intolerable nuisance and greatest fool in Hampton!" Captain Carrington exploded.

"A red flag to a bull isn't in it with Miss Erskine and father," Miss Carrington observed.

"But I hide it pretty well—while she's here," he protested.

"If she's not here too long—and you can get away, in time."

When the two men left the Carrington place, darkness had fallen. As they approached Clarendon, the welcoming brightness of a well-lighted house sprang out to greet them. It was Croyden's one extravagance—to have plenty of illumination. He had always been accustomed to it, and the gloom, at night, of the village residence, bright only in library or living room—with, maybe, a timid taper in the hall—set his nerves on edge. He would have none of it. And Moses, with considerable wonder at, to his mind, the waste of gas, and much grumbling to himself and Josephine, obeyed.

They had finished dinner and were smoking their cigars in the library, when Croyden, suddenly bethinking himself of a matter which he had forgotten, arose and pulled the bell.

"Survent, seh!" said old Mose a moment later from the doorway.

"Moses, who is the best carpenter in town?" Croyden asked.

"Mistah Snyder, seh—he wuz heah dis arfternoon, yo knows, seh!"

"I didn't know it," said Croyden.

"Why yo sont 'im, seh."

"*I* sent him! I don't know the man."

"Dat's mons'us 'culiar, seh—he said yo sont 'im. He com'd 'torrectly arfter yo lef! Him an' a'nudder man, seh—I didn't know the nudder man, hows'ever."

"What did they want?" Croyden asked.

"Dey sed yo warn dem to look over all de place, seh, an' see what repairs wuz necessary, and fix dem. Dey wuz heah a'most two hours, I s'pose."

"This is most extraordinary!" Croyden exclaimed. "Do you mean they were in this house for two hours?"

"Yass, seh."

"What were they doing?"

"'Zaminin the furniture everywhere. I didn't stays wid em, seh—I knows Mistah Snyder well; he's bin heah off'n to wuk befo' yo cum, seh. But I seed dem gwine th'oo de drawers, an' poundin on the floohs, seh. Dey went down to de cellar, too, seh, an wuz dyar quite a while."

"Are you sure it was Snyder?" Croyden asked.

"Sut'n'y! seh, don't you t'inks I knows 'im? I knows 'im from de time he wuz so high."

Croyden nodded. "Go down and tell Snyder I want to see him, either to-night or in the morning."

The negro bowed, and departed.

Croyden got up and went to the escritoire: the drawers were in confusion. He glanced at the book-cases: the books were disarranged. He turned and looked, questioningly, at Macloud—and a smile slowly overspread his face.

"Well, the tall gentleman has visited us!" he said.

"I wondered how long you would be coming to it!" Macloud remarked. "It's the old ruse, in a slightly modified form. Instead of a telephone or gas inspector, it was a workman whom the servant knew; a little more trouble in disguising himself, but vastly more satisfactory in results."

"They are clever rogues," said Croyden—"and the disguise must have been pretty accurate to deceive Moses."

"Disguise is their business," Macloud replied, laconically. "If they're not proficient in it, they go to prison—sure."

"And if they *are* proficient, they go—sometimes."

"Certainly!—sometimes."

"We'll make a tour of inspection—they couldn't find what they wanted, so we'll see what they took."

They went over the house. Every drawer was turned upside down, every closet awry, every place, where the jewels could be concealed, bore evidence of having been inspected—nothing, apparently, had been missed. They had gone through the house completely, even into the garret, where every board that was loose had evidently been taken up and replaced—some of them carelessly.

Not a thing was gone, so far as Croyden could judge—possibly, because there was no money in the house; probably, because they were looking for jewels, and scorned anything of moderate value.

"Really, this thing grows interesting—if it were not so ridiculous," said Croyden. "I'm willing to go to almost any trouble to convince them I haven't the treasure—just to be rid of them. I wonder what they will try next?"

"Abduction, maybe," Macloud suggested. "Some night a black cloth will be thrown over your head, you'll be tossed into a cab—I mean, an automobile—and borne off for ransom like Charlie Ross of fading memory."

"Moral—don't venture out after sunset!" laughed Croyden.

"And don't venture out at any time without a revolver handy and a good pair of legs," added Macloud.

"I can work the legs better than I can the revolver."

"Or, to make sure, you might have a guard of honor and a gatling gun."

"You're appointed to the position—provide yourself with the gun!"

"But, seriously!" said Macloud, "it would be well to take some precaution. They seem obsessed with the idea that you have the jewels, here—and they evidently intend to get a share, if it's possible."

"What precaution, for instance?" scoffed Croyden.

Macloud shrugged his shoulders, helplessly.

"I wish I knew," he said.

XVI

THE MARABOU MUFF

The next two weeks passed uneventfully. The thieves did not manifest themselves, and the Government authorities did nothing to suggest that they had been informed of the Parmenter treasure.

Macloud had developed an increasing fondness for Miss Carrington's society, which she, on her part, seemed to accept with placid equanimity. They rode, they drove, they walked, they sailed when the weather warranted—and the weather had recovered from its fit of the blues, and was lazy and warm and languid. In short, they did everything which is commonly supposed to denote a growing fondness for each other.

Croyden had been paid promptly for the Virginia Development Company bonds, and was once more on "comfortable street," as he expressed it. But he spoke no word of returning to Northumberland. On the contrary, he settled down to enjoy the life of the village, social and otherwise. He was nice to all the girls, but showed a marked preference for Miss Carrington; which, however, did not trouble his friend, in the least.

Macloud was quite willing to run the risk with Croyden. He was confident that the call of the old life, the memory of the girl that was, and that was still, would be enough to hold Geoffrey from more than firm friendship. He was not quite sure of himself, however—that he wanted to marry. And he was entirely sure she had not decided whether she wanted him—that was what gave him his lease of life; if she decided *for* him, he knew that he would decide for her—and quickly.

Then, one day, came a letter—forwarded by the Club, where he had left his address with instructions that it be divulged to no one. It was dated Northumberland, and read:

"My dear Colin—

"It is useless, between us, to dissemble, and I'm not going to try it. I want to know whether Geoffrey Croyden is coming back to Northumberland? You are with him, and should know. You can tell his inclination. You can ask him, if necessary. If he is not coming and there is no one else—won't you tell me where you are? (I don't ask you to reveal his address, you see.) I shall come down—if only for an hour, between trains—and give him his chance. It is radically improper, according to accepted notions—but notions don't bother me, when they stand (as I am sure they do, in this case), in the way of happiness.

"Sincerely,

"Elaine Cavendish."

At dinner, Macloud casually remarked:

"I ought to go out to Northumberland, this week, for a short time, won't you go along?"

Croyden shook his head.

"I'm not going back to Northumberland," he said.

"I don't mean to stay!" Macloud interposed. "I'll promise to come back with you in two days at the most."

"Yes, I suppose you will!" Croyden smiled. "You can easily find your way back. For me, it's easier to stay away from Northumberland, than to go away from it, *again*."

And Macloud, being wise, dropped the conversation, saying only:

"Well, I may not have to go."

A little later, as he sat in the drawing-room at Carringtons', he broached a matter which had been on his mind for some time—working around to it gradually, with Croyden the burden of their talk. When his opportunity came —as it was bound to do—he took it without hesitation.

"You are right," he replied. "Croyden had two reasons for leaving Northumberland: one of them has been eliminated; the other is stronger than ever."

She looked at him, shrewdly.

"And that other is a woman?" she said.

He nodded. "A woman who has plenty of money—more than she can ever spend, indeed."

"And in looks?"

"The only one who can approach yourself."

"Altogether, most desirable!" she laughed. "What was the trouble—wouldn't she have him?"

"He didn't ask her."

"Useless?"

"Anything but useless."

"You mean she was willing?"

"I think so."

"And Croyden?"

"More than willing, I take it."

"Then, what was the difficulty?"

"Her money—she has so much!—So much, that, in comparison, he is a mere pauper:—twenty millions against two hundred thousand."

"If she be willing, I can't see why he is shy?"

"He says it is all right for a poor girl to marry a rich man, but not for a poor man to marry a rich girl. His idea is, that the husband should be able to maintain his wife according to her condition. To marry else, he says, is giving hostages to fortune, and is derogatory to that mutual respect which should exist between them."

"We all give hostages to fortune when we marry!" Miss Carrington exclaimed.

"Not all!" replied Macloud, meaningly.

She flushed slightly.

"What is it you want me to do?" she asked hastily—"or can I do anything?"

"You can," he answered. "You can ask Miss Cavendish to visit you for a few days."

"Can you, by any possibility, mean Elaine Cavendish?"

"That's exactly who I do mean—do you know her?"

"After a fashion—we went to Dobbs Ferry together."

"Bully!" exclaimed Macloud. "Why didn't you tell me?"

"You never mentioned her before."

"True!" he laughed. "This is fortunate, very fortunate! Will you ask her down?"

"She will think it a trifle peculiar."

"On the contrary, she'll think it more than kind—a positive favor. You see, she knows I'm with Croyden, but she doesn't know where; so she wrote to me at my Club and they forwarded it. Croyden left Northumberland without a word—and no one is aware of his residence but me. She asks that I tell her where *I* am. Then she intends to come down and give Croyden a last chance. I want to help her—and your invitation will be right to the point—she'll jump at it."

"You're a good friend!" she reflected.

"Will you do it?" he asked.

She thought a moment before she answered.

"I'll do it!" she said at length. "Come, we'll work out the letter together."

"Would I not be permitted to kiss you as Miss Cavendish's deputy?" he exclaimed.

"Miss Cavendish can be her own deputy," she answered.—"Moreover, it would be premature."

The second morning after, when Elaine Cavendish's maid brought her breakfast, Miss Carrington's letter was on the tray among tradesmen's circulars, invitations, and friendly correspondence.

She did not recognize the handwriting, and the postmark was unfamiliar, wherefore, coupled with the fact that it was addressed in a particularly stylish hand, she opened it first. It was very brief, very succinct, very informing, and very satisfactory.

> "Ashburton,
>
> "Hampton, Md.

"My dear Elaine:—

"Mr. Macloud tells me you are contemplating coming down to the Eastern Shore to look for a country-place. Let me advise Hampton—there are some delightful old residences in this vicinity which positively are crying for a purchaser. Geoffrey Croyden, whom you know, I believe, is resident here, and is thinking of making it his home permanently. If you can be persuaded to come, you are to stay with me—the hotels are simply impossible, and I shall be more than delighted to have you. We can talk over old times at Dobbs, and have a nice little visit together. Don't trouble to write—just wire the time of your arrival—and come before the good weather departs. Don't disappoint me.

> "With lots of love,
>
> "Davila Carrington."

Elaine Cavendish read the letter slowly—and smiled.

"Clever! very clever!" she mused. "Colin is rather a diplomat—he managed it with exceeding adroitness—and the letter is admirably worded. It tells me everything I wanted to know. I'd forgotten about Davila Carrington, and I reckon she had forgotten me, till he somehow found it out and jogged her memory. Surely! I shall accept."

To-morrow would be Thursday. She went to her desk and wrote this wire, in answer:

"Miss Davila Carrington,

   "Hampton, Md.

"I shall be with you Friday, on morning train. You're very, very kind.

                                "Elaine Cavendish."

Miss Carrington showed the wire to Macloud.

"Now, I've done all that I can; the rest is in your hands," she said. "I'll coöperate, but you are the general."

"Until Elaine comes—she will manage it then," Macloud answered.

And on Friday morning, a little before noon, Miss Cavendish arrived. Miss Carrington, alone, met her at the station.

"You're just the same Davila I'd forgotten for years," said she, laughingly, as they walked across the platform to the waiting carriage.

"And you're the same I had forgotten," Davila replied.

"But it's delightful to be remembered!" said Elaine, meaningly.

"And it's just as delightful to be able to remember," was the reply.

Just after they left the business section, on the drive out, Miss Carrington saw Croyden and Macloud coming down the street. Evidently Macloud had not been able to detain him at home until she got her charge safely into Ashburton. She glanced at Miss Cavendish—she had seen them, also, and, settling back into the corner of the phaeton, she hid her face with her Marabou muff.

"Don't stop!" she said.

Miss Carrington smiled her understanding.

"I won't!" she answered. "Good morning!" as both men raised their hats— and drove straight on.

"Who was the girl with Miss Carrington?" Croyden asked. "I didn't see her face."

"I couldn't see it!" said Macloud. "I noticed a bag in the trap, however, so I reckon she's a guest."

"Unfortunate for you!" Croyden sympathized. "Your opportunity, for the solitariness of two, will be limited."

"I'll look to you for help!" Macloud answered.

"Humph! You may look in vain. It depends on what she is—I'm not sacrificing myself on the altar of general unattractiveness." Then he laughed. "Rest easy, I'll fuss her to the limit. You shan't have her to plead for an excuse."

"An excuse for what?"

"For not winning the Symphony in Blue."

"You're overly solicitous. I'm not worried about the guest," Macloud remarked.

"There was a certain style about as much of her as I could see which promised very well," Croyden remarked. "I think this would be a good day to drop in for tea."

"And if you find her something over sixty, you'll gallantly shove her off on me, and preëmpt Miss Carrington. Oh! you're very kind."

"She's not over sixty—and you know it. You're by no means as blind as you would have me believe. In fact, now that I think of it, there was something about her that seems familiar."

"You're an adept in many things," laughed Macloud, "but, I reckon, you're not up to recognizing a brown coat and a brown hat. I think I've seen the combination once or twice before on a woman."

"Well, what about tea-time—shall we go over?" demanded Croyden.

"I haven't the slightest objection——"

"Really!"

"——to your going along with me—I'm expected!"

"Oh! you're expected, are you! pretty soon it will be: 'Come over and see us, won't you?'"

"I trust so," said Macloud, placidly.—"But, as you're never coming back to Northumberland, it's a bit impossible."

"Oh! damn Northumberland!" said Croyden.

"I've a faint recollection of having heard that remark before."

"I dare say, it's popular there on smoky days."

"Which is the same as saying it's popular there any time."

"No, I don't mean that; Northumberland isn't half so bad as it's painted. We may make fun of it—but we like it, just the same."

"Yes, I suppose we do," said Macloud. "Though we get mighty sick of seeing every scatterbrain who sets fire to the Great White Way branded by the newspapers as a Northumberland millionaire. We've got our share of fools, but we haven't a monopoly of them, by any means."

"We had a marvelously large crop, however, running loose at one time, recently!" laughed Croyden.

"True!—and there's the reason for it, as well as the fallacy. Because half a hundred light-weights were made millionaires over night, and, top heavy, straightway went the devil's pace, doesn't imply that the entire town is mad."

"Not at all!" said Croyden. "It's no worse than any other big town—and the fellows with unsavory reputations aren't representative. They just came all in a bunch. The misfortune is, that the whole country saw the fireworks, and it hasn't forgot the lurid display."

"And isn't likely to very soon," Macloud responded, "with the whole Municipal Government rotten to the core, councilmen falling over one another in their eagerness to plead *nolle contendere* and escape the penitentiary, bankers in jail for bribery, or fighting extradition; and graft! graft! graft! permeating every department of the civic life—and published by the newspapers' broadcast, through the land, for all the world to read, while the people, as a body, sit supine, and meekly suffer the robbers to remain. The trouble with the Northumberlander is, that so long as he is not the immediate victim of a hold up, he is quiescent. Let him be touched direct—by burglary, by theft, by embezzlement—and the yell he lets out wakes the entire bailiwick."

"It's the same everywhere," said Croyden.

"No, it's not,—other communities have waked up—Northumberland hasn't. There is too much of the moneyed interest to be looked after; and the councilmen know it, and are out for the stuff, as brazen as the street-walker, and vastly more insistent.—I'm going in here, for some cigarettes—when I come out, we'll change the talk to something less irritating. I like Northumberland, but I despise about ninety-nine one hundredths of its inhabitants."

When he returned, Croyden was gazing after an automobile which was disappearing in a cloud of dust.

"Ever see a motor before?" he asked.

Croyden did not hear him. "The fellow driving, unless I am mightily fooled, is the same who stopped me on the street, in front of Clarendon," he said.

"That's interesting—any one with him?"

"A woman."

"A woman! You're safe!" said Macloud. "He isn't travelling around with a petticoat—at least, if he's thinking of tackling you."

"It isn't likely, I admit—but suppose he is?"

The car was rapidly vanishing in the distance. Macloud nodded toward it.

"He is leaving here as fast as the wheels will turn."

"I've got a very accurate memory for faces," said Croyden. "I couldn't well be mistaken."

"Wait and see. If it was he, and he has some new scheme, it will be declared in due time. Nothing yet from the Government?"

"No!"

"It's a bluff! So long as they think you have the jewels, they will try for them. There's Captain Carrington standing at his office door. Suppose we go over."

"Sitting up to grandfather-in-law!" laughed Croyden. "Distinctly proper, sir, distinctly proper! Go and chat with him; I'll stop for you, presently."

—————

Meanwhile, the two women had continued on to Ashburton.

"Did he recognize me?" Elaine asked, dropping her muff from before her face, when they were past the two men.

"I think not," answered Davila.

"Did he give any indication of it?"

"None, whatever."

"It would make a difference in my—attitude toward him when we met!" she smiled.

"Naturally! a very great difference." Elaine was nervous, she saw. The fact that Croyden did not come out and stop them, that he let them go on, was sufficient proof that he had not recognized her.

"You see, I am assuming that you know why I wanted to come to Hampton,"

Elaine said, when, her greeting made to Mrs. Carrington, she had carried Davila along to her room.

"Yes, dear," Davila responded.

"And you made it very easy for me to come."

"I did as I thought you would want—and as I know you would do with me were I in a similar position."

"I'm sadly afraid I should not have thought of you, were you——"

"Oh, yes, you would! If you had been in a small town, and Mr. Croyden had told you of my difficulty——"

"As *Mr. Macloud* told you of mine—I see, dear."

"Not exactly that," said Davila, blushing. "Mr. Macloud has been very attentive and very nice and all that, you know, but you mustn't forget there are not many girls here, and I'm convenient, and—I don't take him seriously."

"How does he take you?" Elaine asked.

"I don't know—sometimes I think he does, and sometimes I think he doesn't!" she laughed. "He is an accomplished flirt and difficult to gauge."

"Well, let me tell you one fact, for your information: there isn't a more indifferent man in Northumberland. He goes everywhere, is in great demand, is enormously popular, yet, I've never known him to have even an affair. He is armor-plated—but he is a dear, a perfect dear, Davila!"

"I know it!" she said, with heightening color—and Elaine said no more, then.

"Shall you prefer to meet Mr. Croyden alone, for the first time, or in company?" Davila asked.

"I confess I don't know, but I think, however, it would be better to have a few words with Colin, first—if it can be arranged."

Miss Carrington nodded. "Mr. Macloud is to come in a moment before luncheon, if he can find an excuse that will not include Mr. Croyden."

"Is an excuse difficult to find—or is any, even, needed?"

Elaine smiled.

"He doesn't usually come before four—that's the tea hour in Hampton."

"Tea!" exclaimed Elaine. "If you've got him into the tea habit, you can do what you want with him—he will eat out of your hand."

"I never tried him with tea," said Davila. "He chose a high ball the first time

154

—so it's been a high ball ever since."

"With gratifying regularity?"

"I admit it!" laughed Davila.

Elaine sat down on the couch and put her arm about Davila.

"These awful men!" she said. "But we shall be good friends, better friends than ever, Davila, when you come to Northumberland to live."

"That is just the question, Elaine," was the quick answer; "whether I shall be given the opportunity, and whether I shall take it, if I am. I haven't let it go so far, because I don't feel sure of him. Until I do, I intend to keep tight hold on myself."

"Do it—if you can. You'll find it much the happier way."

Just before luncheon, Macloud arrived.

"Bully for you!" was his greeting to Miss Cavendish. "I'm glad to see you here."

"Yes, I'm here, thanks to you," said Elaine—and Davila not being present, she kissed him.

"I'm more than repaid!" he said.

"But you wish it were—another?"

"No—but I wish the other—would, too!" he laughed.

"Give her the chance, Colin."

"You think I may dare?" eagerly.

"You're not wont to be so timid," she returned.

"I wish I had some of your bravery," he said.

"Is it bravery?" she demanded. "Isn't it impetuous womanliness."

"Not a bit! There isn't a doubt as to his feelings."

"But there is a doubt as to his letting them control—I see."

"Yes! And you alone can help him solve it—if any one can. And I have great hopes, Elaine, great hopes!" regarding her with approving eyes. "How any chap could resist you is inconceivable—I could not."

"You could not at one time, you mean."

"You gave me no encouragement,—so I must, perforce, fare elsewhere."

"And now?" she asked.

"How many love affairs have you come down here to settle?" he laughed. "By the way, Croyden is impatient to come over this afternoon. The guest in the trap with Miss Carrington has aroused his curiosity. He could see only a long brown coat and a brown hat, but the muff before your face, and his imagination, did the rest."

"Does he suspect?" she inquired, anxiously.

"That it's you? No! no! It's simply the country town beginning to tell on him. He is curious about new guests, and Miss Carrington hadn't mentioned your coming! He suggested, in a vague sort of way, that there was something familiar about you, but he didn't attempt to particularize. It was only a momentary idea."

She looked her relief.

"Shall you meet him alone?"

"I think not—we shall all be present."

"And *how* shall you meet him?"

"It depends on how he meets me."

"I reckon you don't know much about it—haven't any plans?"

"No, I haven't. Everything depends on the moment. He will know why I'm here, and whether he is glad or sorry or displeased at my coming, I shall know instantly. I shall then have my cue. It's absurd, this notion of his, and why let it rule him and me! I've always got what I wanted, and I'm going to get Geoffrey. A Queen of a Nation must propose to a suitor, so why not a Queen of Money to a man less rich than she—especially when she is convinced that that alone keeps them apart. I shall give him a chance to propose to me first; several chances, indeed!" she laughed. "Then, if he doesn't respond—I shall do it myself."

XVII

A HANDKERCHIEF AND A GLOVE

Miss Cavendish was standing behind the curtains in the window of her room, when Croyden and Macloud came up the walk, at four o'clock.

She was waiting!—not another touch to be given to her attire. Her gown, of shimmering blue silk, clung to her figure with every movement, and fell to the floor in suggestively revealing folds. Her dark hair was arranged in simple fashion—the simplicity of exquisite taste—making the fair face below it, seem fairer even than it was. She was going to win this man.

She heard them enter the lower hall, and pass into the drawing-room. She glided out to the stairway, and stood, peering down over the balustrade. She heard Miss Carrington's greeting and theirs—heard Macloud's chuckle, and Croyden's quiet laugh. Then she heard Macloud say:

"Mr. Croyden is anxious to meet your guest—at least, we took her to be a guest you were driving with this morning."

"My guest is equally anxious to meet Mr. Croyden," Miss Carrington replied.

"Why does she tarry, then?" laughed Croyden.

"Did you ever know a woman to be ready?"

"You were."

"I am the hostess!" she explained.

"Mr. Croyden imagined there was something familiar about her," Macloud remarked.

"Do you mean you recognized her?" Miss Carrington asked.

(Elaine strained her ears to catch his answer.)

"She didn't let me have the chance to recognize her," said he—"she wouldn't let me see her face."

(Elaine gave a little sigh of relief.)

"Wouldn't?" Miss Carrington interrogated.

"At least, she didn't."

"She couldn't have covered it completely—she saw you."

"Don't raise his hopes too high!" Macloud interjected.

"She can't—I'm on the pinnacle of expectation, now."

"Humpty-Dumpty risks a great fall!" Macloud warned.

"Not at all!" said Croyden. "If the guest doesn't please me, I'm going to talk to Miss Carrington."

"You're growing blasé," she warned.

"Is that an evidence of it?" he asked. "If it is, I know one who must be too blasé even to move," with a meaning glance at Macloud.

A light foot-fall on the stairs, the soft swish of skirts in the hallway, Croyden turned, expectantly—and Miss Cavendish entered the room.

There was an instant's silence. Croyden's from astonishment; the others' with watching him.

Elaine's eyes were intent on Croyden's face—and what she saw there gave her great content: he might not be persuaded, but he loved her, and he would not misunderstand. Her face brightened with a fascinating smile.

"You are surprised to see me, messieurs?" she asked, curtsying low.

Croyden's eyes turned quickly to his friend, and back again.

"I'm not so sure as to Monsieur Macloud," he said.

"But for yourself?"

"Surprised is quite too light a word—stunned would but meekly express it."

"Did neither of you ever hear me mention Miss Carrington?—We were friends, almost chums, at Dobbs Ferry."

"If I did, it has escaped me?" Croyden smiled.

"Well, you're likely not to forget it again."

"Did you know that I—that we were here?"

"Certainly! I knew that you and Colin were both here," Elaine replied, imperturbably. "Do you think yourself so unimportant as not to be mentioned by Miss Carrington?"

"What will you have to drink, Mr. Croyden?" Davila inquired.

"A sour ball, by all means."

"Is that a reflection on my guest?" she asked—while Elaine and Macloud laughed.

"A reflection on your guest?" he inflected, puzzled.

158

"You said you would take a *sour* ball."

Croyden held up his hands.

"I'm fussed!" he confessed. "I have nothing to plead. A man who mixes a high ball with a sour ball is either rattled or drunk, I am not the latter, therefore——"

"You mean that my coming has rattled you?" Elaine inquired.

"Yes—I'm rattled for very joy."

She put her hands before her face.

"Spare my blushes, Geoffrey!"

"You could spare a few—and not miss them!" he laughed.

"Davila, am I?" she demanded.

"Are you what?"

"Blushing?"

"Not the slightest, dear."

"Here's your sour ball!" said Macloud, handing him the glass.

"Sweetened by your touch, I suppose!"

"No! By the ladies' presence—God save them!"

"Colin," said Croyden, as, an hour later, they walked back to Clarendon, "you should have told me."

"Should have told you what?" Macloud asked.

"Don't affect ignorance, old man—you knew Elaine was coming."

"I did—yesterday."

"And that it was she in the trap."

"The muff hid her face from me, too."

"But you knew."

"I could only guess."

"Do you think it was wise to let her come?" Croyden demanded.

"I had nothing to do with her decision. Miss Carrington asked her, she accepted."

"Didn't you give her my address?"

159

"I most assuredly did not."

Croyden looked at him, doubtfully.

"I'm telling you the truth," said Macloud. "She tried to get your address, when I was last in Northumberland, and I refused."

"And then, she stumbles on it through Davila Carrington! The world *is* small. I reckon, if I went off into some deserted spot in Africa, it wouldn't be a month until some fellow I knew, or who knows a mutual friend, would come nosing around, and blow on me."

"Are you sorry she came?" Macloud asked.

"No! I'm not sorry she came—at least, not now, since she's here.—I'll be sorry enough when she goes, however."

"And you will let her go?"

Croyden nodded. "I must—it's the only proper thing to do."

"Proper for whom?"

"For both!"

"Would it not be better that *she* should decide what is proper for her?"

"Proper for me, then."

"Based on your peculiar notion of relative wealth between husband and wife —without regard to what she may think on the subject. In other words, have you any right to decline the risk, if she is willing to undertake it?"

"The risk is mine, not hers. She has the money. Her income, for three months, about equals my entire fortune."

"Can't you forget her fortune?"

"And live at the rate of pretty near two hundred thousand dollars a year?" Croyden laughed. "Could you?"

"I think I could, if I loved the girl."

"And suffer in your self-respect forever after?"

"There is where we differ. You're inclined to be hyper-critical. If you play *your* part, you won't lose your self-respect."

"It is a trifle difficult to do—to play my part, when all the world is saying, 'he married her for her money,' and shows me scant regard in consequence."

"Why the devil need you care what the world says!"

"I don't!"

"What?" Macloud exclaimed.

"I don't—the world may go hang. But the question is, how long can the man retain the woman's esteem, with such a handicap."

"Ah! that is easy! so long as he retains her love."

"Rather an uncertain quantity."

"It depends entirely on yourself.—If you start with it, you can hold it, if you take the trouble to try."

"You're a strong partisan!" Croyden laughed, as they entered Clarendon.

"And what are you?" Macloud returned.

"Just what I should like to know——"

"Well, I'll tell you what you are if you don't marry Elaine Cavendish," Macloud interrupted—"You're an unmitigated fool!"

"Assuming that Miss Cavendish would marry me."

"You're not likely to marry her, otherwise," retorted Macloud, as he went up the stairs. On the landing he halted and looked down at Croyden in the hall below. "And if you don't take your chance, the chance she has deliberately offered you by coming to Hampton, you are worse than——" and, with an expressive gesture, he resumed the ascent.

"How do you know she came down here just for that purpose?" Croyden called.

But all that came back in answer, as Macloud went down the hall and into his room, was the whistled air from a popular opera, then running in the Metropolis.

"Ev'ry little movement has a meaning all its own,

Ev'ry thought and action——"

The door slammed—the music ceased.

"I won't believe it," Croyden reflected, "that Elaine would do anything so utterly unconventional as to seek me out deliberately.... I might have had a chance if—Oh, damn it all! why didn't we find the old pirate's box—it would have clarified the whole situation."

As he changed into his evening clothes, he went over the matter, carefully, and laid out the line of conduct that he intended to follow.

He would that Elaine had stayed away from Hampton. It was putting him to too severe a test—to be with her, to be subject to her alluring loveliness, and, yet, to be unmoved. It is hard to see the luscious fruit within one's reach and to refrain from even touching it. It grew harder the more he contemplated it....

"It's no use fighting against it, here!" he exclaimed, going into Macloud's room, and throwing himself on a chair. "I'm going to cut the whole thing."

"What the devil are you talking about?" Macloud inquired, pausing with his waistcoat half on.

"What the devil do you think I'm talking about?" Croyden demanded.

"Not being a success at solving riddles, I give it up."

"Oh, very well!" said Croyden. "Can you comprehend this:—I'm going to leave town?"

"Certainly—that's plain English. When are you going?"

"To-morrow morning."

"Why this suddenness?"

"To get away quickly—to escape."

"From Elaine?"

Croyden nodded.

Macloud smiled.

"He is coming to it, at last," he thought. What he said was:—"You're not going to be put to flight by a woman?"

"I am.—If I stay here I shall lose."

"You mean?"

"I shall propose."

"And be refused?"

"Be accepted."

"Most people would not call that *losing*," said Macloud.

"I have nothing to do with most people—only, with myself."

"It seems so!—even Elaine isn't to be considered."

"Haven't we gone over all that?"

"I don't know—but, if we have, go over it again."

"You assume she came down here solely on my account—because I'm here?"

"I assume nothing," Macloud answered, with a quiet chuckle. "I said you have a chance, and urged you not to let it slip. I should not have offered any suggestion—I admit that——"

"Oh, bosh!" Croyden interrupted. "Don't be so humble—you're rather proud of your interference."

"I am! Certainly, I am! I'm only sorry it is so unavailing."

"Who said it was unavailing!"

"You did!—or, at least, I inferred as much."

"I'm not responsible for your inferences."

"What are you responsible for?" asked Macloud.

"Nothing! Nothing!—not even for my resolution—I haven't any—I can't make any that holds. I'm worse than a weather-cock. Common sense bids me go. Desire clamors for me to stay—to hasten over to Ashburton—to put it to the test. When I get to Ashburton, common sense will be in control. When I come away, desire will tug me back, again—and so on, and so on—and so on."

"You're in a bad way!" laughed Macloud. "You need a cock-tail, instead of a weather-cock. Come on! if we are to dine at the Carringtons' at seven, we would better be moving. Having thrown the blue funk, usual to a man in your position, you'll now settle down to business."

"To be or not to be?"

"Let future events determine—take it as it comes," Macloud urged.

"Sage advice!" returned Croyden mockingly. "If I let future events decide for me, the end's already fixed."

The big clock on the landing was chiming seven when they rang the bell at Ashburton and the maid ushered them into the drawing-room. Mrs. Carrington was out of town, visiting in an adjoining county, and the Captain had not appeared. He came down stairs a moment later, and took Macloud and Croyden over to the library.

After about a quarter of an hour, he glanced at his watch a trifle impatiently. —Another fifteen minutes, and he glanced at it again.

"Caroline!" he called, as the maid passed the door. "Go up to Miss Davila's room and tell her it's half-after-seven."

Then he continued with the story he was relating.

Presently, the maid returned; the Captain looked at her, interrogatingly.

"Mis' Davila, she ain' deah, no seh," said the girl.

"She is probably in Miss Cavendish's room,—look, there, for her," the Captain directed.

"No, seh! I looks dyar—she ain' no place up stairs, and neither is Mis' Cav'dish, seh. Hit's all dark, in dey rooms, seh, all dark."

"Very singular," said the Captain. "Half-after-seven, and not here?"

"They were here, two hours ago," said Croyden. "We had tea with them."

"Find out from the other servants whether they left any word."

"Dey didn', seh! no, seh! I ax'd dem, seh!"

"Very singular, indeed! excuse me, sirs, I'll try to locate them."

He went to the telephone, and called up the Lashiels, the Tilghmans, the Tayloes, and all their neighbors and intimates, only to receive the same answer: "They were not there, and hadn't been there that afternoon."

"This is amazing, sirs!" he exclaimed. "I will go up myself and see."

"We are at your service, Captain Carrington," said Macloud instantly.—"At your service for anything we can do."

"They knew, of course, you were expected for dinner?" he asked, as he led the way upstairs.—"I can't account for it."

The Captain inspected his granddaughter's and Miss Cavendish's rooms, Macloud and Croyden, being discreet, the rooms on the other side of the house. They discovered nothing which would explain.

"We will have dinner," said the Captain. "They will surely turn up before we have finished."

The dinner ended, however, and the missing ones had not returned.

"Might they have gone for a drive?" Macloud suggested.

The Captain shook his head. "The keys of the stable are on my desk, which shows that the horses are in for the night. I admit I am at a loss—however, I reckon they will be in presently, with an explanation and a good laugh at us for being anxious."

But when nine o'clock came, and then half-after-nine, and still they did not appear, the men grew seriously alarmed.

The Captain had recourse to the telephone again, getting residence after residence, without result. At last he hung up the receiver.

"I don't know what to make of it," he said, bewildered. "I've called every place I can think of, and I can't locate them. What can have happened?"

"Let us see how the matter stands," said Macloud. "We left them here about half-after-five, and, so far as can be ascertained, no one has seen them since. Consequently, they must have gone out for a walk or a drive. A drive is most unlikely, at this time of the day—it is dark and cold. Furthermore, your horses are in the stable, so, if they went, they didn't go alone—some one drove them. The alternative—a walk—is the probable explanation; and that remits us to an accident as the cause of delay. Which, it seems to me, is the likely explanation."

"But if there were an accident, they would have been discovered, long since; the walks are not deserted," the Captain objected.

"Possibly, they went out of the town."

"A young woman never goes out of town, unescorted," was the decisive answer. "This is a Southern town, you know."

"I suppose you don't care to telephone the police?" asked Croyden.

"No—not yet," the Captain replied. "Davila would never forgive me, if nothing really were wrong—besides, I couldn't. The Mayor's office is closed for the night—we're not supposed to need the police after six o'clock."

"Then Croyden and I will patrol the roads, hereabout," said Macloud.

"Good! I will go out the Queen Street pike a mile or two," the Captain said. "You and Mr. Croyden can take the King Street pike, North and South. We'll meet here not later than eleven o'clock. Excuse me a moment——"

"What do you make of it?" said Macloud.

"It is either very serious or else it's nothing at all. I mean, if anything *has* happened, it's far out of the ordinary," Croyden answered.

"Exactly my idea—though, I confess, I haven't a notion what the serious side could be. It's safe to assume that they didn't go into the country—the hour, alone, would have deterred them, even if the danger from the negro were not present, constantly, in Miss Carrington's mind. On the other hand, how could anything have happened in the town which would prevent one of them from telephoning, or sending a message, or getting some sort of word to the Captain."

"It's all very mysterious—yet, I dare say, easy of solution and explanation. There isn't any danger of the one thing that is really terrifying, so I'm not inclined to be alarmed, unduly—just disquieted."

At this moment Captain Carrington returned.

"Here! take these," he said, giving each a revolver. "Let us hope there won't be any occasion to use them, but it is well to be prepared."

They went out together—at the intersection of Queen and King Streets, they parted.

"Remember! eleven o'clock at my house," said the Captain. "If any one of us isn't there, the other two will know he needs assistance."

Croyden went north on King Street. It was a chilly November night, with frost in the air. The moon, in its second quarter and about to sink into the waters of the Bay, gave light sufficient to make walking easy, where the useless street lamps did not kill it with their timid brilliancy. He passed the limits of the town, and struck out into the country. It had just struck ten, when they parted —he would walk for half an hour, and then return. He could do three miles— a mile and a half each way—and still be at the Carrington house by eleven. He proceeded along the east side of the road, his eyes busy lest, in the uncertain light, he miss anything which might serve as a clue. For the allotted time, he searched but found nothing—he must return. He crossed to the west side of the road, and faced homeward.

A mile passed—a quarter more was added—the feeble lights of the town were gleaming dimly in the fore, when, beside the track, he noticed a small white object.

It was a woman's handkerchief, and, as he picked it up, a faint odor of violets was clinging to it still. Here might be a clue—there was a monogram on the corner, but he could not distinguish it, in the darkness. He put it in his pocket and hastened on. A hundred feet farther, and his foot hit something soft. He groped about, with his hands, and found—a woman's glove. It, also, bore the odor of violets.

At the first lamp-post, he stopped and examined the handkerchief—the monogram was plain: E. C.—and violets, he remembered, were her favorite perfume. He took out the glove—a soft, undressed kid affair—but there was no mark on it to help him. He glanced at his watch. His time had almost expired. He pushed the feminine trifles back into his pocket, and hurried on.

He was late, and when he arrived at Ashburton, Captain Carrington and Macloud were just about to start in pursuit.

"I found these!" he said, tossing the glove and the handkerchief on the table —"on the west side of the road, about half a mile from town."

Macloud picked them up.

"The violets are familiar—and the handkerchief is Elaine's," said he. "I recognize the monogram as hers."

"What do you make of it?" Captain Carrington demanded.

"Nothing—it passes me."

His glance sought Croyden's.

A shake of the head was his answer.

The Captain strode to the telephone.

"I'm going to call in our friends," he said. "I think we shall need them."

XVIII

When Croyden and Macloud left the Carrington residence that evening, after their call and tea, Elaine and Davila remained for a little while in the drawing-room rehearsing the events of the day, as women will. Presently, Davila went over to draw the shades.

"What do you say to a walk before we dress for dinner?" she inquired.

"I should like it, immensely," Elaine answered.

They went upstairs, changed quickly to street attire, and set out.

"We will go down to the centre of the town and back," said Davila. "It's about half a mile each way, and there isn't any danger, so long as you keep in the town. I shouldn't venture beyond it unescorted, however, even in daylight."

"Why?" asked Elaine. "Isn't Hampton orderly?"

"Hampton is orderly enough. It's the curse that hangs over the South since the Civil War: the negro."

"Oh! I understand," said Elaine, shuddering.

"I don't mean that all black men are bad, for they are not. Many are entirely trustworthy, but the trustworthy ones are much, very much, in the minority. The vast majority are worthless—and a worthless nigger is the worst thing on earth."

"I think I prefer only the lighted streets," Elaine remarked.

"And you will be perfectly safe there," Davila replied.

They swung briskly along to the centre of the town—where the two main thoroughfares, King and Queen Streets, met each other in a wide circle that, after the fashion of Southern towns, was known, incongruously enough, as "The Diamond." Passing around this circle, they retraced their steps toward home.

As they neared Ashburton, an automobile with the top up and side curtains on shot up behind them, hesitated a moment, as though uncertain of its destination and then drew up before the Carrington place. Two men alighted, gave an order to the driver, and went across the pavement to the gate, while the engine throbbed, softly.

Then they seemed to notice the women approaching, and stepping back from the gate, they waited.

"I beg your pardon!" said one, raising his hat and bowing, "can you tell me if this is where Captain Carrington lives?"

"It is," answered Davila.

"Thank you!" said the man, standing aside to let them pass.

"I am Miss Carrington—whom do you wish to see?"

"Captain Carrington, is he at home?"

"I do not know—if you will come in, I'll inquire."

"You're very kind!" with another bow.

He sprang forward and opened the gate. Davila thanked him with a smile, and she and Elaine went in, leaving the strangers to follow.

The next instant, each girl was struggling in the folds of a shawl, which had been flung over her from behind and wrapped securely around her head and arms, smothering her cries to a mere whisper. In a trice, despite their struggles —which, with heads covered and arms held close to their sides, were utterly unavailing—they were caught up, tossed into the tonneau, and the car shot swiftly away.

In a moment, it was clear of the town, the driver "opened her up," and they sped through the country at thirty miles an hour.

"Better give them some air," said the leader. "It doesn't matter how much they yell here."

He had been holding Elaine on his lap, his arms keeping the shawl tight around her. Now he loosed her, and unwound the folds.

"You will please pardon the liberty we have taken," he said, as he freed her, "but there are——"

Crack!

Elaine had struck him straight in the face with all her strength, and, springing free, was on the point of leaping out, when he seized her and forced her back, caught her arms in the shawl, which was still around her, and bound them tight to her side.

"Better be a little careful, Bill!" he said. "I got an upper cut on the jaw that made me see stars."

"I've been very easy with mine," his companion returned. "She'll not hand me one." However, he took care not to loosen the shawl from her arms.

"There you are, my lady, I hope you've not been greatly inconvenienced."

"What do you mean by this outrage?" said Davila.

"Don't forget, Bill!—mum's the word!" the chief cautioned.

"At least, you can permit us to sit on the floor of the car," said Elaine. "Whatever may be your scheme, it's scarcely necessary to hold us in this disgusting position."

"Will you make no effort to escape?" the chief asked.

"No!"

"I reckon that is a trifle overstated!" he laughed. "What about you, Miss Carrington?"

Davila did not answer—contenting herself with a look, which was far more expressive than words.

"Well, we will take pleasure in honoring your first request, Miss Cavendish."

He caught up a piece of rope, passed it around her arms, outside the shawl, tied it in a running knot, and quietly lifted her from his lap to the floor.

"I trust that is satisfactory?" he asked.

"By comparison, eminently so."

"Thank you!" he said. "Do you, Miss Carrington, wish to sit beside your friend?"

"If you please!" said Davila, with supreme contempt.

He took the rope and tied her, likewise.

"Very good, Bill!" he said, and they placed her beside Elaine.

"If you will permit your legs to be tied, we will gladly let you have the seat ——" "No!——
"

"Well, I didn't think you would—so you will have to remain on the floor; you see, you might be tempted to jump, if we gave you the seat."

They were running so rapidly, through the night air, that the country could scarcely be distinguished, as it rushed by them. To Elaine, it was an unknown land. Davila, however, was looking for something she could recognize—some building that she knew, some stream, some topographical formation. But in the faint and uncertain moonlight, coupled with the speed at which they travelled, she was baffled. The chief observed, however.

"With your permission!" he said, and taking two handkerchiefs from his pocket, he bound the eyes of both.

"It is only for a short while," he explained—"matter of an hour or so, and you suffer no particular inconvenience, I trust."

Neither Elaine nor Davila condescended to reply.

After a moment's pause, the man went on:

"I neglected to say—and I apologize for my remissness—that you need fear no ill-treatment. You will be shown every consideration—barring freedom, of course—and all your wants, within the facilities at our command, will be gratified. Naturally, however, you will not be permitted to communicate with your friends."

"How nice of you!" said Elaine. "But I should be better pleased if you would tell us the reason for this abduction."

"That, I regret, I am not at liberty to discuss."

"How long are we to remain prisoners?" demanded Davila.

"It depends."

"Upon what?"

"Upon whether something is acceded to."

"By whom?"

"I am not at liberty to say."

"And if it is not acceded to?" Elaine inquired.

"In that event—it would be necessary to decide what should be done with you."

"Done with us! What do you mean to imply?"

"Nothing!—the time hasn't come to imply—I hope it will not come."

"Why?" said Davila.

"Because."

"Because is no reason."

"It is a woman's reason!" said he, laughing lightly.

"Do you mean that your failure would imperil our lives?"

"Something like it?" he replied, after a moment's thought.

"Our lives!" Davila cried. "Do you appreciate what you are saying!"

The man did not answer.

"Is it possible you mean to threaten our lives?" Davila persisted.

"I threaten nothing—yet."

"Oh, you threaten nothing, yet!" she mocked. "But you will threaten, if——"

"Exactly! if—you are at liberty to guess the rest."

"I don't care to guess!" she retorted. "Do you appreciate that the whole Eastern Shore will be searching for us by morning—and that, if the least indignity is offered us, your lives won't be worth a penny?"

"We take the risk, Miss Carrington," replied the man, placidly.

Davila shrugged her shoulders, and they rode in silence, for half an hour.

Then the speed of the car slackened, they ran slowly for half a mile, and stopped. The chief reached down, untied the handkerchiefs, and sprang out.

"You may descend," he said, offering his hand.

Elaine saw the hand, and ignored it; Davila refused even to see the hand.

They could make out, in the dim light, that they were before a long, low, frame building, with the waters of the Bay just beyond. A light burned within, and, as they entered, the odor of cooking greeted them.

"Thank goodness! they don't intend to starve us!" said Elaine. "I suppose it's scarcely proper in an abducted maiden, but I'm positively famished."

"I'm too enraged to eat," said Davila.

"Are you afraid?" Elaine asked.

"Afraid?—not in the least!"

"No more am I—but oughtn't we be afraid?"

"I don't know! I'm too angry to know anything."

They had been halted on the porch, while the chief went in, presumably, to see that all was ready for their reception. Now, he returned.

"If you will come in," he said, "I will show you to your apartment."

"Prison, you mean," said Davila.

"Apartment is a little better word, don't you think?" said he. "However, as you wish, Miss Carrington, as you wish! We shall try to make you comfortable, whatever you may call your temporary quarters.—These two rooms are yours," he continued, throwing open the door. "They are small, but quiet and retired; you will not, I am sure, be disturbed. Pardon me, if I remove these ropes, you will be less hampered in your movements. There! supper will be served in fifteen minutes—you will be ready?"

"Yes, we shall be ready," said Elaine, and the man bowed and retired. "He has some manners!" she reflected.

"They might be worse," Davila retorted.

"Which is some satisfaction," Elaine added.

"Yes!—and we best be thankful for it."

"The rooms aren't so bad," said Elaine, looking around.

"We each have a bed, and a bureau, and a wash-stand, and a couple of chairs, a few chromos, a rug on the floor—and bars at the window."

"I noticed the bars," said Davila.

Elaine crossed to her wash-stand.

"They've provided us with water, so we may as well use it," she said. "I think my face needs—Heavens! what a sight I am!"

"Haven't you observed the same sight in me?" Davila asked. "I've lost all my puffs, I know—and so have you—and your hat is a trifle awry."

"Since we're not trying to make an impression, I reckon it doesn't matter!" laughed Elaine. "We will have ample opportunity to put them to rights before Colin and Geoffrey see us."

She took off her hat, pressed her hair into shape, replaced a few pins, dashed water on her face, and washed her hands.

"Now," she said, going into the other room where Miss Carrington was doing likewise, "if I only had a powder-rag, I'd feel dressed."

Davila turned, and, taking a little book, from the pocket of her coat, extended it.

"Here is some Papier Poudre," she said.

"You blessed thing!" Elaine exclaimed, and, tearing out a sheet, she rubbed it over her face. "Is my nose shiny?" she ended.

A door opened and a young girl appeared, wearing apron and cap.

"The ladies are served!" she announced.

The two looked at each other and laughed.

"This is quite some style!" Davila commented.

"It is, indeed!" said Elaine as she saw the table, with its candles and silver (plated, to be sure), dainty china, and pressed glass.

"If the food is in keeping, I think we can get along for a few days. We may as well enjoy it while it lasts."

Davila smiled. "You always were of a philosophic mind."

"It's the easiest way."

She might have added, that it was the only way she knew—her wealth having made all roads easy to her.

The meal finished, they went back to their apartment, to find the bed turned down for the night, and certain lingerie, which they were without, laid out for them.

"Better and better!" exclaimed Elaine. "You might think this was a hotel."

"Until you tried to go out."

"We haven't tried, yet—wait until morning." A pack of cards was on the table. "See how thoughtful they are! Come, I'll play you Camden for a cent a point."

"I can't understand what their move is?" said Davila, presently. "What can they hope to accomplish by abducting us—or me, at any rate. It seems they don't want anything from us."

"I make it, that they hope to extort something, from a third party, through us —by holding us prisoners."

"Captain Carrington has no money—it can't be he," said Davila, "and yet, why else should they seize me?"

"The question is, whose hand are they trying to force?" reflected Elaine. "They will hold us until something is acceded to, the man said. Until *what* is acceded to, and *by whom*?"

"You think that we are simply the pawns?" asked Davila.

"Undoubtedly!"

"And if it isn't acceded to, they will kill us?"

"They will doubtless make the threat."

"Pleasant prospect for us!"

"We won't contemplate it, just yet. They may gain their point, or we may be rescued; in either case, we'll be saved from dying!" Elaine laughed. "And, at the worst, I may be able to buy them off—to pay our own ransom. If it's money they want, we shall not die, I assure you."

"You would pay what they demand?" Davila asked, quickly.

"If I have to choose between death and paying, I reckon I'll pay."

"But can you pay?"

"Yes, I think I can pay," she said quietly. "I'm not used to boasting my wealth, but I can draw my check for a million, and it will be honored without a moment's question. Does that make you feel easier, my dear?"

"Considerably easier," said Davila, with a glad laugh. "I couldn't draw my check for much more than ten thousand cents. I am only——" She stopped, staring.

"What on earth is the matter, Davila?" Elaine exclaimed.

"I have it!—it's the thieves!"

"Have you suddenly lost your mind?"

"No! I've found it! I've come out of my trance. It's Parmenter's chest."

"Parmenter's chest?" echoed Elaine. "I reckon I must be in a trance, also."

"Hasn't Mr. Croyden told you—or Mr. Macloud?"

"No!"

"Then maybe I shouldn't—but I will. Parmenter's chest is a fortune in jewels."

"A what?"

"A fortune in jewels, which Mr. Croyden has searched for and not found— and the thieves think——"

"You would better tell me the story," said Elaine, pushing back the cards.

And Davila told her....

"It is too absurd!" laughed Elaine, "those rogues trying to force Geoffrey to divide what he hasn't got, and can't find, and we abducted to constrain him. He couldn't comply if he wanted to, poor fellow!"

"But they will never believe it," said Davila.

"And, meanwhile, we suffer. Well, if we're not rescued shortly, I can advance the price and buy our freedom. They want half a million. Hum! I reckon two hundred thousand will be sufficient—and, maybe, we can compromise for one hundred thousand. Oh! it's not so bad, Davila, it's not so bad!"

She smiled, shrewdly. Unless she were wofully mistaken, this abduction would release her from the embarrassment of declaring herself to Geoffrey.

She could handle the matter, now.

"What is it?" asked Davila. "Why are you smiling so queerly?"

"I was thinking of Colin and Geoffrey—and how they are pretty sure to know their minds when this affair is ended."

"You mean?"

"Exactly! I mean, if this doesn't bring Colin to his senses, he is hopeless."

"And Mr. Croyden?" Davila queried. "How about him?"

"He will surrender, too. All his theoretical notions of relative wealth will be forgotten. I've only to wait for rescue or release. On the whole, Davila, I'm quite satisfied with being abducted. Moreover, it is an experience which doesn't come to every girl." She looked at her friend quizzically. "What are you going to do about Colin? I rather think you should have an answer ready; the circumstances are apt to make him rather precipitate."

The next morning after breakfast, which was served in their rooms, Elaine was looking out through the bars on her window, trying to get some notion of the country, when she saw, what she took to be, the chief abductor approaching. He was a tall, well-dressed man of middle age, with the outward appearance of a gentleman. She looked at him a moment, then rang for the maid.

"I should like to have a word with the man who just came in," she said.

"I will tell him, Miss."

He appeared almost immediately, an inquiring look on his face.

"How can I serve you, Miss Cavendish?" he said, deferentially.

"By permitting us to go out for some air—these rooms were not designed, apparently, for permanent residence."

"It can be arranged," he answered. "When do you wish to go?"

"At once!"

"Very good!" he said. "You will have no objection to being attended, to make sure you don't stray off too far, you know?"

"None whatever, if the attendant remains at a reasonable distance."

He bowed and stood aside.

"You may come," he said.

"Is the locality familiar?" Elaine asked, when they were some distance from the house.

Davila shook her head. "It is south of Hampton, I think, but I can't give any reason for my impression. The car was running very rapidly; we were, I reckon, almost two hours on the way, but we can't be more than fifty miles away."

"If they came direct—but if they circled, we could be much less," Elaine observed.

"It's a pity we didn't think to drop something from the car to inform our friends which way to look for us."

"I did," said Elaine. "I tossed out a handkerchief and a glove a short distance from Hampton—just as I struck that fellow. The difficulty is, there isn't any assurance we kept to that road. Like as not, we started north and ended east or south of town. What is this house, a fishing club?"

"I rather think so. There is a small wharf, and a board-walk down to the Bay, and the house itself is one story and spread-out, so to speak."

"Likely it's a summer club-house, which these men have either rented or preëmpted for our prison."

"The country around here is surely deserted!" said Davila.

"Hence, a proper choice for our temporary residence."

"I can't understand the care they are taking of us—the deference with which we are treated, the food that is given us."

"Parmenter's treasure, and the prize they think they're playing for, has much to do with it. We are of considerable value, according to their idea."

After a while, they went back to the house. The two men, who had remained out of hearing, but near enough to prevent any attempt to escape, having seen them safely within, disappeared. As they passed through the hall they encountered the chief. He stepped aside.

"You enjoyed your walk, I trust?" he said.

Davila nodded curtly. Elaine stopped.

"I feel sorry for you!" she said, smiling.

"You are very kind," he replied. "But why?"

"You are incurring considerable expense for nothing."

He grinned. "It is a very great pleasure, I assure you."

"You are asking the impossible," she went on. "Mr. Croyden told you the

177

simple truth. He *didn't* find the Parmenter jewels."

The man's face showed his surprise, but he only shrugged his shoulders expressively, and made no reply.

"I know you do not believe it—yet it's a fact, nevertheless. Mr. Croyden couldn't pay your demands, if he wished. Of course, we enjoy the experience, but, as I said, it's a trifle expensive for you."

The fellow's grin broadened.

"You're a good sport!" he said—"a jolly good sport! But we're dealing with Mr. Croyden and Mr. Macloud, so, you'll pardon me if I decline to discuss the subject."

XIX

In half-an-hour from the time Captain Carrington strode to the telephone to arouse his friends, all Hampton had the startling news: Davila Carrington and her guest, Miss Cavendish, had disappeared.

How, when, and where, it could not learn, so it supplied the deficiency as best pleased the individual—by morning, the wildest tales were rehearsed and credited.

The truth was bad enough, however. Miss Carrington and Miss Cavendish were not in the town, nor anywhere within a circuit of five miles. Croyden, Macloud, all the men in the place had searched the night through, and without avail. Every horse, and every boat had been accounted for. It remained, that they either had fallen into the Bay, or had gone in a strange conveyance.

Croyden and Macloud had returned to Clarendon for a bite of breakfast—very late breakfast, at eleven o'clock. They had met by accident, on their way to the house, having come from totally different directions of search.

"It's Parmenter again!" said Croyden, suddenly.

"It's what?" said Macloud.

"Parmenter:—Pirate's gold breeds pirate's ways. The lawyer villain has reappeared. I told you it was he I saw, yesterday, driving the automobile."

"I don't quite understand why they selected Elaine and Miss Carrington to abduct," Macloud objected, after a moment's consideration. "Why didn't they take you?"

"Because they thought we would come to time more quickly, if they took the women. They seem to be informed on everything, so, we can assume, they are acquainted with your fondness for Miss Carrington and mine for Elaine. Or, it's possible they thought that we both were interested in Davila—for I've been with her a lot this autumn—and then, at the pinch, were obliged to take Elaine, also, because she was with her and would give the alarm if left behind."

"A pretty fair scheme," said Macloud. "The fellow who is managing this business knew we would do more for the women than for ourselves."

"It's the same old difficulty—we haven't got Parmenter's treasure, but they refuse to be convinced."

The telephone rang, and Croyden himself answered it.

"Captain Carrington asks that we come over at once," he said, hanging up the receiver. "The Pinkerton men have arrived."

They finished their breakfast and started. Half way to the gate, they met the postman coming up the walk. He handed Croyden a letter, faced about and trudged away.

Croyden glanced at it, mechanically tore open the envelope, and drew it out. As his eyes fell on the first line, he stopped, abruptly.

"Listen to this!" he said.

> "On Board The Parmenter,
>
> "Pirate Sloop of War,
>
> "Off the Capes of the Chesapeake.

"Dear Sir:—

"It seems something is required to persuade you that we mean business. Therefore, we have abducted Miss Carrington and her friend, Miss Cavendish, in the hope that it will rouse you to a proper realization of the eternal fitness of things, and of our intention that there shall be a division of the jewels—or their value in money. Our attorney had the pleasure of an interview with you, recently, at which time he specified a sum of two hundred and fifty thousand dollars, as being sufficient. A further investigation of the probable value of the jewels, having convinced us that we were in slight error as to their present worth, induces us to reduce the amount, which we claim as our share, to two hundred thousand dollars. This is the minimum of our demand, however, and we have taken the ladies, aforesaid, as security for its prompt payment.

"They will be held in all comfort and respect (if no effort at rescue be attempted—otherwise we will deal with them as we see fit), for the period of ten days from the receipt of this letter, which will be at noon to-morrow. If the sum indicated is not paid, they will, at the expiration of the ten days, be turned over to the tender mercies of the crew.—Understand?

"As to the manner of payment—You, yourself, must go to Annapolis, and, between eleven and twelve in the morning, proceed to the extreme edge of Greenberry Point and remain standing, in full view from the Bay, for the space of fifteen minutes. You will, then, face about, step ten paces, and bury the money, which must be in thousand dollar bills, under a foot of sand. You will then, immediately, return to Annapolis and take the first car to Baltimore, and, thence, to Hampton.

"In the event that you have not reduced the jewels to cash, we will be content with such a division as will insure us a moiety thereof. It will be useless to try deception concerning them,—though a few thousand dollars, one way or the other, won't matter. When you have complied with these terms, the young women will be released and permitted to return to Hampton. If not—they will wish they were dead, even before they are. We are, sir, with deep respect,

"Y'r h'mbl. and ob'dt. serv'ts,

"Robert Parmenter's Successors.

"Geoffrey Croyden, Esq'r.

   "Hampton, Md."

"Where was it mailed?" Macloud asked.

Croyden turned over the envelope. It was postmarked Hampton, 6.30 A.M., of that day.

"Which implies that it was mailed some time during the night," said he.

"What do you make of it?"

"Do you mean, will they carry out their threat?"

Croyden nodded.

"They have been rather persistent," Macloud replied.

"It's absurd!" Croyden exclaimed. "We haven't the jewels. Damn Parmenter and his infernal letter!"

"Parmenter is not to blame," said Macloud. "Damn the thieves."

"And damn my carelessness in letting them pick my pocket! there lies the entire difficulty."

"Well, the thing, now, is to save the women—and how?"

"Pay, if need be!" exclaimed Croyden. "The two hundred thousand I got for the Virginia Development bonds will be just enough."

Macloud nodded. "I'm in for half, old man. Aside from any personal feelings we may have for the women in question," he said, with a serious sort of smile, "we owe it to them—they were abducted solely because of us—to force us to disgorge."

"I'm ready to pay the cash at once."

"Don't be hasty!" Macloud cautioned. "We have ten days, and the police can take a try at it."

"*That*, for the police!" said Croyden, snapping his fingers. "They're all bunglers—they will be sure to make a mess of it, and, then, no man can foresee what will happen. It's not right to subject the women to the risk. Let us pay first, and punish after—if we can catch the scoundrels. How long do you think Henry Cavendish will hesitate when he learns that Elaine has been abducted, and the peril which menaces her?"

"Thunder! we have clean forgot her father!" exclaimed Macloud. "He should be informed at once."

"Just what he shouldn't be," Croyden returned. "What is the good in alarming him? Free her—then she may tell him, or not, as it pleases her."

Macloud held out his hand.

"Done!" he said. "Our first duty *is* to save the women, the rest can bide until they are free. How about the money? Are your stocks readily convertible? If not, I'll advance your share."

"Much obliged, old man," said Croyden, "but a wire will do it—they're all listed on New York."

"Will you lose much, if you sell now?" asked Macloud. He wished Croyden would let him pay the entire amount.

"Just about even; a little to the good, in fact," was the answer.

And Macloud said no more—he knew it was useless.

At Ashburton, they found Captain Carrington pacing the long hall, in deep distress—uncertain what course to pursue, because there was no indication as to what had caused the disappearance. He turned, as the two men entered.

"The detectives are quizzing the servants in the library," he said. "I couldn't sit still.—You have news?" he exclaimed, reading Croyden's face.

"I have!" said Croyden, and gave him the letter.

He seized it. As he read, concern, perplexity, amazement, anger, all showed in his countenance.

"They have been abducted!—Davila and Miss Cavendish, and are held for ransom!—a fabulous ransom, which you are asked to pay," he said, incredulously. "So much, at least, is intelligible. But why? why? Who are Robert Parmenter's Successors?—and who was he? and the jewels?—I cannot understand——"

"I'm not surprised," said Croyden. "It's a long story—too long to tell—save that Parmenter was a pirate, back in 1720, who buried a treasure on Greenberry Point, across the Severn from Annapolis, you know, and died, making Marmaduke Duval his heir, under certain conditions. Marmaduke, in turn, passed it on to his son, and so on, until Colonel Duval bequeathed it to me. We searched—Mr. Macloud and I—for three weeks, but did not find it. Our secret was chanced upon by two rogues, who, with their confederates, however, are under the conviction we *did* find it. They wanted a rake-off. I laughed at them—and this abduction is the result."

"But why abduct the women?" asked the old man.

"Because they think I can be coerced more easily. They are under the impression that I am—fond of Miss Carrington. At any rate, they know I'm enough of a friend to pay, rather than subject her to the hazard."

"Pay! I can't pay! My whole fortune isn't over twenty thousand dollars. It I will gladly sacrifice, but more is impossible."

"You're not to pay, my old friend," said Croyden. "Mr. Macloud and I are the ones aimed at and we will pay."

"I won't permit it, sir!" the Captain exclaimed. "There is no reason for you ——"

"Tut! tut!" said Croyden, "you forget that we are wholly responsible; but for us, Miss Carrington and Miss Cavendish would not have been abducted. The obligation is ours, and we will discharge it. It is our plain, our very plain, duty."

The old man threw up his hands in the extremity of despair.

"I don't know what to do!" he said. "I don't know what to do!"

"Do nothing—leave everything to us. We'll have Miss Carrington back in three days."

"And safe?"

"And safe—if the letter is trustworthy, and I think it is. The police can't do as well—they may fail entirely—and think of the possible consequences! Miss Carrington and Miss Cavendish are very handsome women."

"My God, yes!" exclaimed the Captain. "Anything but that! If they were men, or children, it would be different—they could take some chances. But women!"—He sank on a chair and covered his face with his hands. "You must let me pay what I am able," he insisted. "All that I have——"

Croyden let his hand fall sympathizingly on the other's shoulder.

"It shall be as you wish," he said quietly. "We will pay, and you can settle with us afterward—our stocks can be converted instantly, you see, while yours will likely require some time."

The Captain pulled himself together and arose.

"Thank you," he said. "I've been sort of unmanned—I'm better now. Shall you show the detectives the letter—tell them we are going to pay the amount demanded?"

"I don't know," said Croyden, uncertainly. "What's your opinion, Colin?"

"Let them see the letter," Macloud answered, "but on the distinct stipulation, that they make no effort to apprehend 'Robert Parmenter's Successors' until the women are safely returned. They may pick up whatever clues they can obtain for after use, but they must not do anything which will arouse suspicion, even."

"Why take them into our confidence at all?" asked Croyden.

"For two reasons: It's acting square with them (which, it seems to me, is always the wise thing to do). And, if they are not let in on the facts, they may blunder in and spoil everything. We want to save the women at the earliest moment, without any possible handicaps due to ignorance or inadvertence."

"But can we trust them?" Croyden asked, doubtfully.

"It's the lesser of two evils."

"We will have to explain the letter, its reference to the Parmenter jewels, and all that it contains."

"I can see no objection. We didn't find the treasure, and, I reckon, they're welcome to search, if they think there is a chance."

"Well, let it be exactly as you wish—you're quite as much concerned for success as I am," said Croyden.

"Possibly, more so," returned Macloud, seriously.

And Croyden understood.

Then, they went into the library. The two detectives arose at their entrance. The one, Rebbert, was a Pinkerton man, the other, Sanders, was from the Bureau at City Hall. Both were small men, with clean shaven faces, steady, searching eyes, and an especially quiet manner.

"Mr. Croyden," said Rebbert, "we have been questioning the servants, but have obtained nothing of importance, except that the ladies wore their hats and coats (at least, they have disappeared). This, with the fact that you found Miss Cavendish's glove and handkerchief, on a road without the limits of Hampton, leads to the conclusion that they have been abducted. But why? Miss Carrington, we are informed, has no great wealth—how as to Miss Cavendish?"

"She has more than sufficient—in fact, she is very rich——"

"Ah! then we *have* a motive," said the detective.

"There is a motive, but it is not Miss Cavendish," Croyden answered. "You're correct as to the abduction, however—this will explain," and he handed him the letter.

The two men read it.

"When did you receive this?" said one.

"At noon to-day," replied Croyden, passing over the envelope.

They looked carefully at the postmark.

"Do you object to explaining certain things in this letter?" Rebbert asked.

"Not in the least," replied Croyden. "I'll tell you the entire story.... Is there anything I have missed?" he ended.

"I think not, sir."

"Very well! Now, we prefer that you should take no measures to apprehend the abductors, until after Miss Cavendish and Miss Carrington have been released. We are going to pay the amount demanded."

"Going to pay the two hundred thousand dollars!" cried the detectives, in one breath.

Croyden nodded. "Afterward, you can get as busy as you like."

A knowing smile broke over the men's faces, at the same instant.

"You too think we found the treasure?" Croyden exclaimed.

"It looks that way, sir," said Rebbert; while Sanders acquiesced, with another smile.

Croyden turned to Macloud and held up his hands, hopelessly.

"If we only had!" he cried. "If we only had!"

XX

On the second morning after their abduction, when Elaine and Davila arose, the sky was obscured by fog, the trees exuded moisture, and only a small portion of the Bay was faintly visible through the mist.

"This looks natural!" said Elaine. "We must have moved out to Northumberland, in the night."

Davila smiled, a feeble sort of smile. It was not a morning to promote light-heartedness, and particularly under such circumstances.

"Is this anything like Northumberland?" she asked.

"Yes!—Only Northumberland is more so. For a misty day, this would be remarkably fine.—With us, it's midnight at noon—all the lights burning, in streets, and shops, and electric cars, bells jangling, people rushing, pushing, diving through the dirty blackness, like devils in hell. Oh, it's pleasant, when you get used to it.—Ever been there?"

"No," said Davila, "I haven't."

"We must have you out—say, immediately after the holidays. Will you come?"

"I'll be glad to come, if I'm alive—and we ever get out of this awful place."

"It *is* stupid here," said Elaine. "I thought there was something novel in being abducted, but it's rather dreary business. I'm ready to quit, are you?"

"I was ready to quit before we started!" Davila laughed.

"We will see what can be done about it. We'll have in the head jailer." She struck the bell. "Ask the chief to be kind enough to come here a moment," she said, to the girl who attended them.

In a few minutes, he appeared—suave, polite, courteous.

"You sent for me, Miss Cavendish?" he inquired.

"I did. Sit down, please, I've something to say to you, Mr.——"

"Jones, for short," he replied.

"Thank you!" said Elaine, with a particularly winning smile. "Mr. Jones, for short—you will pardon me, I know, if I seem unduly personal, but these quarters are not entirely to our liking."

"I'm very sorry, indeed," he replied. "We tried to make them comfortable. In what are they unsatisfactory?—we will remedy it, if possible."

"We would prefer another locality—Hampton, to be specific."

"You mean that you are tired of captivity?" he smiled. "I see your point of view, and I'm hopeful that Mr. Croyden will see it, also, and permit us to release you, in a few days."

"It is that very point I wish to discuss a moment with you," she interrupted. "I told you before, that Mr. Croyden didn't find the jewels and that, therefore, it is impossible for him to pay."

"You will pardon me if I doubt your statement.—Moreover, we are not privileged to discuss the matter with you. We can deal only with Mr. Croyden, as I think I have already intimated."

"Then you will draw an empty covert," she replied.

"That remains to be seen, as I have also intimated," said Mr. Jones, easily.

"But you don't want to draw an empty covert, do you—to have only your trouble for your pains?" she asked.

"It would be a great disappointment, I assure you."

"You have been at considerable expense to provide for our entertainment?"

"Pray do not mention it!—it's a very great pleasure."

"It would be a greater pleasure to receive the cash?" she asked.

"Since the cash is our ultimate aim, I confess it would be equally satisfactory," he replied.

"Then why not tell me the amount?"

He shook his head.

"Such matters are for Mr. Croyden," he said.

"Just assume that Mr. Croyden cannot pay," she insisted. "Are *we* not to be given a chance to find the cash?"

"Mr. Croyden can pay."

"But assume that he cannot," she reiterated, "or won't—it's the same result."

"In that event, you——"

"Would be given the opportunity," she broke in.

He bowed.

"Then why not let us consider the matter in the first instance?" she asked. "The money is the thing. It can make no difference to you whence it comes— from Mr. Croyden or from me."

"None in the world!" he answered.

"And it would be much more simple to accept a check and to release us when it is paid?"

"Checks are not accepted in this business!" he smiled.

"Ordinarily not, it would be too dangerous, I admit. But if it could be arranged to your satisfaction, what then?"

"I don't think it can be arranged," he replied. "The amount is much too great."

"And that amount is——" she persisted, smiling at him the while.

"Two hundred thousand dollars," he replied.

"With what per cent. off for cash?"

"None—not a fraction of a penny!"

She nodded, slightly. "Why can't it be arranged?"

"You're thinking of paying it?" he asked, incredulously.

"I want to know why you think it can't be arranged?" she repeated.

"The danger of detection. No bank would pay a check for that amount to an unknown party, without the personal advice of the drawer."

"Not if it were made payable to self, and properly indorsed for identification?"

"I fear not."

"You can try it—there's no harm in trying. You have a bank that knows you?"

"But scarcely for such large amounts."

"What of it? You deposit the check for collection only. They will send it through. When it's paid, they will pay you. If it's not paid, there is no harm done—and we are still your prisoners. You stand to win everything and lose nothing."

The man looked thoughtfully at the ceiling.

"The check will be paid?" he asked, presently.

"If it isn't paid, you still have us," said Elaine.

"It might be managed."

"That is your part. If the check is presented, it will be paid—you may rest easy, on that score."

Jones resumed his contemplation of the ceiling.

"But remember," she cautioned, "when it is paid, we are to be released, instantly. No holding us for Mr. Croyden to pay, also. If we play square with you, you must play square with us. I risk a fortune, see that you make good."

"Your check—it should be one of the sort you always use——"

"I always carry a few blank checks in my handbag—and fortunately, I have it with me. You were careful to wrap it in with my arms. I will get it."

She went into her room. In a moment she returned, the blank check in her fingers, and handed it to him. It was of a delicate robin's-egg blue, with "The Tuscarora Trust Company" printed across the face in a darker shade, and her monogram, in gold, at the upper end.

"Is it sufficiently individual to raise a presumption of regularity?" she said.

"Undoubtedly!" he answered.

"Then, let us understand each other," she said.

"By all means," he agreed.

"I give you my check for two hundred thousand dollars, duly executed, payable to my order, and endorsed by me, which, when paid, you, on behalf of your associates and yourself, engage to accept in lieu of the amount demanded from Mr. Croyden, and to release Miss Carrington and myself forthwith."

"There is one thing more," he said. "You, on your part, are to stipulate that no attempt will be made to arrest us."

"We will engage that *we* will do nothing to apprehend you."

"Directly or indirectly?" he questioned.

"Yes!—more than that is not in our power. You will have to assume the general risk you took when you abducted us."

"We will take it," was the quiet answer.

"Is there anything else?" she asked.

"I think not—at least, everything is entirely satisfactory to us."

"Despite the fact that it couldn't be made so!" she smiled.

"I didn't know we had to deal with a woman of such business sense and—

wealth," he answered gallantly.

She smiled. "If you will get me ink and pen, I will sign the check," she said.

She filled it in for the amount specified, signed and endorsed it. Then she took, from her handbag, a correspondence card, embossed with her initials, and wrote this note:

"Hampton, Md.

"Nov. —'10.

"My dear Mr. Thompson:—

"I have made a purchase, down here, and my check for Two Hundred Thousand dollars, in consideration, will come through, at once. Please see that it is paid, promptly.

"Yours very sincerely,

"Elaine Cavendish.

"To James Thompson, Esq'r., "Treasurer, The Tuscarora Trust Co., "Northumberland."

She addressed the envelope and passed it and the card across to Mr. Jones, together with the check.

"If you will mail this, to-night, it will provide against any chance of non-payment," she said.

"You are a marvel of accuracy," he answered, with a bow. "I would I could always do business with you."

"At two hundred thousand the time? No! no! monsieur, I pray thee, no more!"

There was a knock on the door; the maid entered and spoke in a low tone to Jones. He nodded.

"I am sorry to inconvenience you again," he said, turning to them, "but I must trouble you to go aboard the tug."

"The tug—on the water?" Elaine exclaimed.

"On the water—that is usually the place for well behaved tugs!" he laughed.

"Now!" Elaine persisted.

"Now—before I go to deposit the check!" he smiled. "You will be safer on the tug. There will be no danger of an escape or a rescue—and it won't be for long, I trust."

"Your trust is no greater than ours, I assure you," said Elaine.

Their few things were quickly gathered, and they went down to the wharf, where a small boat was drawn up ready to take them to the tug, which was lying a short distance out in the Bay.

"One of the Baltimore tugs, likely," said Davila. "There are scores of them, there, and some are none too chary about the sort of business they are employed in."

"Witness the present!" commented Elaine.

They got aboard without accident. Jones conducted them to the little cabin, which they were to occupy together—an upper and a lower bunk having been provided.

"The maid will sleep in the galley," said he. "She will look after the cooking, and you will dine in the small cabin next to this one. It's a bit contracted quarters for you, and I'm sorry, but it won't be for long—as we both trust, Miss Cavendish."

"And you?" asked Elaine.

"I go to deposit the check. I will have my bank send it direct for collection, with instructions to wire immediately if paid. I presume you don't wish it to go through the ordinary course."

"Most assuredly not!" Elaine answered.

"This is Thursday," said Jones. "The check, and your note, should reach the Trust Company in the same mail to-morrow morning; they can be depended upon to wire promptly, I presume?"

"Undoubtedly!"

"Then, we may be able to release you to-morrow night, certainly by Saturday."

"It can't come too soon for us."

"You don't seem to like our hospitality," Jones observed.

"It's excellent of its sort, but we don't fancy the sort—you understand, monsieur. And then, too, it is frightfully expensive."

"We have done the best we could under the circumstances," he smiled. "Until Saturday at the latest—meanwhile, permit me to offer you a very hopeful farewell."

Elaine smiled sweetly, and Mr. Jones went out.

"Why do you treat him so amiably?" Davila asked. "I couldn't, if I would."

"Policy," Elaine answered. "We get on better. It wouldn't help our case to be sullen—and it might make it much worse. I would gladly shoot him, and hurrah over it, too, as I fancy you would do, but it does no good to show it, now—when we *can't* shoot him."

"I suppose not," said Davila. "But I'm glad I don't have to play the part." She hesitated a moment. "Elaine, I don't know how to thank you for my freedom ——"

"Wait until you have it!" the other laughed. "Though there isn't a doubt of the check being paid."

"My grandfather, I know, will repay you with his entire fortune, but that will be little——"

Elaine stopped her further words by placing a hand over her mouth, and kissing her.

"That's quite enough, dear!" she said. "Take it that the reward is for my release, and that you were just tossed in for good measure—or, that it is a slight return for the pleasure of visiting you—or, that the money is a small circumstance to me—or, that it is a trifling sum to pay to be saved the embarrassment of proposing to Geoffrey, myself—or, take it any way you like, only, don't bother your pretty head an instant more about it. In the slang of the day: 'Forget it,' completely and utterly, as a favor to me if for no other reason."

"I'll promise to forget it—until we're free," agreed Davila.

"And, in the meantime, let us have a look around this old boat," said Elaine. "You're nearer the door, will you open it? Two can't pass in this room."

Davila tried the door—it refused to open.

"It's locked!" she said.

"Oh, well! we will content ourselves with watching the Bay through the port hole, and when one wants to turn around the other can crawl up in her bunk. I'm going to write a book about this experience, some time.—I wonder what Geoffrey and Colin are doing?" she laughed—"running around like mad and stirring up the country, I reckon."

———————

XXI

Macloud went to New York on the evening train. He carried Croyden's power of attorney with stock sufficient, when sold, to make up his share of the cash. He had provided for his own share by a wire to his brokers and his bank in Northumberland. A draft would be awaiting him. He would reduce both amounts to one thousand dollar bills and hurry back to Annapolis to meet Croyden.

But they counted not on the railroads,—or rather they did count on them, and they were disappointed. A freight was derailed just south of Hampton, tearing up the track for a hundred yards, and piling the right of way with wreckage of every description. Macloud's train was twelve hours late leaving Hampton. Then, to add additional ill luck, they ran into a wash out some fifty miles further on; with the result that they did not reach New York until after the markets were over and the banks had closed for the day.

He wired the facts to Croyden. The following day, he sold the stocks, the brokers gave him the proceeds in the desired bills, after the delivery hour, and he made a quick get-away for Annapolis, arriving there at nine o'clock in the evening.

Croyden was awaiting him, at Carvel Hall.

"I'm sorry, for the girls' sake," said he, "but it's only a day lost. We will deliver the goods to-morrow. And, then, pray God, they be freed before another night! That lawyer thief is a rogue and a robber, but something tells me he will play straight."

"I reckon we will have to trust him," returned Macloud. "Where is the Pinkerton man?"

"He is in town. He will be over on the Point in the morning, disguised as a negro and chopping wood, on the edge of the timber. There isn't much chance of him identifying the gang, but it's the best we can do. It's the girls first, the scoundrels afterward, if possible."

At eleven o'clock the following day, Croyden, mounted on one of "Cheney's Best," rode away from the hotel. There had been a sudden change in the weather, during the night; the morning was clear and bright and warm, as happens, sometimes, in Annapolis, in late November. The Severn, blue and placid, flung up an occasional white cap to greet him, as he crossed the bridge. He nodded to the draw-keeper, who recognized him, drew aside for an automobile to pass, and then trotted sedately up the hill, and into the woods beyond.

He could hear the Band of the Academy pounding out a quick-step, and catch a glimpse of the long line of midshipmen passing in review, before some notable. The "custard and cream" of the chapel dome obtruded itself in all its hideousness; the long reach of Bancroft Hall glowed white in the sun; the library with its clock—the former, by some peculiar idea, placed at the farthest point from the dormitory, and the latter where the midshipmen cannot see it—dominated the opposite end of the grounds. Everywhere was quiet, peace, and discipline—the embodiment of order and law,—the Flag flying over all.

And yet, he was on his way to pay a ransom of very considerable amount, for two women who were held prisoners!

He tied his horse to a limb of a maple, and walked out on the Point. Save for a few trees, uprooted by the gales, it was the same Point they had dug over a few weeks before. A negro, chopping at a log, stopped his work, a moment, to look at him curiously, then resumed his labor.

"The Pinkerton man!" thought Croyden, but he made no effort to speak to him.

Somewhere,—from a window in the town, or from one of the numerous ships bobbing about on the Bay or the River—he did not doubt a glass was trained on him, and his every motion was being watched.

For full twenty minutes, he stood on the extreme tip of the Point, and looked out to sea. Then he faced directly around and stepped ten paces inland. Kneeling, he quickly dug with a small trowel a hole a foot deep in the sand, put into it the package of bills, wrapped in oil-skin, and replaced the ground.

"There!" said he, as he arose. "Pirate's gold breeds pirate's ways. May we have seen the last of you—and may the devil take you all!"

He went slowly back to his horse, mounted, and rode back to town. They had done their part—would the thieves do theirs?

Adhering strictly to the instructions, Croyden and Macloud left Annapolis on the next car, caught the boat at Baltimore, and arrived in Hampton in the evening, in time for dinner. They stopped a few minutes at Ashburton, to acquaint Captain Carrington with their return, and then went on to Clarendon.

Both men were nervous. Neither wanted the other to know and each endeavored to appear at ease.

Croyden gave in first. He threw his cigarette into his coffee cup, and pushed his chair back from the table.

"It's no use, Colin!" he laughed. "You're trying to appear nonchalant, and you're doing it very well, too, but you can't control your fingers and your eyes—and neither can I, I fancy, though I've tried hard enough, God knows! We are about all in! These four days of strain and uncertainty have taken it all out of us. If I had any doubt as to my affection for Elaine, it's vanished, now. ——I don't say I'm fool enough to propose to her, yet I'm scarcely responsible, at present. If I were to see her this minute, I'd likely do something rash."

"You're coming around to it, gradually," said Macloud.

"Gradually! Hum! I don't know about the 'gradually.' I want to pull myself together—to get a rein on myself—to—what are you smiling at; am I funny?"

"You are!" said Macloud. "I never saw a man fight so hard against his personal inclinations, and a rich wife. You don't deserve her!—if I were Elaine, I'd turn you down hard, hard."

"Thank God! you're not Elaine!" Croyden retorted.

"And hence, with a woman's unreasonableness and trust in the one she loves, she will likely accept you."

"How do you know she loves me?"

Macloud blew a couple of smoke rings and watched them sail upward.

"I suppose you're equally discerning as to Miss Carrington, and her love for you," Croyden commented.

"I regret to say, I'm not," said Macloud, seriously. "That is what troubles me, indeed. Unlike my friend, Geoffrey Croyden, I'm perfectly sure of my own mind, but I'm not sure of the lady's."

"Then, why don't you find out?"

"Exactly what I shall do, when she returns."

"It's sure as fate!" said Croyden.

"Thanks! We each seem to be able to answer the other's uncertainty," he remarked, calmly.

Presently, Macloud arose.

"I'm going over to Ashburton, and talk with the Captain a little—sort of cheer him up. Come along?"

Croyden shook his head.

"Go on!" said he. "It's a very good occupation for you, sitting up to the old gent. I'll give you a chance by staying away, to-night. Make a hit with grandpa, Colin, make a hit with grandpa!"

"And you make a hit with yourself—get rid of your foolish theory, and come down to simple facts," Macloud retorted, and he went out.

"Get rid of your foolish theory," Croyden soliloquized. "Well, maybe—but *is* it foolish, that's the question? I'm poor, once more—I've not enough even for Elaine Cavendish's husband—there's the rub! she won't be Geoffrey Croyden's wife, it's I who will be Elaine Cavendish's husband. 'Elaine Cavendish *and her husband* dine with us to-night!'—'Elaine Cavendish *and her husband* were at the horse show!' 'Elaine Cavendish *and her husband* were here!—or there!—or thus and so!'"

He could not endure it. It would be too belittling, too disparaging of self-respect.—Elaine Cavendish's husband!—Elaine Cavendish's husband! Might he out-grow it—be known for himself? He glanced up at the portrait of the gallant soldier of a lost cause, with the high-bred face and noble bearing.

"You were a brave man, Colonel Duval!" he said. "What would you have done?"

He took out a cigar, lit it very deliberately, and fell to thinking.... Presently, worn out by fatigue and anxiety, he dozed....

And as he dozed, the street door opened softly, a light step crossed the hall, and Elaine Cavendish stood in the doorway.

She was clad in black velvet, trimmed in sable. Her head was bare. A blue cloak was thrown, with careless grace, about her gleaming shoulders. One slender hand lifted the gown from before her feet. She saw the sleeping man and paused, and a smile of infinite tenderness passed across her face.

A moment she hesitated, and at the thought, a faint blush suffused her face. Then she glided softly over, bent and kissed him on the lips.

He opened his eyes, and sprang up! Startled! She was there, before him, the blush still on cheek and brow.

"Elaine! sweetheart!" he cried. And, straightway took her, unresisting, in his arms....

"Tell me all about yourself," he said, at last, drawing her down into the chair and seating himself on the arm. "Where is Miss Carrington—safe?"

"Colin's with her—I reckon she's safe!" smiled Elaine. "It won't be his fault if she isn't, I'm sure.—I left them at Ashburton, and came over here to—

you."

"Alone!" said Croyden, bending over her.

She nodded, eyes half downcast.

"You foolish girl!"

"I'll go back at once——"

He laughed, joyously.

"Not yet a little while!" and bent again.

"Geoffrey! you're dreadful!" she exclaimed, half smothered. "My hair, dear, —do be careful!"

"I'll be good—if you will kiss me again!" he said.

"But you're not asleep," she objected.

"That's why I want it."

"And you will promise—not to kiss me again?"

"For half an hour."

"Honest?"

"Honest."

She looked up at him tantalizingly, her red lips parted, her bosom fluttering below.

"If it's worth coming half way for, sweetheart—you may," she said. . . .

"Now, if you're done with foolishness—for a little while," she said, gayly, "I'll tell you how we managed to get free."

"You know why you were abducted?" he asked.

"Oh, yes!—the Parmenter jewels. Davila told me the story, and how you didn't find them, though our abductors think you did, and won't believe otherwise."

"You suffered no hurt?" he asked, sharply.

"None—we were most courteously treated; and they released us, as quickly as the check was paid."

"What do you mean?" he demanded.

"I mean, that I gave them my check for the ransom money—you hadn't the jewels, you couldn't comply with the demand. How do you suppose we got free?" she questioned.

"You paid the money?" he asked, again.

"Certainly! I knew you couldn't pay it, so I did. Don't let us think of it, dear! —It's over, and we have each other, now. What is money compared to that?" Then suddenly she, woman-like, went straight back to it. "How did you think we managed to get free—escaped?" she asked.

"Yes!" he answered. "Yes—I never thought of your paying the money."

She regarded him critically.

"No!" she said, "you are deceiving me!—you are—*you* paid the money, also!" she cried.

"What matters it?" he said joyfully. "What matters anything now? Macloud and I *did* pay the ransom to-day—but of what consequence is it; whether you bought your freedom, or we bought it, or both bought it? You and Davila are here, again—that's the only thing that matters!"

"Right you are! Geoffrey, right you are!" came Macloud's voice from the hallway, and Davila and he walked into the room.

Elaine, with a little shriek, sprang up.

"Don't be bashful!" said Macloud. "Davila and I were occupying similar positions at Ashburton, a short time ago. Weren't we, little girl?" as he made a motion to put his arm around her.

Davila eluded him—though the traitor red confirmed his words—and sought Elaine's side for safety.

"It's a pleasure only deferred, my dear!" he laughed. "By the way, Elaine, how did Croyden happen to give in? He was shying off at your wealth—said it would be giving hostages to fortune, and all that rot."

"Shut up, you beggar!" Croyden exclaimed. "I'm going to try to make good."

"Geoffrey," said Elaine, "won't you show us the old pirate's letter—we're all interested in it, now."

"Certainly, I will!" he said. "I'll show you the letter, and where I found it, and anything else you want to see. Nothing is locked, to-night."

They went over to the escritoire. Croyden opened the secret drawer, and took out the letter.

"A Message from the Dead!" he said, solemnly, and handed it to Elaine.

She carried it to the table, spread it out under the lamp, and Davila and she studied it, carefully, even as Croyden and Macloud had done—reading the Duval endorsements over and over again.

"It seems to me there is something queer about these postscripts," she said, at last; "something is needed to make them clear. Is this the entire letter?—didn't you find anything else?"

"Nothing!" said Croyden.

"May I look?" she asked.

"Most assuredly, sweetheart."

"It's a bit dark in this hole. Let me have a match."

She struck it, and peered back into the recess.

"Ah!" she exclaimed. "Here is something!—only a corner visible." She put in her hand. "It has slipped down, back of the false partition. I'll get it, presently. —There!"

She drew out a tiny sheet of paper, and handed it to Croyden.

"Does that help?" she asked.

Croyden glanced at it; then gave a cry of amazed surprise.

"It does!" he said. "It does! It's the key to the mystery. Listen!"

The rest crowded around him while he read:

"Hampton, Maryland.

"5 Oct. 1738.

"Memorandum to accompany the letter of Robert Parmenter, dated 10 May 1738.

"Whereas, it is stipulated by the said Parmenter that the Jewels shall be used only in the Extremity of Need; and hence, as I have an abundance of this world's Goods, that Need will, likely, not come to me. And judging that Greenberry Point will change, in time—so that my son or his Descendants, if occasion arise, may be unable to locate the Treasure—I have lifted the Iron box, from the place where Parmenter buried it, and have reinterred it in the cellar of my House in Hampton, renewing the Injunction which Parmenter put upon it, that it shall be used only in the Extremity of Need. When this Need arise, it will be found in the south-east corner of the front cellar. At the depth of two feet, between two large stones, is the Iron box. It contains the jewels, the most marvelous I have ever seen.

"Marmaduke Duval."

For a moment, they stood staring at one another too astonished to speak.

"My Lord!" Macloud finally ejaculated. "To think that it was here, all the time!"

Croyden caught up the lamp.

"Come on!" he said.

They trooped down to the cellar, Croyden leading the way. Moses was off for the evening, they had the house to themselves. As they passed the foot of the stairs, Macloud picked up a mattock.

"Me for the digging!" he said. "Which is the south-east corner, Davila?"

"There, under those boxes!" said she.

They were quickly tossed aside.

"The ground is not especially hard," observed Macloud, with the first stroke. "I reckon a yard square is sufficient.—At a depth of two feet the memorandum says, doesn't it?"

No one answered. Fascinated, they were watching the fall of the pick. With every blow, they were listening for it to strike the stones.

"Better get a shovel, Croyden, we'll need it," said Macloud, pausing long enough, to throw off his coat.... "Oh! I forgot to say, I wired the Pinkerton man to recover the package you buried this morning."

200

Croyden only nodded—stood the lamp on a box, and returned with the coal scoop.

"This will answer, I reckon," he said, and fell to work.

"It seems absurd!" remarked Macloud, between strokes. "To have hunted the treasure, for weeks, all over Greenberry Point, and then to find it in the cellar, like a can of lard or a bushel of potatoes."

"You haven't found it, yet," Croyden cautioned. "And we've gone the depth mentioned."

"No! we haven't found it, yet!—but we're going to find it!" Macloud answered, sinking the pick, viciously, in the ground, with the last word.

Crack!

It had struck hard against a stone.

"What did I tell you?" Macloud cried, sinking the pick in at another place.

Crack!

Again, it struck! and again! and again! The fifth stroke laid the stone bare— the sixth and seventh loosened it, still more—the eighth and ninth completed the task.

"Give me the shovel!" said he.

When the earth was away and the stone exposed, he stooped and, putting his fingers under the edges, heaved it out.

"The rest is for you, Croyden!" and stepped aside.

The iron box was found!

For a moment, Croyden looked at it, rather dazedly. Could it be the jewels were *there!*—within his reach!—under that lid! Suddenly, he laughed!— gladly, gleefully, as a boy—and sprang down into the hole.

The box clung to its resting place for a second, as though it was reluctant to be disturbed—then it yielded, and Croyden swung it onto the bank.

"We'll take it to the library," he said, scraping it clean of the adhering earth.

And carrying it before them, like the Ark of the Covenant, they went joyously up to the floor above.

He placed it on the table under the chandelier, where all could see. It was of iron, rusty with age; in dimension, about a foot square; and fastened by a hasp, with the bar of the lock thrust through but not secured.

"Light the gas, Colin!—every burner," he said. "We'll have the full effulgence, if you please.".…

For a little time, the lid resisted. Suddenly, it yielded.

"Behold!" he heralded, and flung it back.

The scintillations which leaped out to meet them, were like the rays from myriads of gleaming, glistening, varicolored lights, of dazzling brightness and infinite depth. A wonderful cavern of coruscating splendor—rubies and diamonds, emeralds and sapphires, pearls and opals glowing with all the fire of self, and the resentment of long neglect.

"Heaven! What beauty!" exclaimed Davila.

It broke the spell.

"They are real!" Croyden laughed. "You may touch them—they will not fade."

They put them out on the table—in little heaps of color. The women exclaiming whene'er they touched them, cooingly as a woman does when handling jewels—fondling them, caressing them, loving them.

At last, the box was empty. They stood back and gazed—fascinated by it all: —the color—the glowing reds and whites, and greens and blues.

"It is wonderful! wonderful!" breathed Elaine.

"It is wonderful—and it's true!" said Croyden.

Two necklaces lay among the rubies, alike as lapidary's art could make them. Croyden handed one to Macloud, the other he took.

"In remembrance of your release, and of Parmenter's treasure!" he said, and clasped it around Elaine's fair neck.

Macloud clasped his around Davila's.

"Who cares, now, for the time spent on Greenberry Point or the double reward!" he laughed.